THE MAN IN THE RED OVERCOAT

IAN SKAIR INVESTIGATES
BOOK 5

HILARY PUGH

Housemouse Press

Copyright © 2023 by Hilary Pugh

All rights reserved.

No part of this book may be reproduced in any form or by any electronic or mechanical means, including information storage and retrieval systems, without written permission from the author, except for the use of brief quotations in a book review.

❃ Created with Vellum

1

You are such an idiot.

Boutique hotel owner Mickey Rix's parting sentence still rang in Ian Skair's ears three months later. Mickey, as ever, had been right. So his next question, *Why don't you do something about it?* made perfect sense. Ian should definitely do something about it. Only a fool would argue with that.

But had he done anything? No, he'd carefully avoided even thinking about it. He'd been too busy. No, that was a lie. He had been busy, but only because he made himself so. Professionally, the Dundas Farm case had done him a lot of good. In the last couple of months his client, ex-boyband singer, Gavin Stamper, had sent several cases in Ian's direction with a promise of more to come. Famous people had famous friends. Inevitable, Ian supposed. Of course, not all of them thought, as Stamper's leading lady had, that they were in imminent danger of being murdered. In fact, to date none of them thought that. But many of these friends employed people who required background checks – one couldn't afford to give jobs to just anyone when famous, nor could one ignore security. And all of that meant that Ian was kept busy.

Murder at the Dundas Farm production of *Carmen* had simultaneously been averted both in the opera and in real life. An irony that had not escaped the notice of the media. Ian's role in the arrest of the unsuccessful murderer earned him enough coverage to make him something of a celebrity in the world of private investigation and had led to so much work that he'd been able to contract out some of the less interesting cases. Ian could now afford a team, mainly of ex-coppers like himself, that he employed on short contracts to protect the aforementioned rich and famous. All Ian had to do now was sit in his office and arrange things. The work kept him busy and also away from situations that could turn out to be dangerous. He mused over the scars he'd collected recently; shards of glass in his left arm after falling through a window in the line of duty, a reminder of his fear of heights after talking someone down from a roof, and further back, the gunshot wound in his leg that had ended his police career and caused him several years of pain, not to mention the end of his marriage.

Ian rarely felt any pain in his leg now, although the end of the marriage still rankled. Those were the scars that really hurt. Cuts from broken glass, even gunshot wounds, healed eventually. Broken marriages took longer and led to the kind of idiocy that Mickey had correctly, and much to Ian's discomfort, accused him of.

Financially he was doing well. He and his assistant, Molly, had enough cases to bring in a steady income. He lived in a house that was entirely his own. Bought and paid for and now also his place of work. Commuting involved no more than a flight of stairs. Molly took on boring stuff like VAT and tidying the office, leaving him to concentrate on the more interesting aspects of the work.

In his leisure time Ian could enjoy a stunning view over the Tay estuary. He shared his home with Lottie, a dog of small stature but huge personality, whose need for regular exercise ensured that Ian, too, kept fit. He had a next-door neighbour, Lainie, who kept him supplied with home-baked cakes and biscuits, and on whom he could always rely for a friendly chat over the fence, and who, when he needed it, looked after Lottie for him.

There were other friends nearby. His best friend was a maths teacher called Caroline Gillespie, a feisty mixture of straightforward good sense and extreme resourcefulness under pressure. Was she more than a friend? This was something Ian could never quite work out. She had declared a determination to remain single forever, something he respected. But that didn't mean they didn't share some highly enjoyable, not to say intimate, times together. It was a friendship that many men would give their right arm for, and it suited him very well. Or it had until recently.

But right now, Caroline was on the other side of the world. He put her out of his mind for the moment and thought about another close friend. An ex-colleague, now a DI in St Andrews and who had kept in touch over many years since they had worked together for Police Scotland in Leith. Duncan Clyde's promotion to St Andrews had been a stroke of luck for Ian. It was always good for a PI to have a friendly contact in the local police, and Duncan had been able to help him out with information and occasional short contract work. Ian was also fond of Duncan's wife, Jeanie, a relentless matchmaker, whose main object in life was to pair him off, if possible with a ring on his finger and preferably with Caroline. Ian and Caroline both suffered this with affectionate tolerance.

Ian's parents lived in Aberdeen where they mostly, to his relief, ignored him. He was the family disappointment, having failed to impress career-wise, provide grandchildren or even remain married. But should he feel the need for family, his brother Stewart lived a short distance away with a very charming wife and two children. Stewart Skair had a dazzling and highly remunerative career, first on the oil rigs, later in offshore wind and now working in biofuels. He'd also provided their parents with two grandchildren, which took the pressure off Ian himself. Or perhaps they had just given up. Ian, now in his forties with one failed marriage behind him and a noticeable lack of offspring, was no doubt, in their eyes, beyond hope. Which suited him just fine.

Ian had very little to worry about. But that didn't stop him worrying. Mickey was right. He was an idiot whose love life hovered somewhere between messy and non-existent. Ian had only himself to blame and he should sort it out. He had spent the last three months avoiding the issue, which had by no means made it any better. In fact, it had probably made it worse. The trouble was he had no idea what he wanted or, for that matter, what the lady in question wanted. Elsa worked for Mickey. And Mickey was a caring employer, hence the severe reprimand he had hurled in Ian's direction. And with all that going on there was only one thing to do. Avoid it for a little longer and hope it would resolve itself. In the meantime, he would concentrate on work, although to be honest, that had become just a little dull recently. Sitting behind a desk waiting for the fees to come in was okay. But what he really needed was a case that would fire up his imagination, get him out of the office and introduce a bit of excitement into his life. And as he was wondering how exactly he was going to achieve it, his landline rang. The only people who used the landline these days wanted to sell him double glazing, which he already had, or a funeral plan, which he didn't have but preferred not to think about. He tried to ignore the insistent ringing. Where was Molly when he needed her? Not here today, he remembered, pushing a pile of papers off his desk and reaching reluctantly for the handset. But it was neither funeral plans nor double glazing. He should be more careful what he wished for.

2

'I need you to find this man.'

The woman reached into a small leather handbag with a gloved hand and pulled out a photograph. She stared at it for a moment and then pushed it across the desk in Ian's direction with the tip of her finger.

Photographs played a huge part in Ian's business. Usually they were taken by Ian himself and used as evidence of misdemeanours such as adultery or pilfering at work. But he rarely printed them. Very few people did these days. They were all stored on smartphones or in the cloud. The number of pictures floating around up there was mind-blowing. How big exactly was cyberspace? Were they in danger of running out of room at some time in the future? And if they did, what would become of all the photographs? Although most of them were probably rubbish ones. All those hurried snaps of scowling relatives, the hindquarters of pets as they disappeared from the frame a second too soon, or blurred holiday pictures taken after one too many piña coladas.

Ian dragged himself back from his musing and stared down at the picture in front of him. Then he looked at the woman seated on the other side of his desk. Her visit had been a surprise. He was wondering if he should have just let the phone ring out. But he knew the moment he heard her voice that this case was going to be different. Most of his clients contacted him by email or through his website, or increasingly by word of mouth. This woman insisted on making an appointment to call on him in person, which as far as Ian was concerned meant that it wasn't going to be the usual run-of-the-mill type of case. He'd admitted to himself that work had become a little dull recently, so a case that was a bit out of the ordinary was what he wanted, wasn't it? But looking at the woman seated on the other side of his desk, he wasn't so sure. Was he imagining it or was there something rather odd about her? Sinister, even. She told him her name was Felicity Bright and he had no reason not to believe her. Whether she was Mrs, Miss or even Ms, he didn't know. She'd said nothing about who she was and what she wanted from him. Even when phoning, people usually gave some hint of the kind of case they were bringing him. She'd not even told him where she lived or what she did for a living. Only that she would come to his office at ten o'clock this morning. Appearance and body language usually gave him clues about who people were and what their problem might be and he'd put the phone down feeling sure he would know everything once they were face to face.

Now, sitting here in front of him, Felicity Bright still gave nothing away. She defied classification. At least not in today's world. She could have walked out of a nineteen-fifties film. She was dressed in a slim-fitting, grey and navy blue pin-striped suit, black shoes with heels, a small felt hat and, as he'd already noticed, leather gloves, also navy blue. She could be any age from thirty to a well preserved sixty. He'd watched *Brief Encounter* a year or two previously on an ancient DVD player in a holiday cottage, and now he was reminded of Celia Johnson on her way to change her library books. Felicity Bright had the same pensive expression and, as far as her hat allowed him to see, a very similar hairstyle.

Was she equally baffled by him? Was there anything about his own appearance that said *private detective?* General scruffiness perhaps, or an air of being, as Mickey had hurtfully reminded him recently, an idiot where relationships with women were concerned.

Better not go there. Not when interviewing a potential client.

How had she found her way to him? To this out of the way office in a little-known commuter village on the banks of the Tay. She was not from around here; he was sure of that. No Scottish accent for one thing. And no protection against the biting east coast wind. Had she consulted a list of investigators, his name happening to be where her pin landed? Had she checked him out online or seen articles about him in the local press? Or had a friend recommended him? He thought that was unlikely. He couldn't imagine Felicity Bright fitting into any of his recent scenarios. She didn't look like a performer of opera, or someone who mixed with ex-members of boy bands. Neither did she look like an advocate of wellness and all its attendant mind-soothing activities. She'd fit in at genteel tea parties and visits to stately homes. Perhaps she knew his mother. Not likely. His mother barely acknowledged his existence, and she had never once encouraged him in his current profession.

But here Felicity Bright undoubtedly was, and she deserved his attention. He took out his phone and aimed it at the photograph. 'May I copy this?' he asked. 'And can you confirm that you are willing for me to keep a record of our interview?' She nodded. Ian took the photo then tapped the record button on the phone and pushed it to one side. He looked again at the printed photograph. The man was tall, with dark hair curling towards the velvet collar of a red overcoat. Ian was a stranger to upmarket gentleman's attire, but this he was sure was an expensive coat. He could tell by the way it hung from padded shoulders, a generous pleat falling to the hemline. The fabric was not bright pillar-box red, but a rich burgundy, and it looked soft to the touch. Alpaca perhaps, or cashmere, and, he was sure, with a pure silk lining in black or purple. The man was standing with his back to the camera in front of a painting of a couple dancing – Renoir, Ian thought – with his arm raised, as if demonstrating something in the picture and revealing a set of gold cuff buttons while doing so.

Was Ian about to be contracted to find a man who, at some time in the past, had visited a gallery, probably in Paris, and who owned an expensive overcoat? It was not much to go on. The man hadn't even bothered to turn around to be photographed. How easy was it to find someone when all one had was a view of his back? Although in the past he'd found people with less information than that. The sender of cryptic postcards, for example, or a sister who had been missing for fifty years.

He reached for a notebook and pen. 'Perhaps you could give me some details,' he suggested. 'His name?'

'Julian,' she said, removing her gloves and placing them on the desk in front of her, revealing ringless fingers, and nails that were cared for but free of coloured polish.

'His last name?'

She shrugged. 'I know him only as Julian.'

He noted the soft *J* as she pronounced his name. 'French?' he asked.

She nodded.

'And when did you last see him?' Had she actually met him at all, or had she just taken a fancy to him from a photograph? But she knew his name, so there must have been some communication between them, however slight.

'A few weeks ago,' she said. 'We were to have met under the glass dome at Waverley Station in Edinburgh last Friday at midday. But he was not there and now I must find him.'

Ian didn't know what to make of that. What was she asking him to do? And why? If this had been a date, the guy in the red coat had every right to change his mind. Not the kindest way of showing it, perhaps, but hardly enough to trigger a man hunt. He picked up the notepad and, for want of a better idea, scribbled the date on it. 'His age?' he asked.

She shrugged. 'Maybe early fifties. I didn't ask.'

Ian tried to imagine the man's face. 'Colour of eyes? Clean shaven? Good looking?'

'No beard,' she said. 'Brown eyes, bushy greying eyebrows, a genial plumpish face, good complexion; a light tan, not ruddy or pale. And yes, good looking.'

She'd clearly taken more than a passing glance at the man. 'I don't suppose you'd be able to draw him?' he asked, smiling.

She shook her head, looking at him with a strange smile on her face. 'I know what you're thinking,' she said. 'Just a drab, middle-aged woman getting desperate because she can't keep a man. I can assure you that this is not the case.'

'You need to tell me more about the circumstances of your meeting,' said Ian. 'Unless you can persuade me otherwise, I can't search for someone who might not want to be found.'

She sighed loudly. 'Why not? The police do it all the time.'

He shook his head. 'Only if they are wanted in connection with a crime. They can appeal for people to come forward, for example as witnesses, but we live in a free country. Everyone has a right to come and go as they please.'

'So if I told you he'd committed a crime, you would look for him?'

'No, I'd tell you to report it to the police.' But she had piqued his interest. 'Has he committed a crime?' he asked.

'Not as far as I know,' she said, looking down at her hands, leading Ian to wonder if she might be lying about that. 'But I can assure you that I need to find him urgently.'

'Whether he wants to be found or not?'

'What makes you think he doesn't want to be found?'

The fact that he hadn't turned up when he was supposed to? 'I can't possibly know,' he said. 'Unless you tell me more about the whole situation.'

She studied her fingernails then tapped the desk impatiently with them. Her expression, he thought, growing mutinous.

He stared back at her with what he hoped was an equally stubborn look. They were playing a staring game that Ian knew he was going to win. She needed him a lot more than he needed her. He had a diary full of cases and one more or less would not make much difference. All the same, he hoped she would give in and tell him what it was all about. She'd intrigued him.

She sighed and fiddled with the clasp on her handbag.

Ian took pity on her. 'Perhaps you could start by telling me a bit about yourself,' he suggested. 'Are you local? Do you work around here?'

'I moved here from London four years ago. I lived with my mother in Sevenoaks and commuted to a job in the city.'

'What kind of work were you doing?'

'Just an office job,' she said. 'Until he died, I worked for my stepfather, who dealt in antiques. After his death, we sold up. I didn't want to carry it on without him. I didn't really care what I did so I took what was available. I worked in an insurance office as a loss adjuster. Not the most exciting job. It was a relief to leave it when we moved here.'

'You left London for a new job?'

'Not exactly. Mother had a stroke and we needed to downsize to somewhere more convenient. The house we lived in was large and old. It had uneven floors and draughty windows. It was not an appropriate environment for a frail, elderly lady. But it was in the stockbroker belt. House prices in the Home Counties are ridiculous so we decided to leave the area. We bought a very nice house in St Andrews and raised a sizeable amount in capital.'

St Andrews was probably a good place in which to be an elderly person with spare cash. 'Does your mother like living there?' he asked.

'She died eighteen months ago.'

'I'm so sorry,' he said, wondering how he could have been so tactless.

'You needn't be,' she said. 'Sometimes there are worse things than being dead. She did enjoy the garden and pottering around the town for a while, but then she had a second stroke from which she never recovered.'

'And you've not considered returning to London?'

'No, I'm quite happy here. I have a good job and an easy commute. No mortgage and enough money to lead a comfortable life.'

'And recently you were in Paris,' he said, tapping the photo that still lay in front of them.

She looked at him, surprised. 'You knew that was taken in Paris?'

'I recognise the painting. It's in the Musée d'Orsay, isn't it?'

She looked grudgingly impressed. To be honest, he felt impressed with himself. It was a lucky coincidence. His host on a recent trip to the south of France had a laptop bag with a reproduction of the same painting. He'd liked the two dancers and had asked about them. One day, perhaps he would travel to Paris and visit the gallery for himself.

'After mother died,' Felicity continued, 'I took a holiday. I no longer had to pay for carers so there was money to spare. I had always wanted to visit Paris and thought I would do it in style. I loved my mother, but my life with her was restricting. I felt I deserved a break. I flew to London and travelled premium class on the Eurostar. I stayed in an hotel near the Opera, and that's where I met Julian. I suppose you could say he picked me up in the bar. At L'Hotel Didier Pierre.'

Really? She didn't look the type to be picked up by men in bars. On the other hand, single middle-aged women were well-known targets for men of dubious character set on robbing them of their savings. He looked again at the shot of Julian's back. Did he look like a con man? Hard to say. Ian wasn't sure what the back view of a con man would look like. He wasn't too sure about the front view, either, but he guessed they exuded an air of confidence and Julian, even in a photograph and without showing his face, certainly did that.

Felicity suddenly laughed in a way he found unsettling. 'I know what you are thinking,' she said. 'And I can assure you that you are wrong. Julian was not after my money. He has plenty of his own.'

'So you met in the bar, and then what?'

'We enjoyed Paris, of course. In style. Julian is an art lover, something of an expert, I understand.'

He hesitated to enquire further into the kind of relationship they had developed, although he would probably need to know if only to understand her urgent need to find him. 'How long did you stay in Paris?' he asked.

'For a few days. Then Julian told me he had things to sort out.

Some dark corners in his life, he told me. But he would be in Edinburgh soon and we arranged to meet under the glass dome in Waverley station at midday last Friday.'

'But he wasn't there.'

'Exactly.'

'You're sure you had the correct date?'

She gave him a withering look. 'Of course.'

He hated to suggest it, but perhaps the guy had just changed his mind. Searching for him could be seen as stalking. He was wondering how to suggest it tactfully when she spoke again.

'He must be found,' she said. 'He is in danger.'

'What kind of danger?'

'I... I don't know. Perhaps I was too hasty saying that. But I am worried about him.'

Once again, Ian had the impression that she wasn't telling him everything. She'd said the man was in danger and then suddenly backtracked. Why would she do that? 'Look,' he said, standing up ready to escort her to the door. 'We are rather busy at the moment. I need to discuss this with my partner. Can I contact you in a day or two?' He passed her a notepad and asked her to write down her contact details. She wrote down a number. A landline with a local code and an email. No mobile number or any clue about where she lived. 'I'll need an address,' he said. 'Also a mobile number.'

'I'll give you my address if you take the case,' she said. 'I do not use a mobile phone.'

Absolutely her choice, he supposed. But she was possibly the only person under the age of about ninety in the whole of Fife who didn't use a smartphone.

AFTER SHE LEFT, Ian took Lottie for a stroll down to the waterside to think. Thinking was something he did best with a pint in his hand, so they called in at the Pigeon, a pub conveniently close to the Greyport harbour wall. He bought his pint and then thought that while he was here, he might just as well have some lunch, so he ordered a ham sandwich and a packet of crisps – bacon flavour, Lottie's favourite. The bar was crowded with regulars and although there was a fresh autumn breeze, he wanted to think uninterrupted, so he carried everything outside, pulled his coat collar around his ears, sat down on the wall and thought about that morning's meeting. Lottie hopped up onto the wall next to him, not taking her eyes off the packet of crisps. Lottie was a good judge of character. Ian had been known to turn down clients simply because Lottie had growled at them. But she had barely acknowledged Felicity. A cursory bark when she rang the doorbell, a quick uninterested glance, then an hour spent snoozing in her bed next to the boiler in the kitchen. Ian was on his own here.

What had he really made of Felicity Bright? She intrigued him and repelled him at the same time. No, repelled was too strong. But he definitely mistrusted her. He was sure she had not been telling him the truth, at least, not the whole truth. She'd not said anything about the nature of this friendship with the man called Julian. Had they simply met, chatted and discussed art? Or had there been more to it?

He fed a handful of crisps to Lottie, who had huddled close to him for warmth – he'd never been a believer in coats for dogs. Then he drained his pint and walked home, back to the office. He'd talk it through with Molly. She was generally far better than he was with people. It was a pity she had been out of the office today, but he'd play her the recording he'd made and see what she thought. Whether it was a case they should take or not.

3

The next day Molly was back in the office. She'd been working on what they had called the 'catnapper of Tayport' case. Their client was a woman by the name of Dorothy Spriggs, who lived on her own in the village with a cat called Ferdinand the Special. Ferdy, as Ian and Molly renamed him for convenience, had upped sticks and moved in with a Mr Jones who lived three doors down. Ms Spriggs accused him of luring Ferdy into his house with expensive snacks of smoked salmon and fresh cream. She had reported the matter to the local police, who recommended Ian and Molly as being more appropriate to handle the matter. Occasionally, Ian was forced to reassess the convenience of working closely with the local police, and on this occasion was all set to turn it down. But Molly was all for taking the case. 'We need to have the local community on our side,' she insisted.

'Okay,' said Ian. 'But it's all yours.'

It took two days for Molly to sort it. She visited Mr Jones, who insisted, 'That blasted cat strolls in whenever it feels like it and helps itself. And if it prefers my house to hers, well it's a free country. It's up to the bloody cat where it lives.'

At that point there was no sign of the cat in Mr Jones' house, so

Molly concealed herself in a nearby hedge and kept watch. The cat appeared and duly entered Mr Jones' house by the front door, which he'd left open. There was no evidence of any luring or bribery. A fact she reported back to Ms Spriggs.

'Cat sorted?' Ian asked as she came into the office.

'All settled,' she said. 'Ms Spriggs coughed up for a can of stuff that repels cats and watched while Mr Jones sprayed his front garden with it. And in return he promised to carry Ferdy back to her should he cross the barrier and turn up in his kitchen again.'

'I hope you're invoicing her for that.'

'Of course. She agreed to a fee before I started.'

Molly was definitely an asset, he thought as she went into the kitchen to make coffee. He doubted he would have dared to suggest cat negotiations were a fee-paying matter. As others had pointed out, he was probably too nice for hard-nosed negotiations over fees.

Molly put a cup of coffee down in front of him and opened a packet of chocolate biscuits. Ian took one with a slight feeling of disappointment. Molly usually baked shortbread or brownies. He didn't dislike chocolate biscuits, and with recent remarks concerning his waistline, he was probably lucky to get anything. But chocolate was bad for dogs. He couldn't remember why, but it meant that however much Lottie drooled and rolled her eyes at him, she couldn't have one.

'How did it go yesterday?' Molly asked. 'Was it a new case?'

'Possibly. I said I'd get back to her in a day or two. I'm not sure what she wants is ethical.' He outlined Felicity Bright's visit and played the recording he'd made.

Molly bit into a second biscuit and played the recording again, looking thoughtful. 'My first reaction is that she gave him money and he walked out on her. You hear about that sort of thing, don't you? Lonely women targeted by unscrupulous men.'

'I thought so too, but she was adamant that she hadn't given him anything.'

'Is she stalking him?'

'I did wonder that. If there's any hint of it, we can't take the case.'

In fact, stalking was an offence. He'd have to report her to the police. 'Did you notice how she told me he was in danger and then changed that to just being worried about him?'

'That was odd,' said Molly. 'As if she suddenly thought she'd told you too much.'

'Or perhaps she felt she'd told me a lie too far.'

'Either way, we can't know if it's true or not without finding out a lot more.' Molly started to clear away the coffee things. 'So what are you planning to do?'

He'd spent a sleepless night wondering that. He didn't want to turn away a client with a genuine need to find someone. He just had no idea if this was genuine or not. Eventually, at around four in the morning, he'd got up and made a cup of tea, spent an hour trawling the Internet, and finally made a plan, which he'd scribbled down on the back on an envelope. Then he went back to sleep.

Now he pulled the envelope out of his pocket and read it to Molly.

1. *Find out all there is to know about Felicity Bright.*
2. *Discover why she thinks Julian is in danger.*
3. *Search for men wearing red overcoats.*
4. *If, unlikely as it seems, we find Julian, offer to act as a go between and deliver a letter to her explaining his non-appearance.*

Molly read the list. 'The first is easy. Not sure about the second. She didn't give you any details, did she?'

'She barely gave me a description until I pressed her for it.'

'We need to know if she has any evidence that he is in danger. I suppose the second step would be to look at what she has and then try to find out if it's genuine.'

Ian agreed. 'We'll only take the case if she can tell us why she said that.'

'Three looks impossible,' said Molly, running her finger down the list. 'We'd need to find men who *own* red coats. I guess Julian doesn't wear his all the time. I can't think where you'll even start with that.'

Ian idly tapped *red coat societies* into Google. All that came up was a group of women of a certain age who wore red hats and went out in them in noisy groups to have fun. Interesting but not helpful.

'And four,' Molly continued, 'won't happen unless three does.' She handed the list back to him.

'You think it's a non-starter? Shall I just tell her we can't do it?'

'And spend all our time on wandering spouses and employment checks? Absolutely not. This sounds like fun.'

She was right, of course. It had been dull since their return from Dundas Farm. It would be a challenge, but this case might be just what they needed to spice things up again. 'Let's get started then,' he said, rubbing his hands enthusiastically. 'Clear a space on the board and we'll do some brainstorming.'

Molly checked some old cases with him. 'We don't need those any more, do we? It's all saved electronically.' He nodded and she wiped them off with a damp cloth. Then she picked up a pen. 'What shall we call the case?' she asked.

'The man in the red overcoat,' he said, not having to think very hard about it.

Molly wrote it at the top of the board and then divided it into two columns. 'Shall I start with Felicity?' she asked. 'What do we know already?'

'That she left a dull but apparently well-paid job in London a few years ago and now works in Dundee. Her mother died recently, leaving her a house in St Andrews and a fair bit of capital. And she went on holiday to Paris a couple of weeks ago.'

Molly wrote it on the board and then stared at it. 'Would it be worth asking Duncan if there was anything suspicious about the mother's death?'

Ian laughed . 'You're thinking like a detective,' he said. 'And it's always worth keeping the local police inspector up to speed, so we'll give Duncan a call. The woman had a stroke so it's unlikely to be on his radar, but he'd probably like to know what we're looking into.'

Molly made a note of everything Ian said. 'Do you know what she does now? And where she works?' she asked.

'She didn't say. But before he died, she worked with her stepfather in an antiques business. She sold it after his death and got a job as a loss adjuster in an insurance company.'

'If she has experience in insurance, perhaps that's where she's working now.'

'Could be, although she more or less said it was a dull job. Perhaps she's gone back to antiques.'

'We know that she's working in Dundee, so we could check out antique dealers and insurance companies there. I'll make a list of likely places and we can call them.'

'And when we've done that, we'll nose around a bit. See if we can chum up with some of her colleagues. Hopefully it will be in the city centre or waterside. They'll use local coffee shops and sandwich bars.'

'Definitely good places to catch up with any gossip,' Molly agreed. 'Shall we take a look at where she lives?'

'She wouldn't give me her address. Said she'd wait until I accepted the case.'

'That shouldn't be a problem,' said Molly. 'There can't be that many Brights in St Andrews. We can check the voter rolls.'

That was why he liked working with Molly. She got a buzz out of trawling lists for information. Something he was happy to hand over to her. 'Okay,' he said. 'I'll check out the mother's death certificate while you make lists of possible businesses in Dundee. Then I'll call them while you go through voter rolls. When you find her, you can go and chat to the neighbours.'

By the end of the day, they had an address in St Andrews and confirmed that Mrs Bright had died from a stroke. She'd been seeing her doctor regularly and there had been no reason to suspect it as anything other than a natural, even expected, death. They hadn't discovered where Felicity Bright worked. But Ian thought he had narrowed it down to a dozen possibilities. He could have called them and asked to speak to Felicity, but he wanted to avoid actually being put through to her, so he kept each call to an anonymous enquiry about whether or not she worked there. Most of the businesses he called told him that no one of that name worked for them and he crossed them off his list. Four of them, two insurance companies and two antique outlets, had told him they were not able to disclose information about their employees. More than likely, he thought, that she worked at one of them. 'We'll go to Dundee tomorrow,' he said. 'Ask around at these four places and then get some lunch there.'

'It's a pity we don't have a contact in Paris,' said Molly. 'We could ask about both her and Julian at the hotel she stayed in. I don't suppose our budget would run to a weekend in Paris, would it?' She fluttered her eyelashes at him. 'I could go on my own to keep the cost down.'

He laughed. They were doing well, but not that well. 'Nice try,' he said. 'But no. At least not right now.'

Felicity had told him the name of the hotel she'd stayed in. L'Hotel Didier Pierre. He checked it out online. A rather kitsch-looking place with modern chandeliers and frilly curtains. He clicked on the gallery and found photos of bedrooms with flounced bedcovers and a bar furnished with brass tables and pink lampshades, presumably where Julian had picked her up. Had she, in all innocence, wandered into the kind of establishment where men prowled for gullible women with money to spare? He was probably being unfair to the hotel. The décor might be tawdry, but that simply meant that whoever was in charge of it had questionable taste. He checked for contact details and found an email booking form and a phone number. Would they respond to an email from him if he was merely asking about one of their guests and didn't actually want to book a room? Or should he call them? But what would he ask? They wouldn't give any details of who had been staying there, particularly if he didn't even know the name of one of the people he was interested in. In any case he doubted his French was up to it. His enquiries would have to be email ones. But he could hardly send an email and expect them to send the name and address of a man who had been seen in the bar wearing a red overcoat.

It was time to finish work for the day. They had made some progress and had a plan that would keep them busy for a couple of days. Unpaid days. But it looked as if they would take the case as long as Felicity didn't have a criminal record for stalking or had been suspected of murdering her mother. Assuming they found out more about her, he'd contact her in a day or two, offer to look for Julian and act as a go-between.

4

Ian liked living in Greyport. His decision to move there had been a random one based on cursory searches around one or two property websites. But as things turned out it had been an excellent choice. Greyport had kept its village feel while still being a fun mix of commuters and families, quite often commuters with families. It had changed very little since he'd moved there three years ago. One of the attractions for him had been its closeness to Dundee, with the likelihood of PI work for him. Unlike Greyport, Dundee *had* changed. It had become a city of many parts; the old town with its sandstone buildings and dingy passageways, a tourist centre with the V&A and the Discovery, and further along the waterfront a burgeoning of high-rise luxury flats, hotels and office blocks. It was also in competition with Glasgow for the title of Scotland's drugs capital, but apart from a brief clash with one of its major drug dealers, Ian usually had more to do with Dundee's respectable residents.

Yesterday's phone calls had narrowed down Felicity's possible workplaces to four. Two, the antique dealers, were in the old town and two insurance offices were on the waterfront. Before they left, he and Molly studied a street map of the city. He circled the four places they planned to watch. We'll park here,' he said, tapping the Gellatley

Street car park with his finger. 'It's an easy walk for both of us from there. You do the waterside and I'll take the old town.'

Molly tapped the addresses of the two insurance companies into her phone.

He wanted to keep this enquiry low key. It would just be surveillance, he told Molly. A chance to observe Felicity. To see where she worked and the kind of people she mixed with. He would take the two antique dealers in the old part of the city and Molly would explore the newer, glitzy companies on the waterfront. It would be easier for Molly. She'd not met Felicity so she could mingle with employees as they came and went from the offices. Felicity would be easy to spot. All Molly had to do was watch out for someone who looked like an extra in a nineteen-fifties film and then note which building she entered or left. They consulted Google Maps and found a coffee shop conveniently placed on a corner with views of the two large office blocks. Molly would take her laptop and look as if she was working. He would lurk around the back streets of the older part of the city and watch people arriving for a day's work at the gloomy sandstone buildings that housed the city's antique dealers.

'What if she doesn't work at any of them?' Molly asked.

'We'll have to think of something else,' he said, hoping that *something else* would come to mind.

BY LATE MORNING Ian's feet were hurting and he was becoming hyper on multiple cups of coffee. He'd found an old-style café with a view of the city square, close to a car park and with a good view of both antique dealers. One was housed in what used to be a bank. It had big windows, and he had a clear view of the interior and the kind of stock they were dealing in, mostly furniture, paintings, silverware and crockery. The other was in an old department store that had been converted into smaller businesses; charity shops, places that unlocked mobile phones, cheap clothing stores and one that sold bric-a-brac. Somehow he didn't see Felicity selling bric-a-brac. He could be wrong, but it didn't feel like a venue that employed someone who wore tailored suits and gloves.

He bought his first cup of coffee, watched an encouraging number of people emerge from the car park and make their way into the buildings, but not Felicity. He sat there for a couple of hours before deciding it was a waste of time. Was he wrong to focus on the antique shops? He moved on to more coffee shops outside more offices and shops hoping to catch the lunch trade. But then he thought about Felicity and decided she was probably more of a sandwich lunch at her desk type. He couldn't see her with the groups of chatty young women with long glossy hair and short dresses who gathered in hipster type coffee bars for a chat over chai latte and avocado wraps, or whatever was currently the go-to lunch. He texted Molly to tell her he'd had no luck at all and it was probably time to get back to the office. *Lunch first* was her reply. *Meet at that sandwich place near where we parked.*

He knew the one. Nice crusty rolls filled with fresh mackerel or locally grown tomatoes. His mouth was already watering as he texted her a thumbs up.

SHE'S LOOKING *pleased with herself*, Ian thought as Molly arrived and settled next to him at the table he had found near the window. They ordered cheese toasties and bottles of sparkling water.

'How did you get on?' Ian asked, while they waited for their food.

'Found her,' said Molly with a grin.

'You met her?'

'No, but I saw her and then had a long chat with some of her workmates. Staff, I should probably call them. Turns out she's quite important.'

'You're sure it was her?'

'Definitely. Like you said, she was easy to recognise – black suit, court shoes, hat and gloves,' said Molly as their toasties arrived.

'You saw her arrive at work?' he asked, taking a bite of his toastie and burning his mouth on the cheese. He reached for a glass of water.

Molly shook her head. 'No, I watched her leave. She was picked up in a black Mercedes at eleven. I've got the number.' She handed him a piece of paper. He put it into his wallet ready to check when they got back to the office. 'Just after that, a crowd of girls left the same building and came over for coffee. It was quite busy, so I offered to share my table with them and got them talking about work. I said I was thinking of applying for a job in insurance and asked what it was like working there and if the boss was nice.'

'They work for Felicity?'

Noticing his discomfort, she took a cautious bite of her own toastie. 'She more or less runs the place. She's an area manager.'

Ian took another gulp of water, got out his notebook and wrote down the name of the company. 'Do they like working for her?'

'I think they're a bit scared of her. She's away for the rest of the day, they said, so they were taking an early lunch. I think they kind of respect her but mock her at the same time.'

'Did they say what the work was?'

'Just insurance. Cars, house contents and travel, they said. Sounds very boring.'

Ian was wondering if that might just be cover for something else. He'd check out the company when they got back to the office, but he wasn't likely to find anything. He'd no real reason to think that Felicity was anything more than a high-powered loss adjuster. Being driven away in a big black car probably just meant she was off for a spot of high-level loss adjusting. 'Did they know anything about her personal life?' he asked.

'Mostly speculation. One of them said they'd seen her at a bar in town in evening dress with a man in a dinner jacket. But she doesn't talk about anything outside work and doesn't encourage them to talk about themselves, either.'

'So, no hobbies that she wants to share?'

'Like what?'

'I don't know. Singing in a choir, perhaps, or amateur dramatics. Something she might try to encourage people to go to.'

'Selling raffle tickets for guide dogs?'

'Does she do that?'

'Not as far as I know. It was just an idea.'

Ian poured himself another glass of water and took a bite from the now cooling toastie. 'Well, you've done a lot better than me,' he said. 'Well done.'

'What are we doing now?' Molly asked as she finished her toastie. 'We could go to St Andrews and have a look at her house, maybe talk to the neighbours.'

He'd prefer to get back to the office and follow up on the car Molly had seen, maybe check out the company Felicity worked for. 'It's probably best if you go on your own,' he said. 'We don't want her to know we're checking up on her.'

'But she won't be there. She's gone off for the day in a posh car.'

'Which might drop her off at home. Or the neighbours might see me and come up with a recognisable description. No, you should go on your own. And you need to think of a reason for knocking on people's doors.'

'Go undercover again?' Molly asked, looking enthusiastic. She'd enjoyed her undercover work at Murriemuir.

'Can you think of a cover?'

'I've got just the thing,' she said. 'There's a fundraiser for the Greyport school in a couple of weeks. Dad's printed a load of flyers for it. I could do a leaflet drop in her road.'

'A bit out of the way, isn't it? Won't St Andrews schools have their own fundraisers?'

'Ours is a bit different,' she said. 'Gav is coming as a celebrity guest.'

'Oh yeah, a special favour?' Having an ex-rock star as a friend clearly had its uses. Even if his boy-band days were a distant memory.

Molly blushed. 'Most of the school mums are about my age so they'll remember him, and he said he might bring an alpaca or two for the kids to stroke.' She opened her bag and pulled out a pack of leaflets with a picture of Gavin Stamper, his arms around the necks of two alpacas.

That could work, he thought. Even if they did take Felicity on as a client and she recognised Molly as a hawker of leaflets, it would just be a coincidence. 'Go this afternoon,' he said. 'I'll follow up on one or two things from this morning and then start searching for Julian.'

'How are you going to do that?' Molly asked.

'I've absolutely no idea,' he said.

5

Once back in Greyport, Molly headed off in her car to St Andrews while Ian phoned Duncan and asked him for the name of the owner of the black Mercedes that had picked Felicity up from work that morning.

While he waited for Duncan to reply, he did some background checks on the insurance company that employed Felicity. He wasn't sure what he'd expected to find but was nevertheless a little disappointed to discover that it was a long-standing and highly respected company. It was, and always had been, solvent. There were very few recorded disputes or complaints made to the regulator. Its rates were considered fair, and its settlement of claims was timely. Its employees were treated well, and its pension fund was in excellent order. So if Felicity turned out to be involved in anything disreputable it was not on company time.

The car turned out to be only slightly more interesting.

'It belongs to a Douglas Craigie,' said Duncan, dictating an address to Ian.

'Do you know anything about him?' Ian asked. That would be interesting. If this man had been involved with the police, what was his connection to Felicity?

'He's a semi-retired lawyer,' said Duncan.

'Semi-retired?'

'He used to work in a large company in Edinburgh but now does a bit of freelance work and sits on various committees.'

'And he's local?'

'Lives quietly on his own in a big house just outside Anstruther. A widower.'

'Not in any way suspicious then?'

'Not at all. I'd probably not have heard of him,' said Duncan, 'only he was burgled a couple of weeks ago.'

That would be his connection to Felicity. A couple of weeks, Duncan had said, so no doubt still in the process of finalising an insurance claim. He ended the call with a twinge of disappointment. Perhaps his misgivings about Felicity were unfounded. She was a blameless, slightly lonely, middle-aged woman with a disappointing love life. He'd just wasted a whole day spying on her and was no nearer deciding whether or not to take the case. He'd no idea what to do about her. Or, for that matter, Julian, who still intrigued him.

He'd take Lottie for a walk. He could let his mind wander and perhaps inspiration would strike. He put Lottie's lead on her, and they walked down to the harbour under gloomy clouds which, by the time they arrived, had become a thin but persistent drizzle. He led Lottie into the harbourside tearoom and ordered a pot of tea – having sunk a week's worth of coffee that morning – and a currant bun.

Just suppose, he thought, *that I was sitting in a bar in a hotel in Paris wearing an expensive and distinctive red overcoat. Who would I be and why am I there? I'm someone in the art world, perhaps.* What was it Felicity had said? *An art lover, something of an expert.* Not an artist, he thought. An artist who could afford expensive coats, not to mention wining and dining well-off ladies, would probably be well known, like Damian Hirst. He wasn't sure who the French equivalent would be. He pulled out his phone and googled *famous French artists living now,* but hadn't heard of any of them. And none were called Julian. He made a list in his notebook; Google well known dealers and critics called Julian. Was that even his real name? He'd have to assume for now that it was. He didn't think googling *art critic with red overcoat* would get him very far.

It might be worth checking the Edinburgh art world, since that was where the mysterious Julian was supposed to have been a few days ago. Unless, of course, he'd never intended being there. Then he remembered that Felicity said he was in danger. Could he perhaps be a forger? Or a dealer in stolen artworks? Duncan would be the person to ask about that. He'd mention it at their next pub meeting.

Lottie was getting restless, so he walked her home and settled down for an evening of likely futile Google searching. He tapped in *French artists* omitting the word *famous*. There were several artists living in Paris called Julian but none of them fitted the description. He did find a photo of one of them wearing a well-cut overcoat. He couldn't tell whether or not it was red, and in any case the guy had died in 1910. Dealers were no better and there was no gallery in either Paris or Edinburgh owned by anyone called Julian. He yawned and shut down his computer for the night, downloaded a book that claimed to be a fast-paced psychological thriller onto his Kindle and settled down in his living room with a bowl of linguine alle vongole – bought from the farm shop and made with local clams – and a can of beer.

IAN WAS UP EARLY the next morning, his sleep having been disturbed in equal parts by unscrupulous men in red coats and the fate of the young detective from the novel that he had fallen asleep over, and who was about to, inadvisably in his opinion, enter a dark and gloomy deserted warehouse on the outskirts of Birmingham.

He watched from the office window as Molly made her way up the path in a raincoat and battling with an umbrella.

'Any luck yesterday afternoon?' Ian asked, as she sank into a chair and took her boots off.

'Quite a lot of interest in the school event. I'm not sure I found out much about Felicity, although her next-door neighbour had quite a lot to say about her mother. Most of it not very complimentary.'

'No mention of Felicity?'

'Only that she was a bit of a recluse. The neighbour hadn't seen much of her, but she did say she had her hands full with work and looking after what she described as *that bad-tempered old bat.*'

'And she'd not become more sociable after her mother died?'

'Apparently not. Some of the neighbours asked if she needed any help with the funeral and stuff, but she didn't take them up on it. They said she was quite stand-offish. But it didn't seem like the kind of road where people are in and out of each other's houses all the time.'

'What's the house like?'

'Modern town house. Quite upmarket with very tidy lawns at the front and separate drives. No fences, but I don't think it's the kind of road where kids go out and play together. There were neighbourhood watch signs on some of the windows and notices saying *no cold callers or salespeople.*'

'Not a student area then.'

'No families either. I should think it's all dinkies.'

'Dinkies?'

'Double income, no kids. You know, young working couples on the make. No children until they can afford a nanny.'

'And a move to a bigger house?'

'Yeah, there were several houses with sale boards outside.'

'An area for the upwardly mobile then. I wonder if Felicity plans to stay there.'

'That might depend on where Julian fits in, don't you think?'

'Hard to say until we can find out more about him.'

'Did you find anything useful?' she asked.

He'd made some discoveries. He wasn't sure how useful they were. 'The car you saw yesterday belongs to a man who was burgled recently.'

'She was probably just going to his house to sort out a claim then.'

'Looks like it.'

Molly looked disappointed. 'I thought big black cars meant rich criminals, Mafia types perhaps, or drug barons.'

'You were hoping she was some kind of female equivalent of the Godfather?'

'It's your fault,' she said, laughing. 'You were the one who said you didn't trust her.'

Fair enough. He had said that. He should be more careful when making assumptions about prospective clients.

'Did you find out anything about Julian?' she asked.

'Not a thing. But I do have one idea.'

'Are you going to tell me about it?'

He grinned at her. 'Not yet. There's someone I need to contact first.'

WHEN WAS IT? Ian wondered, delving into the depths of his email. He'd archived it somewhere and forgotten about it. He cast his mind back over the last few months. It would have been after he returned from France but before he went to Dundas Farm. That narrowed it down to a couple of weeks. His email contained a number of folders. Easier, he'd always thought, to find things. But it seemed he was wrong. He had family folders, client folders and business folders, but Anna Lymington didn't fit into any of those. What about his folders for old cases. Would he put a recent email from Anna into that? He clicked on the one called *Drumlychtoun* and found that was exactly what he'd done. And because it was some time since the Drumlychtoun case, Anna's email was right at the top.

The day they'd met, Anna had turned up on his doorstep demanding to know why he was working for her grandmother, a forceful lady by the name of Ailish Lyton. He wasn't working for her. He was working for her brother, Xander, who had hired him to find Ailish. The sister he had not seen for more than fifty years. At that point in time Xander knew nothing at all about Anna. Or even the fact that his sister had given birth to a son, now deceased, who was Anna's father. The day Anna hurled herself into Ian's life, he had recently returned from London where he had tracked down Ailish, visited her at her flat in Kensington and left his card on a table in her living room. Anna, at the time an excitable student, had travelled from St Andrews by train for a party and decided while in London to call on the grandmother she had never met. Returning to Scotland, she landed on his doorstep and fell in love with Lottie. They worked as a team for the rest of that day and compared notes. He was able to tell her about family she had never heard of. And she filled him in with details of her own father. A huge surprise for Xander, who had only ever expected to find a sister.

He'd been sorry that, because of the pandemic, Anna had returned to her home in France and hadn't come back to complete her degree at St Andrews. During the Drumlychtoun case she had become more than merely the great-niece of his client. They'd kept in touch all through the pandemic. Anna sending multiple pictures of her life, most of which involved dogs. Ian replying with what he thought were probably boring uncle type emails with pictures of Lottie. But however fond one was of a dog, there were limited photo opportunities. His pictures lacked variety; Lottie running on the beach, Lottie shaking off water after a plunge into the sea, Lottie asleep. That was about the limit of her photographic repertoire. His emails had trailed off until he was unexpectedly invited to spend a week's holiday with Anna's family at their home near Carcassonne. And while there, he learnt of Anna's plans to return to Scotland that autumn to work with her great-uncle on the Drumlychtoun estate.

Her latest email had arrived after his return home and brought the news that Great-uncle Xander, otherwise known as the Laird of Drumlychtoun, had suffered a stroke. A minor one, Ian was relieved to hear, and while he'd made a good recovery, his vision was still affected. If that had been all, Xander would now be back at work with as much energy as ever. But a few weeks before he'd planned to return to full-time running of the estate, his wife Bridget had slipped on some rocks while gathering seaweed and broken her leg in several places. Anna had brought her return to Drumlychtoun forward by a month, and if Ian had not been so tied up at Dundas, he'd probably be able to remember exactly when she said she was arriving. But there was something else in her email that was jangling around in his head, hence his need to find it.

He clicked open the email and found what he was looking for. He looked at his calendar and realised that Anna would be back in Scotland quite soon. It was not that that interested him so much as her itinerary. She was going to take the train to Paris and spend a few days there with a cousin. Then she would take a flight to Edinburgh. She asked Ian to meet her at the airport and drive her to Drumlychtoun, Bridget being unable to drive on account of her broken leg and Xander having been advised not to drive until his eyes had made a full recovery and he'd been supplied with distance glasses. Ian had been about to depart for Dundas but sent her a short reply saying that he'd be happy to meet her and to text him her flight time.

Now he read the email again and studied the dates on his calendar. In two days she would be in Paris, shopping and nattering in bars, she said. Plenty of time then for her to visit both the Musée d'Orsay, not that he thought she'd learn much there, and to drink in the bar of L'Hotel Didier Pierre. He'd happily foot the bill for both Anna and her cousin.

Anna had once appointed herself his assistant for one day. A role for which she'd shown huge enthusiasm and Ian hoped she would feel as keen about helping him once again. He sent her an email reminding her that if she wanted him to meet her at the airport, she would need to send him some flight details, and then asking if she'd be willing to do a little work for him while she was in Paris. Nothing too onerous, he explained. Just a visit to an art gallery or two and an evening drinking in the over-embellished bar of a hotel near the opera.

Her reply came quickly. *You bet,* she told him. *Always fancied doing more as your assistant. Give me all the gen. BTW I'm on an early flight. Shall we go for a posh breakfast in Edinburgh before you drive me to Drumlychtoun?*

He smiled as he read the email and then typed his reply.

We'll go to the Donald of Drummond, he wrote. *I went there once with your grandmother when I was acting as her paid escort at a funeral – not a career move I've pursued since.* He attached a copy of the photo of Julian and explained a little of Felicity's possible case. *Probably too much to expect that Julian is a regular at the hotel, but people might remember seeing him there. Not hopeful that you'll find out much at the gallery, but you might try joining whatever friend scheme they have (I'll reimburse you) and get chatting to people in the members' bar. See if anyone's heard of a critic or a dealer called Julian.*

He clicked send and immediately felt better. So much so that he thought he and Lottie deserved an evening in the pub. He looked at his watch. *Too soon,* he thought. Only someone with a serious drink problem would start drinking at four in the afternoon. And in any case, he wasn't hungry yet. Lottie might be, but one never knew. Lottie was always ready for a meal. He'd work for a couple of hours and then walk down to the village for a pie and a pint.

While he was waiting, he thought he'd try to find out more about Douglas Craigie's burglary. It probably had nothing to do with his search, but it would tell him a little more about the kind of work Felicity was involved in.

Craigie lived close to the small town of Anstruther. A fishing port further down the Fife coast, it was noted for a famous fish and chip shop on the seafront. But that was a hangout for walkers and tourists rather than burglars. He paid a small subscription and gained access to a local newspaper site that covered the Fife area. He typed Douglas Craigie's name into a search box, and it was not long before he found what he was looking for. Craigie appeared in a photograph of a local charity dinner held on the evening of 30th September. Ian then searched for burglaries reported on that night. There were two in the Anstruther area. One was a break in at a mobile phone shop. The other at Stonebridge House. A quick check told him that Stonebridge House was indeed the residence of Douglas Craigie, so he delved further and found details of the crime. The house was broken into at around nine-thirty that evening and a number of valuable items taken; six paintings by Scottish artists dating from eighteenth century to contemporary, a few items of silver and some of the late Mrs Craigie's jewellery. The house was a few miles out of the town and none of the neighbours heard or saw anything suspicious either that evening or in the days before the burglary. Probably, Ian thought, because houses around there had very large gardens and were separated from each other by high walls and fences. It was an area where the residents valued their privacy. Craigie did not own a dog and his burglar alarm was little more than a metal box on the wall that said *burglar alarm,* and which the thieves had disabled by stuffing a sock into it before forcing their way into the house by smashing a downstairs window. It was assumed they left the house the same way.

Ian was curious. Someone must have known that Craigie would be out that evening. And if they knew where he was going, they would also know that they had plenty of time. So why had they not taken more? Unless the paintings were very small, they would have needed a van to transport them, so why hadn't they ransacked the house for laptops and smartphones, and flat-screen TVs, or valuable sets of golf clubs? Ian was sure Craigie played golf. It was pretty much compulsory for men of his standing in this part of Scotland. Why not take all of Mrs Craigie's jewellery and their entire collection of silverware? The answer was obvious. They knew the paintings that were in the house and had targeted them. The extra items were a smokescreen. These were professional art thieves. And since Felicity had been seen getting into Craigie's car, it looked as if she was involved in the theft, if only as its insurer. And Felicity had a connection to the art world, admittedly a tenuous one, through the mysterious Julian.

He was suddenly determined to take the case.

He sat at his desk and drafted an email to Felicity. He offered himself as an intermediary. *At this stage,* he wrote, *anything more would be dubious ethically.* But if she was happy to proceed on those terms, he would take her case.

He saved it for Molly to look at the next day.

Then he looked at his watch. Still too early for the pub, so he searched for more information about Douglas Craigie. He found plenty, but nothing to suggest he was anything other than a fine, upstanding citizen. Craigie was active in charities, a member of the local council and a keen supporter of the National Trust for Scotland.

Ian found a photograph of him handing out awards to students at a school speech day in Cupar. He was a good-looking man, perhaps in his late fifties, with a rugged complexion and a friendly smile, sporting the tie of the Royal St Andrews Golf Club – Ian had been right about the golf. Mrs Craigie had died three years previously after a long illness. They had a daughter, now married to a lawyer in Edinburgh. All interesting stuff, but nothing to suggest he was any more than an innocent victim of a burglary.

Ian shut down his computer, gathered up Lottie and her lead, and headed to the village.

6

Just as well he didn't eat here very often, Ian thought two days later as he studied the menu. The price of breakfast was about what he usually spent on three days' worth of meals, dog food included. But he liked it here. The Donald of Drummond managed to exude good old Scottish aristocratic values, mostly, he suspected, recreated through nostalgic rose-tinted glasses with an eye to the American tourist market; tartan carpets, portraits of posh-looking gentlemen in kilts who were more often than not holding the bleeding corpses of whatever it was they had just shot, and salmon in glass cases. But the food was excellent and celebrating Anna's return was worth splashing out. She smiled at him across the table, suntanned, her curly hair bleached golden by French sun. Ian looked out of the window at a grey, damp Edinburgh morning.

'You'll miss the sun,' he said. 'Scotland must be a bit of a shock.'

'Yeah, that first gulp of damp Scottish air as you get off the plane. But I've packed all my warmest clothes. I *have* spent a winter in Scotland before, remember, so it won't be a complete surprise. Anyway, Xander and Bridget have spent a fortune on the west tower where the estate office is. I'm getting one of the new flats which are all heated and triple-glazed.'

Ian opened the menu. A bulky affair printed on thick paper and encased in a red leather folder with a crest. An embossed gold crest. The Drummond coat of arms, he assumed, although he knew nothing about the Drummond clan or heraldic crests, or their connection to the hotel. For all he knew, it might have been designed by someone in the hotel's publicity department last year. But it didn't matter. Red leather and gold lettering fitted well with the image of ageless opulence that attracted guests to the place.

The breakfast menu was lengthy and descriptive. For Ian it would be a toss-up between eggs benedict made with Ayrshire ham and free range Perthshire eggs, served on an authentic locally sourced brioche and topped with a luscious hollandaise sauce, or grilled sourdough topped with creamy scrambled eggs. He assumed these would be the product of the same Perthshire free range chickens.

'What do you think?' He glanced at Anna, who had closed her menu and put it down on the table next to her plate.

'Crushed avocado.' She grinned at him. 'I can't resist the thought of *Mac's home-baked whole grain and pumpkin seed toast*,' she said, quoting from the menu. 'Not to mention the organically grown baby tomatoes.'

'Good choice,' he said, but deciding that if he had grains and pumpkin seeds, he'd spend the rest of the day picking them out of his teeth. He opted for the eggs benedict. 'Coffee?'

'Of course,' she said, as a woman dressed in a kilt and white blouse took their order and poured coffee from a silver pot.

'I wish you could have brought Lottie,' said Anna, sniffing her coffee appreciatively and taking a sip.

'She'd have been a nuisance. I couldn't have left her in the car at the airport and I don't suppose the valet service here caters for dogs.'

'They might. There will be old ladies with spoiled Pekineses and film stars with tiny lapdogs in their Gucci bags. Did you only suggest coming here because they have someone to park the car for you?' she asked with a grin.

'Of course,' he said. 'The only alternative would have been Starbucks in the arrival lounge and Xander would expect me to treat you better than that.'

'Have you seen him recently?' she asked, as their breakfast arrived.

'No. We spoke on Facetime a couple of days ago. He looks well but he's still not allowed to drive. He's got to have tests first. And of course, Bridget's still hobbling around on crutches.'

'It's such bad luck, isn't it? Both of them out of action at the same time. It's just as well I'm going to be there to help them.'

'They'll be thrilled to have you. They sounded very excited when I spoke to them. Xander told me he has a surprise for you.'

'What is it?' she asked, wide-eyed.

'It wouldn't be a surprise if I told you. Anyway, he didn't tell me what it was. Just that I was to be sure to get you there before dark.'

'Can we go and see Lottie first? It's on the way, isn't it? I can't wait to see her. Do you think she'll remember me?'

'I'm sure she will. Lottie never forgets a friend.'

'Did you leave her on her own?'

'No, she's Molly for company.'

'Molly? Oh, your assistant. I can meet her as well.'

'You'll like her, I think. She's very efficient, excellent with clients as well. She'd probably do perfectly well without me there at all.'

'I bet she wouldn't.' Anna frowned at him. 'You shouldn't do yourself down the way you do. You've built up something really special. You should hear the way Xander and Bridget talk about you.'

She was probably right. Work was fine. The rest of his life? Not too good right now. Since the end of the Dundas case, he'd avoided the two women in his life. Or they'd avoided him. He wasn't sure which, but in a lot of ways it was more comfortable like that. Caroline had signed up for an exchange of maths teachers and was currently teaching for a term in a California high school, while some American guy called Brett was doing her job in Dundee. Not a fair exchange. Caroline was teaching at a well-resourced school in a sunny climate with the prospect of weekends at the beach. Brett was at an inner-city school on the wrong side of Dundee with a Scottish winter to look forward to. But at least, Ian thought, Brett stood less chance of being shot by a deranged gunman with a supermarket Kalashnikov. He should contact Brett and suggest an evening at the pub, sampling some warm Scottish hospitality.

Caroline would be home by Christmas, and they could take things up where they had left them. Perhaps. Elsa was an entirely different matter. He'd messed up. Her boss, Mickey Rix, had laid into him. Suggested he was a heartless, selfish oaf. He'd never thought of himself that way, but Mickey was probably right. And he had absolutely no idea what to do about it. He'd put it out of his mind for weeks and when he did think about Elsa, all he could feel was guilt. She was a lovely person and he'd hurt her.

Anna snapped her fingers under his nose and he blinked. 'Where were you?' she asked.

'Sorry,' he said. 'Just… well, never mind. Tell me how you got on in Paris.'

Anna popped the last tomato into her mouth and pushed her plate aside. 'I made notes,' she said, opening her bag and taking out a green moleskin notebook.

'Nice notebook,' he said. 'Did you buy it specially?'

'Absolutely. I thought if I was working for you, I should be properly equipped.' She opened it at the first page, which Ian could see was covered with writing.

'Looks like you had plenty to write about.'

'Yes and no,' she said. 'Eva, she's my cousin, is studying art history in Paris and she has a pass for the d'Orsay. So we started there and went to look at the painting in the photo. There was no one there that looked like the man in the coat, but you didn't really expect that, did you?'

Ian shook his head. Nothing was ever that easy.

'Eva blagged our way into a members' bar by flashing her student pass and saying she was meeting with a dealer,' Anna continued. 'It was all tight little groups of people dressed in black, drinking tiny cups of coffee and looking look like they didn't want to be interrupted, but we talked to the girl behind the bar, and she recognised the coat. She'd spent some time in the cloakroom and it had been left there a couple of times in the summer. She couldn't tell us any more about the man who'd left it, but she did say it was a Jean de Saul Chesterfield.'

'I thought a Chesterfield was a sofa,' said Ian.

'It's a kind of coat as well. Made fashionable in London in the 1840s by George Stanhope, the sixth earl of Chesterfield. We looked it up.'

'And Jean de Saul?'

'A Parisian maker of bespoke overcoats.'

'So this is a one-off?'

'It's probably not the only one they've made, but it's definitely unusual.'

'And expensive, I'd imagine.'

'You could contact them,' said Anna. 'And ask who they've made them for. I'll do it if you like. My French is better than yours.'

'I could get Molly onto that,' he said, although he had not yet noticed if speaking French was one of Molly's skills. 'But our guy could have bought it second-hand so it might not tell us much.'

Anna turned to the next page of the notebook, which again was covered in writing. 'Eva and I went to the bar at the Didier Pierre the next evening and that's where it started to get a bit confusing.'

'How do you mean?' Either Julian was recognised, or he wasn't.

'Several people recognised the photo,' she said. 'Even with only the back view of him. And they gave us a name.' She pointed to the name she had underlined several times in her notebook. 'Claude Lambert.'

'They were sure that was him?'

'Several people confirmed it.'

'Could they tell you much about him?'

'He lives in Paris. No one seemed to know where, but they said he has a gallery and he's a regular at Didier Pierre.'

'Did they know the name of the gallery?'

'No, but Eva thinks it's probably somewhere on the Left Bank.

That's where all the arty Bohemian stuff is. Eva and I walked around there the next day, but there are quite a few galleries and no way of knowing which was his. We checked online and there's no Lambert gallery.'

'And no sign of him while you and Eva were at the hotel?'

'We did ask when they expected him, but someone said they thought he was out of town for a while. We got the impression they think he's a bit dodgy. He meets quite a lot of people in the bar. Eva and I thought he could be either selling on stolen artworks or perhaps forging them.'

Anna and Eva were two young women who were possibly letting their imaginations run away with them. But this wasn't looking good for Felicity. If she had got herself involved with a shady-sounding character who didn't even tell her his correct name, it was just as well he'd not turned up to meet her. Or could she be the one getting involved in dodgy deals? There were definitely connections, the theft of paintings, insurance and Parisian dealers. The burglary at Stonebridge House happened around the same time as Felicity's visit to Paris. His brain was ticking over with possible scenarios. Some kind of racket where paintings were stolen to order, and once insurance claims had been settled, they were sold on to dealers at an inflated price. Had it really been a chance meeting? Had Felicity then arranged to meet Julian to hand over a painting in Edinburgh? One that he'd known in advance was going to be stolen?

Anna turned to another page in her notebook. 'That's not all,' she said. 'We talked to some of the reception staff. I told them I was going to visit a friend in Scotland who had stayed at the hotel a couple of weeks ago and thought she'd left a pink scarf behind. I said I'd be happy to return it to her.'

'A pink scarf? I don't think Felicity is the kind to wear pink.'

'That doesn't matter. I made it up so they'd check and see if she'd left anything in her room. Of course, they wouldn't find anything, but that way I could ask if they remembered her and if they'd noticed anything about her and this Claude or Julian or whoever he is.'

'And did they notice anything?'

'They had no record of her. They checked the register for the dates you said she was there and found nothing.'

'Could she have been staying there under a false name?'

Anna shook her head. 'Hotels have to check passports when people check in.'

Was his case about to be blown out of the water? Ian didn't think so. If anything, he was more intrigued by it than he had been before.

'I gave them your description of her,' Anna said. 'No one like that stayed there on those dates.'

What was this all about? He was beginning to wonder if he'd imagined the whole thing. But Felicity definitely existed. She worked where she said she did and lived at the address on the voter roll. The man in the red coat also existed. But he wasn't called Julian and while he had been at L'Hotel Didier Pierre, Felicity had not.

'But,' said Anna, turning to yet another page in her notebook. 'She had been in the hotel bar. The barman remembered her from your description. He didn't recall whether or not she was drinking with Julian, or Claude, but he didn't think she'd been drinking on her own. He remembers that she left alone, and he thought she was picked up by someone on a motorbike.'

No, surely not. Try as he might, Ian couldn't imagine Felicity on the back of a motorbike. The man must have mistaken her for someone else. Felicity hadn't told him how she got around Paris, but riding pillion was very unlikely.

Anna closed the notebook and put it back in her bag. She'd done well, but Ian was glad that was the end. He didn't think he could handle any more baffling information. He handed over his credit card to pay for the meal, asked for his car to be brought round and they headed home.

ARRIVING BACK IN GREYPORT, Lottie was beside herself with joy at being reunited with Anna. Dogs had good memories. It must be three years since Anna was last there, but Ian remembered that they been besotted with each other then. And Anna adored dogs, all dogs, whatever shape or size. The feeling, it appeared, was mutual. Ian wondered if she'd get the same rapturous reception from Xander's two Labradors. She seemed to hit it off with Molly as well. But that wasn't a surprise. They were both confident, lively young women and not that different in age.

'I'll make us some tea,' said Molly. 'And you can tell us what you discovered in Paris.'

'You can help me sort it out,' said Ian. 'It's all deeply confusing.'

'Does that mean we won't take the case?' Molly asked.

'Absolutely not. After what Anna found out, I'm more determined than ever to go ahead with it. Let's go through it again,' he said. 'See if Molly can unravel any of it.'

Anna read out the notes she'd made. Molly wrote them up on the board and then stood back to look at what she had written. 'Something's going on, isn't it? I'd really like to find out what it is.'

'Me too,' said Ian. 'Felicity may be who she says she is, but she's been lying to us about something. I mean to find out what and why.'

'We need to know why she really wants to find this man,' said Molly. 'And double check it. He may be in danger from *her*.'

'But then would she have told us that he was in danger?' Ian asked.

'She could have been trying to distract you,' said Anna. 'She'd want you on her side so she might have said that, hoping that you'd concentrate on him rather than looking for more about her.'

'Possibly,' said Ian. 'A bit of a risk, though. Wouldn't she expect us to check up on her?'

'We did,' said Molly. 'We discovered what she told us was true. And until Anna started asking questions in Paris, we were quite happy to accept it.'

'We need to set up another meeting,' said Ian. 'Keep Anna's notes, but wipe it all off the board before she comes here again. We don't want her to know we've been making enquiries in Paris. Can you do that while I drive Anna to Drumlychtoun?'

'Sure,' said Molly. 'I'll make a corkboard for it in Fact Stuffer.'

'Fine,' said Ian. He hated Fact Stuffer. Molly had introduced him to it while they were at Dundas Farm. It had its uses, he supposed. Definitely a good way to store information. But he still hated it. It reminded him that he was out of touch with modern techie stuff, and he'd always rather prided himself on being up to date. It also meant he had to wear his reading glasses. And that made him feel old.

7

After mulling over Anna's discoveries in Paris, Ian and Molly decided against sending the email he had drafted. Instead, Molly sent a revised version containing their terms of service and suggesting that Felicity should make an appointment to discuss the details of her case. She replied quickly, which suggested to Ian that she was anxious to get on with the search. That put him at an advantage. A little show of reluctance on his part might make Felicity open up and tell him things she'd planned to keep quiet about.

On the morning of the appointment Molly arrived early. Felicity was going to call in on her way to work. Ian would have preferred a later time, after he'd had a decent breakfast and time to work through his emails, but he could see that an early visit would be convenient for Felicity, and he didn't want to alienate her more than he had to considering he was about to accuse her of lying.

'Do you want to see her on her own?' Molly asked. 'I can go and work in the back office.'

'No, I'd like you to sit in and take notes. And ask questions if you think she's being inconsistent.'

'It sounds like you expect her to change her story.'

Was that what he expected? Maybe. There was something about her that he didn't trust but he couldn't put his finger on what it was.

She might not be trustworthy, but Ian was sure she would be on time. There was something about her appearance that suggested being late was high on her list of misdemeanours. Odd when she made meeting strange men in Parisian bars sound like a day-to-day activity. But there you go. Everyone has different standards. He wanted to be seated at his desk looking businesslike, even a little intimidating, by the time she arrived. He wasn't too confident about conveying a severe image. The best he'd managed to date was when confronting truanting kids in Leith and trying keep a straight face when they came out with more and more extravagant excuses for missing school. He took Lottie next door to spend the morning with Lainie. Lottie was usually good for business. She had a talent for putting people at ease. Except, of course, dog haters and Ian was reluctant to take them as clients. But a small yapping dog wouldn't do a lot for the image he was trying to create. And she'd leave dog hairs on Felicity's immaculate navy-blue suit.

Molly laughed when she saw he was wearing a tie. 'What's that all about?' she asked. 'You look like a schoolteacher.'

'Just trying to look professional,' he said.

'Then you should probably have a deerstalker and a pipe. Or wear that hat Caroline bought you. The fedora.'

'That was a joke,' he said, although he did quite fancy himself in it.

They were interrupted by the doorbell. Molly went to answer it. She showed Felicity into the office and indicated a chair on the far side of Ian's desk. She sat down at her own desk and picked up a notebook and pen.

Ian kept them waiting for a moment then turned towards Felicity. 'Just checking what we have on the case so far,' he said. His computer screen was open at the Fact Stuffer corkboard on which Molly had entered the notes of his previous interview. He stared at Felicity Bright with what he hoped was a piercing gaze.

Felicity sighed impatiently and glared at Molly.

'Molly will be working with us on your case,' said Ian.

Felicity nodded.

'First,' he said. 'I'd like you to explain why you lied to me.'

She slowly removed her leather gloves and placed them on the table next to her handbag. Then she looked up and returned Ian's stare. 'I don't know what you mean,' she said. 'I thought we were here to discuss details of my case before I sign your contract.'

Ian opened Anna's notebook at the page on which she'd recorded the details of her visit to the hotel. Then he laid it page down on the desk in front of him and returned to the computer screen. 'You told me you met Julian in the bar of L'Hotel Didier Pierre where you were staying. An establishment that I understand is in a street close to the Paris Opera.'

'That's correct.'

Ian clicked on a file he had uploaded to the corkboard. It was the recording he'd made of their initial interview.

I stayed in an hotel near the Opera. And that's where I met Julian. I suppose you could say he picked me up in the bar. L'Hotel Didier Pierre.'

Ian paused the recording at that point.

Felicity frowned at him. 'You recorded our conversation?'

'If you recall,' said Ian. 'I asked you if you were happy for me to keep a record of it.'

'I assumed that referred to the written notes you were making.' For a moment she fidgeted with the clasp on her bag. But then she looked him in the eye. 'It seems you misunderstood me,' she said. 'I did stay in an hotel near the opera. I met Julian in a bar at a different hotel.'

'You met him in the Didier Pierre, or is that where you stayed?'

'I forget now. You're confusing me.'

'Then let me help you out. According to the receptionist at the Didier Pierre, there is no record that you ever stayed there.'

'You've been checking up on me?'

'I asked a colleague to make some enquiries. It's standard practice,' he told her. 'A private investigator has to ensure that the work he takes on complies with ethical standards.' *Not true*, he thought. PIs were some of the most unethical people he'd ever met. Particularly those that worked for journalists. But Felicity didn't need to know that, and he liked to think his own standards were exemplary. 'But you haven't answered my question.'

'I don't recall that you asked me a question. You merely confirmed that I told you I had met Julian in the bar at an hotel. Which is true. There would have been no reason for the receptionist to know that.'

'Do you have the name of the hotel you stayed in?' Molly asked.

'I... I'd need to check my itinerary,' she said.

'Perhaps you could email it to Molly if we decide to go ahead with your case,' he said coldly. He hoped that his use of *if* would suggest to her that they were in some doubt about it. There was nothing like giving the impression of turning one's back to hook clients.

'I assume you also checked the other details I gave you? You've no doubt discovered where I live and where I work?'

'We have, yes.'

'In that case you know that I told you the truth. That the business of the hotel was merely a misunderstanding, and we can now proceed with my request for you to search for Julian.'

'We'll take a short break,' he said, handing her a sheet of paper. 'This is your contract. You will see that I require a deposit. If you are agreeable, Molly will take a payment from you now and then we can discuss the information we have collected.' He stood up. 'Coffee?'

BY THE TIME Ian had poured the coffee and handed round a plate of shortbread, Felicity appeared nervous and edgy, which was exactly how he wanted it. Nervous people talked more and were less guarded about what they said. He'd caught her out. She might or might not have lied to him, but the account of her stay in Paris was muddled. He was sure she hadn't told him everything. He returned to the subject of Julian and why she was so set on finding him.

'You told me you think Julian is in danger,' he said.

'I know he is.'

'What makes you so sure?'

'He told me.'

'What exactly did he say?'

'It's not so much what he said as what I saw.'

Was this another lie? Had Julian told her he was in danger or not?

'What you saw?' Molly asked. 'Was this at the hotel?'

'No, in the gallery. I went to use the cloakroom and when I returned, Julian was talking to someone.'

'Nothing very menacing in that,' said Ian, wondering yet again if she was making it all up.

'You wouldn't say that if you'd seen him,' said Felicity. 'The man had grabbed him by the arm, and they were having an argument. When he saw me, he left in a hurry.'

'Did you ask who he was?'

'Of course. But later, after we had left the gallery. We talked about it over dinner. Julian told me he had become involved in a deal that had gone wrong and he knew that there were people who wanted to harm him. After that he became very wary, always checking to see if we were being followed.'

'Did you notice if anyone was following you?'

'Once or twice. There was a car that drove slowly past us, and Julian pulled us both into a narrow side street, then down into the metro station. A couple of times he had phone calls that he ignored.'

'And he postponed your next meeting until he was in Edinburgh. Did he say why?'

'He told me it would all be over by then.'

Molly looked up, puzzled. 'When he wasn't there to meet you, you assumed he was still in danger. Couldn't something have happened already?'

'I'm not sure what you're getting at,' said Felicity.

'I think what Molly is saying,' said Ian. 'Is that, to put it bluntly, we could be too late. You'd be wasting your money trying to get me to stop something that's already happened.'

'Then I want you to find out if that is the case.'

'It could be a matter for the police.'

'Who, as you said yourself, will only be interested if they know a crime has been committed.'

She was right. Police Scotland would not be in the least interested in the disappearance of an unknown man wearing a red coat who might or might not be in danger from an as yet unknown source. It was time to change direction. 'When you met Julian,' he said, 'how did he introduce himself?'

'How do you mean?'

'Did he offer to buy you a drink and then say something like, "Hi, I'm Julian"?'

'I suppose that's pretty much what happened, yes.'

'I assume he is French? Do you speak French yourself?'

'A little. But Julian speaks very good English.'

'And during the time you spent together he didn't tell you anything more than that? No last name, or address, or any hint of what he did or where he came from?'

'He gave me his phone number,' she said. 'But it's been disconnected.'

'We were able to confirm that the man you described was seen drinking in the hotel bar. We even know that you were seen there at the same time.'

'So you confirmed our meeting. It is what I told you.'

'But the man in the photograph was identified by several people as a Monsieur Claude Lambert.'

Felicity shrugged and looked blank. And what she should have looked was surprised. But she didn't. Did she know that name?

'The name means nothing to me,' she said, as if reading his thoughts.

8

Ian peered into one of the brown paper bags he was carrying, identified a cream cheese and salad wrap and handed it to Molly. He'd gone for the roast beef roll, which he now unwrapped and took a bite of. For a moment the still-warm-from-the-oven roll, filled with the tenderest imaginable roast beef laced with tangy Hebridean mustard, drove all thoughts of Felicity from his head. He took a second bite and then remembered they should be planning how to solve the case of the missing man in the red overcoat.

Felicity had left them with the suggestion that they should concentrate their search for Julian in Scotland. For someone who seemed to know little about the person she wanted to find, this seemed very specific. Once again, Ian had the feeling she was not telling them everything. However, limiting their search to Scotland would keep their expenses down and it was the obvious place to start since Julian was supposed to have been in Edinburgh recently.

Ian and Molly had both been puzzled by Felicity. It was reassuring that Molly thought she was something of an enigma as well, and it wasn't just him being a bit thick. He knew he wasn't good at reading women – or whatever the term was – so having an actual woman thinking the same as he did made him feel better. They had decided the best way to clear their heads was a walk down to the harbour, where they could feel the wind through their hair and indulge in freshly made sandwiches. And if that wasn't a good way of clearing their brains, well, at least it would make their cheeks glow and leave them feeling well fed.

'Did you believe Felicity?' he asked Molly, perching himself next to her on the harbour wall and swinging round so that he could dangle his legs over the edge and look down at the beach. *Not for much longer,* he thought. There was a fresh breeze from the estuary and dark clouds gathering over the horizon. Winter was on the way.

'About the hotel?' Molly asked. 'No, I listened to your recording again and she definitely implied she'd stayed at the Didier Pierre.'

Ian took another bite of his sandwich. 'That's what I thought, too. Do you think she was lying when she said she'd never heard of Claude Lambert?'

'Maybe,' said Molly. 'Why come to us if she has things to hide?'

A good question. She must know they would dig into her own background. So either she'd covered her tracks well, and her slip-up over the hotel didn't suggest she had, or she needed to find Julian more than she needed to keep herself hidden. Did that suggest her motives might not be benevolent? Was she out to find and then damage Julian in some way? He couldn't see how. Felicity was petite. The man in the photo was tall and well built. She'd hardly be able to launch a physical attack. Unless she had henchmen to do the job for her or was planning to poison him. But she'd agreed readily enough to Ian acting as a go-between. If it went further than that and Julian agreed to meet her, Ian would suggest that they do it somewhere public. But he was getting ahead of himself. They had to find Julian first and that was not going to be easy.

Lottie nudged his leg with her nose, having given up trying to wheedle anything from Molly, who was strict where dog diets were concerned. Ian was more of a softie. He broke off a corner of his sandwich and fed it to her. 'Interesting that she wants us to focus on Scotland. She must know more about Julian's movements than she's letting on.'

Molly removed an apple from her bag and took a bite. 'We're assuming Julian is French,' she said. 'At least I was. But she did tell us that or are we just going by his name and the fact that they met in Paris?'

'She didn't actually answer that question. She just said he spoke very good English,' said Ian, reaching for his phone and studying the photo of Julian. 'I think he looks French. God knows why. Is it the dark hair, the way it curls down to his collar? And he looks confident, doesn't he? Even if we are only seeing his back view. He reminds me of that bloke in *Call My Agent*.'

Molly looked blank.

'It's a series on Netflix.' He clicked into Google and found some images of the series.

Molly took the phone from him. 'He's a bit like that guy who was in *Murder in Provence*,' she said. 'He's British but pretending to be French. Elegant but not flashy. Stereotypical French. And we both fell for that, but he could be from anywhere. Just because he's not wearing a kilt doesn't mean that he's not Scottish. How often do you wear a kilt?'

'About once or twice every ten years.'

'There you go then. I'd imagine that if you were standing in a Parisian gallery with your back to me, I might assume you were French.'

'Nah,' he said, laughing. 'I don't have the right kind of coat.' He scrunched up his sandwich bag and threw it into a bin. 'We'd better get back to the office and plan what we're going to do.'

'Brainstorming?'

'We'll do one of those mind maps.'

'On the board with coloured pens?'

'Absolutely.'

. . .

It was raining by the time they got back to the office. Lottie shook herself and scuttled into the kitchen to sit under the boiler and warm up.

'I'll put the kettle on,' said Molly, shaking her jacket and hanging it up. 'Any of that shortbread left or have you and Lottie scoffed the lot?'

He gave her what he hoped was an offended look and patted his stomach. 'I have some restraint,' he said. 'And Lottie doesn't get to choose.'

Molly made the tea and carried it with a plate of shortbread into the office.

'Right,' said Ian, handing her a pack of coloured pens. 'Where do we start?'

Molly wrote Felicity's name in the middle of the board and circled it in purple. Then she wrote Julian and Claude Lambert and circled them in orange, linking them with blue lines to Felicity's name. Then she picked up a green pen and looked at Ian. 'What next?'

'Places. Paris with branches for the d'Orsay and Didier Pierre. Edinburgh, Waverley station. And then Dundee and St Andrews.'

'Felicity came from London,' said Molly.

'Okay,' he said. 'Add London. Then start drawing action arrows. Internet searches for Claude Lambert. Felicity as well. We should go a bit deeper into her background.'

'What about Jean de Saul?'

'Who?'

'The guy who makes bespoke coats.'

'Yeah, add him.'

By the time Molly needed to leave, the board looked colourful and busy. 'I'll make a to-do list for tomorrow,' she said. 'We can do Fact Stuffer corkboards for each of these people and what we discover about them.'

Ian glanced out of the window at the dark clouds on the horizon. 'Looks like tomorrow's going to be wet,' he said. 'So a good day for Internet searching. We'll plan from there.' He hoped this case wouldn't turn out to be weeks of sitting at his computer. The Internet was invaluable. But there was a whole world out there, hopefully with clues and real people who could tell him things.

Molly put her jacket on and left. Ian looked at his watch. Lottie had had a good walk today and wouldn't welcome being dragged out in the rain. He had beer in the fridge and one of Jeanie's casseroles in the freezer. He'd take the evening off. Facetime Drumlychtoun and check on how Anna was settling in. And then trawl Netflix for the latest crime drama and reflect on the joys of living alone; eat what he fancied, watch programmes he'd chosen and with no pressure to *talk*. And definitely not regret the lack of female company.

9

Jeanie could be exasperating with her constant hints about Caroline and marriage, but it was worth keeping in with her because when she wasn't nagging him, she was cooking him delicious meals. She and Duncan had brought up two energetic boys with voracious appetites, which meant she was always cooking. The boys had now grown up and left home, but Jeanie still cooked. 'It's not worth cooking for two,' she'd told him. 'Just as easy to batch cook and keep the freezer stocked up.' The Clyde freezer, Ian knew, was a large chest-type one that stood in their garage. Its contents would keep a small town fed in the event of a lengthy siege. Every so often Jeanie overstretched herself. The freezer would hold no more and Ian would be the beneficiary. Consequently, his own freezer was also well stocked and through no efforts of his own. With Jeanie's casseroles and Lainie's cakes, Ian barely needed to shop at all.

He put a chicken casserole in the oven and sat down to scroll through what Netflix had to offer. He decided on *The Scapegoat*. He knew nothing about the film but had enjoyed Andrew Scott's portrayal of Moriarty in *Sherlock*. But Andrew Scott's role in this film was quite different. He was the rather ineffectual brother of a dodgy character who discovered he had a double, and arranged for the man who looked exactly like him to take his place for a while. A dubious concept, Ian thought. However alike the two men were, surely the family would notice.

T HE FILM FINISHED and he was about to shut down his computer when an email pinged in from Caroline. Since she had been away, they had exchanged weekly emails. Caroline sent him photos of California, where she appeared to be leading an enviable life sitting on sun loungers and sipping drinks garnished with exotic fruit and little paper umbrellas. He sent her some photos he was quite pleased with of sunsets over the Tay and one of Lottie playing with seaweed at low tide. Was there, he wondered, an exchange scheme for private investigators? Probably not. It was no more than a distant daydream. Sunny weather would be nice, but did he really want the lifestyle? The Philip Marlowe-type existence that American movies had led him to believe was usual for PIs. In any case, what would he do with Lottie? He couldn't take her with him, or at least he didn't think so. He didn't know a lot about dog passports, but from what he did know he suspected that it would cost three or four times as much as getting himself over there. It was okay for Caroline. She could leave her dog with her sister in Perth. There was no way he could leave Lottie with Lainie for six months. And he didn't want to leave her for that long. It was three and a half years in dog time. Why was he even thinking about it?

He clicked open Caroline's email. It was very short. No photos, just one sentence saying she had a favour to ask him. Could they Facetime this evening at eleven? Your time, she had added. *Why so late?* he wondered, trying to work out the time difference on his fingers. Or was it early? He could never remember if America was behind or ahead. He checked on Google and discovered that eleven p.m. in the UK would be three o'clock in the afternoon for Caroline. It was ten-thirty now. She'd be waiting for his answer. He clicked reply and said that he would look forward to talking to her. Just time to clear away his meal and be back at his computer ready for her call.

CAROLINE CALLED PROMPTLY from her iPad, which she had propped on her lap. She was sitting in a garden in the shade of a white wall up which grew a plant with purple flowers. *Bougainvillea,* he thought. He'd seen it in the south of France but hadn't expected it to be in flower this late in the year. Caroline was wearing a rather fetching sunshine yellow dress with short sleeves and drinking something with ice from a tall glass. In November! He felt a stab of envy. Here on the east coast of Scotland it was rarely short sleeve weather even in August.

'Looking well,' he commented as she turned the iPad to give him a view of a sparkling blue swimming pool, where some teenagers were playing with a blow-up flamingo.

'Jealous?' she asked.

'Definitely. Where are you? And what are you drinking?'

'It's iced tea. They pretty much live on it here. I'm at the home of one of my students. The kids are cooking a barbecue later.'

With large hunks of local meat, he supposed. And juicy hot dogs dripping with mustard. 'Is that why you called?' he asked. 'To make me jealous?'

'Not exactly, although the glorious all-round summer that you get in these parts is kind of related to it.'

For a fleeting moment he wondered if she was about to invite him to join her. But probably not. 'You said you wanted a favour?'

'Yeah,' she said, taking a lazy sip of her drink. 'Just thought you might be able to help me out.'

'I'll do my best,' he said, smiling. 'Although I'm not sure how much use I'll be when I'm so far away.'

'That's just it,' she said. 'What I need you to do is closer to home. Your home, that is.'

'Tell me more.'

'The thing is, I'm having a really great time here.'

'I can see that,' he said.

'I'm seen as rather exotic. Scottish accents are quite rare. They've heard English ones, of course, in the movies, but because I'm from Scotland they expect me to sound like something out of *Braveheart*. I get invitations to barbecues and parties where people just want to hear me say something typically Scottish.'

'Do they expect you to dress up in full highland gear as well?'

'I get asked about kilts,' she said. 'But I see more here than I ever do in Scotland.'

'Really?'

'Yes, it's part of the uniform at the school I'm teaching in.'

Ian tried to imagine a lot of sporty American teenagers in kilts and couldn't. 'I didn't think American schools wore uniforms.'

'They do in posh private schools. And believe me, this one is the poshest of the posh, where no expense is spared – all the latest IT, links to college websites, all the resources I can possibly want, and kids who are as ambitious as hell and have their hearts set on top college places and then jobs as bankers and lawyers. They work hard and even ask me for more so they can keep their grades up and do extra stuff for their applications.'

'Bit of a change from Dundee,' he said. From any school he'd experienced.

'That's the problem,' said Caroline. 'I'm not sure what Brett thought he was going to but a down-at-heel, inner city state secondary has been a real shock.'

'Brett is your exchange partner?'

'That's right. He thought he'd be mixing with the Scottish kilt-wearing gentry and instead he's got the disaffected youth of Dundee, who'd rather be anywhere than in school. He wants to end the exchange early.'

'And you don't?'

'Absolutely not. I'll be sorry to come home at Christmas. The last thing I want is to leave six weeks early.'

'What do you want me to do?'

'Change his mind,' she said, smiling at him.

How exactly did she think he could do that? He could take Brett to Drumlychtoun, he supposed. He might even be able to persuade

Xander to don his kilt for the occasion. But a storm-ridden castle on the Angus coast was hardly hospitable at this time of year, even with the promise of roast venison and log fires. 'I'm not sure what I can do,' he said lamely.

'Ask him out,' she said.

'On a date? I'm not sure that's—'

'Don't be silly. You know that's not what I mean.'

He did, of course. 'So what do you want me to do with him?'

'He's not made a lot of friends. I think he's been taken out for a few meals, but my colleagues aren't all that exciting and living in my house means he's missing out on any social life there is. I'll send you his phone number. I thought you could take him away from Dundee. A nice country pub, perhaps. Or a day out in Edinburgh. I've told him you are a good friend of mine and he's expecting you to call.'

'Sounds like it's all sorted.'

'You don't mind, do you?'

He supposed not. A day out in Edinburgh taking touristy photos was no problem, and he was planning to visit Drumlychtoun anyway. 'Of course I don't,' he said.

'Good,' she said. 'Just keep him busy for the next few weeks.'

He ended the call and made a note of the number she had sent him. He'd call the next day and talk to the guy.

~

BRETT, as it turned out, was far better company than Ian had expected. In his mind he'd had someone in his twenties, bronzed by Californian sun and muscular from all the beach volleyball and rollerblading, or whatever else they did there. Brett was around his own age, slight and bespectacled. 'Nerdy' was the word Ian would have used to describe him. He wasn't surprised the guy was homesick. He had a class full of bored Scottish teenagers who were probably running rings around him. Caroline ruled them with an iron fist and some of them even passed the occasional exam. Brett, he imagined, would be lucky if he got them to sit still for half an hour. He was probably picking up some ripe Scottish language, but his maths teaching skills would be stretched to the limit. No wonder he wanted to go home at the first possible opportunity.

Ian picked him up from Caroline's house where he had the central heating turned to its highest setting. Was someone paying his expenses, or was Caroline going to be greeted on her return to a monumentally large gas bill? The school had arranged a hire car to pick Brett up every morning, drive him the twelve miles to Dundee and return him at the end of the school day. Cupar was a nice enough town, but without a car of his own Brett was stranded there. Not surprising he was fed up.

Ian drove them the few miles to Leuchars station. He'd decided to take the train to Edinburgh. That way he would be able to point out some of Fife's scenery and the Forth bridge. Brett wasn't overly impressed with the scenery, used, Ian supposed, to something way more spectacular. But he did like the bridge, taking multiple photos on his phone as they crossed it.

'What brings you to Scotland?' Ian asked, feeling stuck for conversation with someone he had very little in common with.

'The teacher exchange programme,' said Brett, turning his attention from the suburbs of Edinburgh back to Ian but still clutching his phone, waiting for more photo opportunities. 'I thought you knew that.'

'Yes, but why now? Why leave what looks like paradise for Scotland in the winter?'

Brett shrugged. 'Messy personal life,' he said, turning to examine the approach into Waverley Station with more than usual interest.

Yeah, thought Ian. *I know all about that.* Brett must have a personal life that was even more of a mess than his own if he needed to travel five thousand miles to get away from it. He felt a sudden sympathy for the man, friendless and cold in a strange country.

LEAVING THE TRAIN, they decided on a coffee before tackling the tourist hotspots. Ian bought two Costa cappuccinos and picked up a free tourist map for Brett. They sat on a bench in the ticket hall and drank their coffee while Brett studied his surroundings, looking down at the marble floor and taking photographs.

'Cool dome,' he said, looking up at the glass roof above them. He clicked into Google. 'Designed by James Bell,' he read. 'Says here there was a timber panelled booking office that was removed in 1970.' He pointed to a bank of ticket machines. 'I guess it was over there,' he said.

Ian looked up at the glass dome. He'd been here many times but hadn't spent much time studying the roof. They were sitting, Ian thought, exactly where Felicity and Julian were supposed to have met. He looked around at the crowds of travellers. Probably more than at midday on a Friday when Felicity was here waiting, but even with the weekend crowd he and Brett were surrounded by, it was unlikely that if both she and Julian were here, they could have missed each other. No, Felicity had been stood up. Plain and simple. He took a few photos of the concourse and the dome. Molly would be interested, and perhaps he'd ask Felicity to show him exactly where they'd planned to meet. Not much use, probably, but it would be evidence that he was actually working on the case. He glanced around and contemplated the layout of the station. Local trains left from platforms in front of them. Long distance ones from platforms down a series of escalators behind where they were sitting. He looked at a group of people with wheeled suitcases heading to the platform for the London train. He envied them. He'd not been to London since, well, sometime before lockdown. He had a standing invitation to stay at Ailish's flat in Kensington and found himself daydreaming about a long weekend there with Caroline, perhaps at New Year. Thoughts of Elsa also flitted into his head but he dismissed them. *Too late for that,* he thought. A weekend with a best friend was a far better, and safer idea.

Suddenly thoughts of either of them were driven from his head. His attention was caught by a man at the far end of the concourse staring up at the departure boards.

Ian jumped up. 'Wait there,' he said to Brett, breathlessly.

'Someone I need to catch.' He barged past people and their cases, scraping his shins on the metal edge of a passing suitcase. 'Sorry,' he muttered to the owner of the case, who was trying to stop it from toppling over. The man scowled at him, but there was no time to help him. Ian pushed on towards the boards. To where he had caught a glimpse of a man wearing a red overcoat. But by the time he got there the man had gone. He scanned the people studying the board and none of them were wearing a red coat, or even carrying one. He looked up at the board. The next train to leave was going to Inverness. Ian pushed his way to the platform, where he was stopped by a ticket barrier. He stared helplessly over it and caught a flash of red as the doors were slammed and the train crawled slowly away. He strained to look through the windows but saw nothing. He returned to where Brett was sitting and flopped down onto the bench, frustrated and breathless.

'Problem?' Brett asked.

'Yeah, thought I saw someone I recognised. A person of interest in one of my cases.' But maybe not. It could have been anyone in a red coat. 'Come on,' he said, standing up. 'Let's go and explore Edinburgh.'

They walked up the steps to the Royal Mile, checked out the castle, listened to a bagpiper and browsed tourist shops. Then they found a bench with a panoramic view over the city. Ian pointed out some of the landmarks and Brett took more photos. He shuffled closer to Ian on the bench and stretched out his phone carrying arm. 'I'll take a selfie of us and send it to Caroline,' he said.

Fair enough. It would be evidence that Ian had kept his promise to entertain Brett and hopefully persuade him to wait out another six weeks.

'What's she like?' Brett asked.

'Who?'

'Caroline. I was only given a few details. No idea what she looks like.'

Ian fished out his own phone and scrolled through his photos, choosing one of the two of them together on holiday a couple of years back.

He handed it to Brett. 'Nice,' he said, winking. 'You look close. How long have you known each other?'

'Must be three years,' said Ian. 'We met over a missing dog. We have very similar dogs. It was a case of mistaken identity.'

'Romantic,' said Brett. 'You don't live together though?'

'Not that sort of relationship,' said Ian.

'Really?' said Brett. 'Not how it looks here.' He handed the phone back to Ian.

'Just good friends,' said Ian.

'Oh yeah,' said Brett, giving Ian a sceptical look. 'You should hang on to that. She looks like a real nice lady.'

'Are you still thinking of leaving early?' Ian asked, keen to change the subject. 'Schools do all kinds of fun stuff at Christmas. You should stay for that.' There would be carol concerts, Christmas dinners and shopping trips on dark afternoons in quaint little old-fashioned shops lit up with Christmas lights.

'Perhaps I will,' said Brett, with a sigh. 'Not much to hurry home for and I've enjoyed today. It's been great to get out of Dundee. Guess I was feeling a bit low a week or so back.'

'Do you have a flight home booked?'

'Not yet.'

Ian checked his calendar. Caroline was due home on a Saturday. He supposed the school term would finish the day before that. 'You could stay a day or two after term finishes and meet Caroline when she gets home.'

'I'd like to meet her.' He chuckled. 'It'll be odd for her to get home and find a strange man in her guest room.'

'Well, she knows you're using her house. It'll hardly be a big surprise.'

Brett shrugged. 'S'pose there's a lot more of Scotland to see. Perhaps I'll email her and ask if she minds me staying a few days longer.'

'Fancy a visit to a laird in a castle?' Ian asked. 'We don't need to wait for the end of term for that. We can go any weekend.'

'You're kidding me?'

'I'm absolutely not. One of my closest friends is the Laird of Drumlychtoun. Just an hour or so north of Dundee. I can drive you there if you like.' Well, he was going anyway and it would please Caroline.

'Is it a very old castle?'

'Not really. It was built to replace the original one that was washed into the sea in a storm.'

'So this new castle, it's what, early twentieth century?'

'Seventeenth, I think.'

'For God's sake. However old was the old one?'

He tried to remember the history of the castle that Xander had told him when he first visited. 'I think it was built in thirteen hundred and something, but I'm not sure. Xander can give you all the details when we visit.'

Brett leaned back on the bench and stared down at the city spread out in front of him. 'I could get to like Scotland,' he said. 'If only it wasn't so cold.'

'We'd better get back to the station,' said Ian. 'The trains will be quite crowded once we hit rush hour.' They walked back down the hill, just missing a train and discovering that the next one was delayed by leaves on the line at Kirkcaldy. Only a forty-five minute wait. Ian bought them both another coffee and they sat down to wait.

'That guy you saw,' said Brett. 'Was he the one in the cool red coat?'

'Yes,' said Ian. 'The person I'm searching for was last seen wearing a similar one.'

'I'd really like a coat like that to keep out the Scotch mist,' said Brett, looking at his phone. 'I got a good photo of it.'

'Can I see?' said Ian, taking the phone from him. An impressive photo. Brett had zoomed in and had a clear image of the man in the coat. A man who, from the rear, was identical to the one in Felicity's photo.

10

The Tuesday morning after his visit to Edinburgh, Ian staggered up the garden to his front door in the first gale of the winter. Worried that the strong wind might blow Lottie back down the path, he clutched her lead and opened the door. After several years' experience of returning from walks with a wet dog, he kept his waxed, knee-length coat on while he reached for a towel and gave Lottie good rub down before she managed the inevitable shaking that would send muddy droplets of rain all over the walls of his entrance hall. Once dry, Ian released Lottie, who still felt obliged to shake but now with less effect. Then she trotted into the kitchen to sit in her bed under the boiler.

Ian hung up his coat, noticing that Molly had already arrived and had bagged the best peg, the one above the radiator, to hang her own coat. 'Wild morning,' he said, as he went into the office and sat down at his desk.

'Aye,' said Molly. 'Real Piglet ears weather.'

'Sorry?' he said, as he booted up his computer.

'Did you never read Winnie the Pooh?' she asked. 'Dad used to read it to me, and he's kept the book to read to Ryan. I loved the drawing of Piglet on a windy day with his ears streaming behind him like banners.' She was tapping at her computer keyboard while she chatted. 'We always talk about Piglet ears weather when it's windy like this. Here, I've found the picture. I'll airdrop it.'

Ian clicked open the screenshot of Piglet battling against a strong wind, and smiled. Yes, it was familiar. He must have known the stories as a child, long ago as that was. And Lottie's ears had looked like that on their walk this morning. He saved the picture and then clicked on his email. Brett had sent a message thanking him for their day out on Sunday and attaching the copy of the photo he'd taken of the man in the red coat. Ian added it to Fact Stuffer and lined it up next to the copy of Felicity's photo. 'Take a look at this,' he said to Molly. 'It looks like the same man, doesn't it?'

'It looks exactly the same,' she said. 'Where did you get it?'

'The guy I was with at the weekend took it at Waverley. I tried to catch up with the bloke, but he slipped through the barrier before I could reach him.'

'Catching a train?'

'The ten-twenty to Inverness.'

'Very interesting,' she said.

They were interrupted by the phone ringing. Ian picked up the receiver and found he was being shouted at by an impatient-sounding Felicity. The plan was to send her a weekly report every Friday. There'd been nothing much to tell her last Friday and as far as he could predict there wasn't going to be much next Friday either, although the sighting of a red coat was going to make it a little more interesting. That had cheered him up, even if it didn't progress their case by a lot. Inverness was the gateway to the Highlands. A tourist hub from where people spread out all over Scotland. Red coat man could be anywhere by now. He might not have been going as far as Inverness. There were other stops he could have got out at. 'You'll get the report as usual on Friday,' he told Felicity. 'We may have something to add this week, but I need to do some follow up before I can give you details.' He hoped that sounded promising, if a little vague.

'Never mind that now,' she said. He could almost feel her impatience buzzing down the phone line. 'What do you know about the body?'

'Body?'

'You know. The one they found on the beach yesterday. You must have heard about it.'

'Yes, of course.' He'd seen the report on a local TV channel the previous evening. A body had been found near the rocks just below the southern end of the railway bridge. Sadly this was not particularly unusual. Admittedly, the railway bridge was not typical. People who wanted to do away with themselves usually chose the road bridge, which had easier access both onto the bridge and then over the barrier. But he supposed climbing up onto the rail bridge and jumping off it was not impossible. He'd shrugged sadly as he watched the item. Just another sad suicide, he assumed. It hadn't made the national news and no names had been mentioned. There had been some gossip among the locals in the pub last night, but no one had known the victim and the subject was soon dropped in favour of whinges about the price of beer and disappointment in some football team Ian had never heard of.

'I think it might be Julian,' said Felicity.

Why did she think that? It hadn't occurred to Ian that it might be the man they were looking for. As far as he knew, Julian, if that was even who he had spotted, had last been seen boarding a train for Inverness. Completely the wrong direction from Dundee. But if it had been Julian, Ian had the sudden chilling thought that he could have been one of the last people to see the man alive. Perhaps he'd changed his mind and taken a different train going in the opposite direction. But he'd have needed to change platforms and Ian would have seen him either returning through the barrier or climbing the stairs to the southbound platform. Red coat man had leapt aboard the train just as it was pulling out of the station. There'd been no time to change his mind, get out again and wait for another train. Ian did some calculations in his head. He'd been at Waverley on Sunday morning. The body had been found in the early hours of Monday. Possible, he supposed, that the man had made a quick visit to Inverness and taken an evening train back to Dundee. But that would have approached the bridge from the north after dark. The train would pull onto the bridge almost immediately after leaving Dundee station and would have been travelling quite slowly. By the time it reached the southern end of the bridge, it would have sped up. It would take a very brave person to jump from a moving train and then hurl himself off the bridge. He could have walked from Dundee, but why wait until he was on the far side of the bridge to jump off? No. Either the dead person was someone entirely different, or it had not been Julian that he'd seen in Edinburgh. 'Why do you think it might be Julian?' he asked.

'I told you he was in danger,' said Felicity. 'I need you to find out more about it. You have contacts in the police, don't you?'

'I do, yes. I'll see if I can get more details for you.' At least that was something he could do for her. He'd not been able to do much else yet.

'You need to find out if they have identified him. Or her,' she added.

'And if they haven't?'

'Then you must ask for a description. And I need to see the body.'

'If it's a man.'

'Yes, of course. I'm not interested if it was a woman.'

He ended the call, promising to make some enquiries.

'Call me back tomorrow,' she'd said rather than a polite goodbye or an even politer thank you for your help.

He looked across his desk at Molly, who had been listening to the conversation and was now hopping up and down in excitement. 'This could be real progress,' she said. 'Shall we go and see Duncan? Or shall I call him?'

'I'm seeing him this evening. Line dancing night.'

Molly looked disappointed.

'It's probably nothing to do with Julian,' said Ian. 'There's no need to waste Duncan's time if they already know who it is. And I promise we'll catch up with everything he tells me first thing tomorrow.'

Duncan took a swig of his beer. 'No,' he said. 'We have no idea who it is. Definitely male though.'

'He had nothing on him that might identify him?'

'No wallet or phone,' said Duncan.

Ian sensed a but...

'Just an empty envelope addressed to a Claude Lambert, at an address in Paris. The local police checked it out and were assured that, although Lambert was currently away, he had called home on Monday afternoon. So definitely not lying dead in the Tay on Monday morning.'

Ian almost choked on his beer. Could this be Felicity's Julian? Or rather, the man she knew as Julian and everyone else seemed to think was Claude Lambert.

'You knew him?' Duncan asked.

'No, well, not exactly.' He briefly explained his latest case. 'Was he wearing a red coat?'

'No, why?'

'That's what he was wearing the last time my client saw him. And I think I spotted him at Waverley on Sunday getting on a train to Inverness.'

'What makes you think it was the same man?'

'Right build, same colour hair, unusual coat.' He opened a file on his phone and showed Duncan the two photos.

Duncan gave them a cursory look. 'The bloke we fished out of the Tay was wearing very little. Just a t-shirt, jeans and a lightweight jacket. No sign of a coat.'

'On a November night?' That wasn't very likely. He took his phone back from Duncan. 'He could have been wearing a coat when he got on the train and perhaps someone robbed him and pushed him out.'

Duncan shook his head. 'Not possible to push someone out of a train and down into the water. Either the guy jumped or was pushed over the edge by someone standing on the track. It would have to have been someone quite strong to heft him over the barrier.'

'How did he die?' Ian asked.

'We don't have the forensic report yet, but it looked like a blow to the head. Either he fell onto the rocks or was hit on the head and then pushed in.'

'What did he look like?'

'About six-foot, dark hair, late forties or early fifties.'

That would fit Felicity's description. 'Would my client be allowed to see the body?' he asked.

'Don't see why not, assuming we haven't ID-ed it first. As long as she has a good reason to think she knows him. Let me see those photos again.'

Ian passed the phone back to Duncan, who studied it for a moment. 'Could be him. Looks like the right build and hair colour. Hard to tell from the back, though.'

'And she knew him as Julian,' said Ian. 'She'd never heard of Claude Lambert.'

'People don't always use their real names. He might have had a very good reason not to tell her. But there is a likeness, and the Paris connection. And of course, your possible sighting of the man. It's enough to allow her to view the body. Let me know when she'll be there, and I'll sort out a family liaison officer to be on hand.'

Best not to leave it too long, Ian thought as he walked home later than evening. He'd call Felicity as soon as he got home and arrange for her to view the body first thing in the morning. What would happen if the body was Julian? Would that be the end of his case, or was he about to be dragged into something sinister?

∼

FELICITY HAD SOUNDED QUITE impressed when Ian called her that evening. He gave her the address of the hospital and they agreed to meet at the main entrance the next morning. They were greeted by the sergeant that Duncan had organised as their family liaison officer. A plump, middle-aged woman with, Ian thought, a kind face. She shook Felicity's hand and introduced herself. Then she led them through miles of hospital corridors, out of a back exit and down some stairs into the concrete block of the building that was the mortuary. 'Take your time,' she said, as she held the door open for them. 'I'll take you in when you're ready. There's no hurry. You will be viewing the deceased through a window. When you signal that you are ready, a member of staff will turn back the sheet to reveal the face. I will ask you if you are able to identify the man. I have to warn you, though, I'm told there is bruising to the face and seeing a body can be extremely upsetting. I'm here to support you, though.'

Felicity nodded. 'I understand,' she said. 'The sooner we do it, the better.' She turned to Ian. 'I would like you to be there as well,' she said.

Ian turned to the sergeant, who nodded, and they were led into the viewing suite, a tastefully decorated room with a row of chairs and a small table on which was placed a box of tissues and small vase of lavender.

A curtain was drawn back and the three of them looked through the window at the body lying on a trolley and covered with a green sheet. The top part of the sheet was folded back to reveal a man's face. Felicity stared at it for a moment. Then she turned to the sergeant. 'It's not him,' she said, with no sign of either relief or any other kind of emotion.

'Are you quite sure?' the sergeant asked. 'As I told you, the face is badly bruised.'

'I realise that,' said Felicity. 'But if you don't believe me, uncover his left arm. Julian had a tattoo of a dove on the inside of his forearm, just below the elbow.'

The sergeant pressed a button on the small intercom device and instructed the orderly to reveal the left arm. He carefully rolled back the sheet. The hand and wrist, like the face, were bruised. The upper arm was bare. No scratches or bruises and no sign of a tattoo.

'A<small>RE YOU OKAY TO DRIVE</small>?' Ian asked as they walked out of the building and into the car park.

'Of course. Why wouldn't I be?'

'It can be a shock,' he said, feeling quite shaken himself. 'Seeing a body, even if you don't know who it is.'

'I'm perfectly fine,' she said, reaching into her bag for her keys.

'And you would like me to continue with the case?'

'Of course. Now you have had a sighting of Julian.'

'I can't be sure it was him,' said Ian, taking out his phone and looking once again at the photo Brett had taken. He handed it to Felicity, who stared at it. She agreed that the man looked very similar to the photo she herself had taken in the gallery in Paris.

'I'm sure it's him,' she said. 'And now we know he was heading for Inverness. That should make your search considerably easier.'

Easier, he supposed, than Paris or even Edinburgh, but that still left a lot of Scotland to search. 'I'll discuss our next steps with Molly,' he said. 'And report to you again at the end of the week.'

HE DROVE BACK to the office, where Molly sat him down with a strong cup of coffee. 'You look shaken up,' she said.

'I am totally confused by this,' he said as Lottie jumped up onto his lap and he stroked her, feeling calmer as his fingers felt the warmth of her fur.

'Let's do one of your visuals,' said Molly, clearing a space on the whiteboard and reaching for a pack of coloured pens. 'What do we actually know so far?'

'We know that Felicity was in Paris,' said Ian. 'And she met up with a man who was either called Julian or Claude Lambert. Who, if we can believe Felicity, has a tattoo of a dove on his left arm. We think that he was in Edinburgh wearing a red coat and catching a train north on Sunday morning. We know that another man answering a similar description was found dead under the Tay rail bridge with Claude Lambert's name on an envelope in his pocket. If Felicity can be trusted, this was not the man she met in Paris because he didn't have a tattoo.'

'Do you think Felicity *can* be trusted?' Molly asked.

'I really don't know. She doesn't give anything away. She was completely unfazed by seeing a dead and bruised body.'

'Do you think she did recognise him?'

'I wondered that. Perhaps she just needed to confirm that he was dead. Perhaps she hired someone to kill him. But then why does she want us to go on searching?'

'Cover, perhaps. If she'd told us to stop, she'd have been admitting that the body really was Julian.'

'So we could be wasting our time.'

'She'll still be paying us,' Molly pointed out.

A good point, but they'd still have to do the work. And if that revealed Felicity as a criminal, they wouldn't see a penny of her money. He finished his coffee and idly fed Lottie half a Hobnob. 'I wonder what happened to the coat,' he mused.

'We should search for it,' said Molly. 'If it was on the train and turned up in lost property the man in the Tay might have been the owner, which doesn't look good for Felicity's reliability. But if we can find someone wearing it, then it will most likely be Julian and Felicity was telling us the truth after all.'

'Or Claude,' said Ian. 'Because if Claude *was* the dead man, why would he have his own name written on an envelope in his pocket?'

'Someone had sent him a letter?'

'And he stuffed the envelope into his pocket? Possible, I suppose. But what happened to the letter?'

'I don't know,' said Molly. 'We should concentrate on finding the coat.'

'I agree, but I haven't the first idea where to start.'

Molly looked at her watch. 'It's getting late,' she said. 'We should take a break and come back to it tomorrow. I'll start by calling the lost property office in Inverness first thing in the morning.'

11

The next morning, Ian looked out of his bedroom window at a clear blue sky, bright sunlight sparkling on the estuary. It wouldn't last. Rain was forecast for later, so he decided to take Lottie for a long early-morning walk. First a run in the park, then down to the village shop to pick up a local paper in case there was any more news of the body. Perhaps it had now been identified and that could make a difference to their enquiry.

The park was empty apart from a squirrel, which Lottie chased up a tree and then stood barking at it. Was she hoping it would come down again for a bit more chasing? She should know better. She'd chased squirrels here for as long as she had lived with Ian and never, to his relief, had she caught one. He wasn't sure which of them would have been more surprised. Squirrels were vicious little things with sharp teeth and claws. Lottie, he was sure, wouldn't come out of it well. But as long as there were trees, the squirrels would be safe. Just in case, he called Lottie and put her on her lead, and they walked down the hill to the shop.

He picked up the paper and then remembered it was the day Lainie's magazine was delivered, so he picked that up as well. He'd drop it off on his way home. She'd want him to join her for a chat, but he'd have to pass on that this morning because by the time he got back Molly would be there with the coffee brewing and a mountain of work for him to do. He'd make sure he found time for Lainie later, perhaps join her for a cup of tea that afternoon. Walking in the cold made him hungry, so he added a bag of buns to take back to the office and share with Molly.

They crossed the road to the harbour wall, where Ian perched himself to flick through the paper. Still no news of who the body was, but there were some photos of where it had been found. He glanced upstream towards Wormit, where a train had just appeared and was now right over the stretch of rocks where the body must have landed. Had he jumped or had he been pushed? If it was their coat-owning man, what had he done with the coat? Nothing had been found near the body, so he must have taken it off. Did that suggest suicide? That he'd valued his coat more than his own life? Not a rational thought, but then did people think clearly when about to kill themselves?

Or was murder more likely? Was there now a red-coat-clad murderer on the loose somewhere in Scotland? But that also seemed unlikely. If you were about to kill someone for whatever reason, did you first invite them to take their coat off? Ian looked at the rocks and shivered. The idea of landing on them from the track above was terrifying. Could anyone be that desperate? He found himself reluctantly hoping that the man had at least been unconscious when he fell. But that would mean someone had pushed or thrown him in, which was an equally terrifying idea.

Ian pushed his hands into his pockets for warmth and he and Lottie walked back to the office. He tapped on Lainie's door and handed her the magazine.

'You've time for a coffee and a wee snack?' she asked.

'I'm sorry,' he said. 'But Molly will have started work and I'd feel bad about leaving her on her own for any longer.'

'She's a good lass,' said Lainie. 'And you're right to take care of her and see she doesn't overwork. But I'll be baking later. How about joining me for a cuppa later this afternoon once Molly's left?'

'Lovely,' he said. 'I'll see you about five.'

'And don't be eating too much lunch,' she said.

He laughed. 'Just a small salad,' he said. 'That won't spoil my appetite for cake.'

MOLLY WAS LOOKING pleased with herself when he and Lottie arrived back in the office. 'I'm going to a vintage clothes shop in Perth later,' she said, rubbing her hands and helping herself to a bun. 'Would you like to come with me?'

There were few things he wanted to do less than that. He hadn't, as far as he could remember, ever been inside a vintage clothes shop and didn't see any reason why he should break the habit of a lifetime. 'Why?' he asked.

Molly grinned at him. 'To look at coats,' she said. 'Well, actually just one coat.'

'You want to buy a new coat?' Although not new, he supposed. If it was a vintage shop it would be second hand, although now it was usually called pre-loved. A term he found irritating.

Since she'd been working for him, Molly's wardrobe had evolved from an unobtrusive librarian look, which involved grey trousers and plain blouses, baggy and buttoned up to the neck, through bright colours and sparkles, home knitting in rainbow stripes paired with tie-dyed T-shirts and skirts, to her current look, which was quirky and involved velvet jackets, dresses his grandmother might have worn, an orange and purple coat, and odd-shaped little hats. A look he liked, and in spite of his lack of experience in the area, he suspected was vintage and probably found on eBay or a site he'd seen as frequently visited on the laptop called Rokit.

Molly sighed. 'It's not a coat for me. It's *the* coat.'

'What? The actual red overcoat? You've found it?'

'Possibly,' she said. 'I've had a busy morning.'

'Clearly. Tell me how it led you to the coat?'

'Possible coat,' she said. 'I can't be sure.'

'Okay, so how did you find a possible coat?'

'I started like we agreed, by phoning the lost property office in

Inverness. They collect up all the stuff people have left on trains on the whole of that stretch of railway. Anything that's not claimed within a month goes to some dealer who sells it on.'

'But I saw the coat on Sunday,' said Ian. 'So it would only just have been handed in. No time to sell it on. It won't turn up in any vintage shops for at least another four weeks.'

'The lost property office didn't have it. The only coats they had in the last week were one or two dark-coloured anoraks, a grubby raincoat and some children's parkas. They told me people don't hand in a lot of clothes. They take them home and sell them on eBay.'

'That doesn't sound very ethical. Imagine you've lost a favourite piece of clothing and see it on eBay. You'd be quite upset, wouldn't you?'

She shrugged. 'Probably, but there's not much you can do about it unless it's got some distinguishing mark on it. Even then... Anyway, I searched eBay for Jean de Saul Chesterfield coats and there weren't any. What I did find were lots of dealers selling vintage stuff. Well, I knew that already. I bought my bag at one of them.' She held up a round leather bag the size of a large goldfish bowl, with a drawstring and elephants embroidered on it.

'Very nice,' he said.

'There were a few in Scotland so I called some of them and said my boyfriend really, really wanted a red overcoat for his birthday but the only ones I'd seen were too expensive and did they have any? Some of them had red coats, but nothing like the one we're looking for until I called this shop in Perth. I've been there, actually. You know my green velvet skirt?'

Ian nodded although he couldn't be sure. He thought he remembered Molly wearing a green skirt with poodles embroidered around the hem. 'The one with the dogs?' he asked.

'That's the one. I bought it a couple of months ago to wear when Dad took me to that posh restaurant in St Andrews for my birthday. I've worn it for work a couple of times as well when I've had clients to meet.'

'Very nice,' he said. 'But what does it have to do with the red coat?'

'I called the shop with the same story about wanting a red coat for my boyfriend. I spoke to a rather gormless boy, work experience probably, and he said they had one in the back, but it wasn't for sale yet. I got him to go and check the label and guess what?'

'Jean de Saul?'

'That's right. I asked who had brought it in and how much they were selling it for. He didn't know who had brought it in because he only does a few hours in the shop and wasn't there when it came in. But he did say it must be in the last day or two because it hadn't been priced yet. The owner was out, so I asked him to keep it for us. Gormless work experience lad said he didn't have the authority to do that, and I'd need to speak to his boss. I thought I would drive up there this afternoon when the boss will be there and see if I can get a description of whoever brought it in.'

And the Edinburgh to Inverness train stops in Perth, Ian thought. 'Good idea,' he said. 'How does this place operate? Do people just hand stuff in and then disappear?'

'For more upmarket items they sell on commission. The shop takes a cut, and they pocket the rest.'

'So if that's what happened,' said Ian, 'they might have a name and contact details of the coat owner.' And if they had, it was going to make their search much easier. 'Do people drop in and collect the cash or is it paid into their bank account?'

'I think it depends on the agreement they have with the shop. I've heard of it being done both ways.'

'Well done, Molly,' he said. 'You've made some real progress.'

She grinned at him. 'So do you want to come with me?'

'Definitely. And we should go as soon as possible. We don't want to risk them selling it before we get there.'

'We could buy it and then wait to see who picks up the cash.'

'Lurk outside the shop, you mean?'

'There a very nice café just across the square. We could wait there.'

'There are two problems with that,' he said. 'First, we could be waiting for days and much as I like cafés, I wouldn't want to take up residence in one. But more importantly, it might have belonged to the guy that was fished out of the Tay. He could have taken the train to Perth, sold his coat and then caught the Dundee train from where he was violently ejected. If that's the case, he won't be picking up the cash.'

'That doesn't work,' said Molly. 'If it's the same man and he wanted to sell his coat, maybe because he was short of cash, why go to Perth? He'd get a better price in Edinburgh. He'd save himself the train fare and could probably sell it outright and not have to wait around for someone to buy it.'

That was a good point. 'Perhaps he had another reason to go to Perth. Maybe he was meeting someone.'

'The killer, perhaps?' Molly suggested.

Ian shook his head. 'According to Felicity, the man who died was not the owner of the coat.'

'She might have been lying.'

'Okay, let's say she was lying and the killer robbed him of his coat, bundled him onto a train, waited until they'd gone all the way to Dundee and then pushed him off the bridge. Doesn't sound likely, does it?'

Molly agreed that it didn't. 'If the murderer had stolen his coat, he could have pushed him into the river at Perth,' she said. 'What time did you see him at Waverley?'

'Just before ten-thirty.'

'And how long does the train take to get from Edinburgh to Perth?'

Ian checked. 'Around an hour and a half.'

'So he'd have been in Perth by midday,' said Molly, opening a map on her computer. 'It's a twenty-minute walk from the station to the shops which have to close at four on Sundays. Do we know what time he died?'

'Not been released yet,' said Ian. 'But the police think it was after dark. Even on a quiet Sunday, people notice when someone goes into the water in daylight.'

'You're probably right,' said Molly, looking disappointed. 'The only thing that links the body with the red coat is that he had a piece of paper with Claude Lambert's name on it in his pocket.'

'But brilliant work, Molly. Remember we're looking for the man who said he was Julian. We're not trying to solve the murder. This is the best lead we've had so far.'

They left Lottie with Lainie and drove to Perth, a town Ian liked, upstream from Dundee on the banks of the Tay and with an agreeable assortment of eating places. They parked his car and Molly led him through a modern shopping mall, out into a wide square and then down a narrow road of small, old-fashioned shops. She pointed to a shop on a corner called Alyson's with two windows either side of a blue door. In the window he could see mannequins wearing dresses with full skirts. What his mother would call cocktail dresses. Although never having been to a cocktail party in his life, he couldn't be sure. It looked like a very small shop so it shouldn't take long to peruse their stock of coats.

He said as much to Molly. 'Wait until you see inside,' she told him. 'There's an enormous conservatory-type thing at the back. It fills up the whole space between this shop and the street that runs behind. And it's all packed with clothes,' she added with a gleam in her eye.

It could be a long day. No doubt Molly would want to restock her entire wardrobe while they were there. 'Shall we have a coffee first?' he suggested, indicating a small café on the other side of the road. 'We can watch the sort of people that use the shop.'

'We should do the shop first,' said Molly. 'We don't want to risk someone buying the coat before we get there.'

She was probably right, and coffee and a slice of cake would be something to look forward to after sifting through God knew how many racks of clothing. They crossed the road and opened the door, which had an old-style bell on a coiled spring that clanged at them as they entered. Molly wasn't wrong. The place was enormous. Where on earth were they going to start?

'We need to go through to the back,' said Molly, who obviously knew her way around. 'The front of the shop is for dresses.'

They walked through the shop, past more clothes than Ian had ever seen. Dresses hanging from rails, hats on stands, scarves and beads draped over the backs of chairs and shelves of jumpers and blouses. They passed racks of shoes and handbags until eventually, having walked, Ian thought, halfway back to Greyport, they reached an iron spiral staircase which led up to a gallery and yet more clothes.

'Don't tell me,' said Ian, pointing up the stairs. 'Menswear is up there.'

'I'm not sure,' said Molly. 'I only ever come here for stuff for me.'

A woman appeared holding an armful of dresses, which she dumped down on a red velvet chaise longue. The owner, Alyson, Ian assumed. *She must get first dibs on the new stock as it arrives,* he thought, noticing her green velvet trousers worn with a cream frilled shirt, flowing silk scarf and a perky little beret. Her wrists jangled with bracelets, and she had baubles the size of light bulbs dangling from her ears. 'Can I help you?' she asked. 'Nice to see you again,' she said, turning to Molly. 'Looking for anything special today?'

'A red coat,' said Molly.

'You'll find coats over there,' she said, pointing. 'Behind the aspidistra.'

Ian glanced in the direction of the plant, which was big enough to conceal a lot of coats.

'It's not for me,' said Molly. 'It's a men's coat. Jean de Saul. I spoke to your assistant this morning and he told me you had one.'

Alyson sighed. 'Stupid boy,' she said. 'I knew I shouldn't have left him in the shop on his own, but I had to get to the bank.'

'So you don't have the coat?' Ian asked.

'I do. It came in on Sunday but...' She seemed uncertain what to say. 'It needs a bit of attention.'

'We don't mind the condition,' said Molly.

'I'm afraid it's not for sale,' said Alyson. 'At least, not yet. I'm keeping it for a customer until he decides what to do with it. My guess is that he's holding out for the right offer. He asked me to call him when someone shows an interest in it.'

'Can we at least see it?' Ian asked.

'I suppose that would be okay.' She disappeared through a door under the staircase and reappeared a few moments later, holding the coat. 'It's a very nice piece,' she said. 'I would expect a good price for it.'

'So let me get this right,' said Ian. 'Someone brought it in but asked you not to sell it. Is that how you usually operate?'

'Sometimes. We don't put our more valuable items on display in the shop.'

'Then how do people know they are here?'

'Like yourselves, they ask.'

'So there is a market for specific items?'

'A small one, yes.'

And lucrative, he assumed. He wondered if it was all honest and above board. He'd never thought that vintage clothing could operate a black market, but what did he know about it?

He took the coat from Alyson and held it up. It looked like the coat in Felicity's photo. Same size, he guessed. He felt in the pockets, but they were empty. What had he expected? Another piece of paper with a name on it? 'Are there many of these around?' he asked.

'Never seen one before,' said Alyson. 'It would have been a bespoke order. Probably around sixty years old.'

'How can you tell that?' he asked.

She reached into one of the pockets and revealed a small silk label. 'It's a 60% Woolmark tag. These were used between 1964 and 1971. Also, it's a style that briefly became popular after the first James Bond film in 1962.'

He'd never realised there was so much to know about clothes. 'And it's been here since Sunday? Can you tell me about the man who brought it in? I assume it was a man. He must have left you his details. Name? Contact number?'

'He was here on Sunday afternoon. And he did, of course, leave his details but I'm afraid I'm not at liberty to give them to you.'

'I understand.' He hadn't really expected her to.

'What did he look like?' asked Molly.

Alyson shrugged. 'Like someone who would own a coat like this. I can't tell you any more than that.'

What did that mean? What sort of person owned an expensive and historically interesting coat? Someone well off and flamboyant, he supposed. Ian handed her his card. 'Could you call me if he comes in again?'

She took the card and put it in her pocket, nodding briefly.

She wasn't going to tell *him* any more. He suspected Molly would have more luck. 'Thank you for your help,' he said to Alyson and headed for the door. He turned to Molly. 'You'll want to shop,' he said. 'Take your time. I'll meet you in the café?'

Molly smiled at him. 'You read my mind,' she said.

Ian left the shop and crossed the road. He was quite happy to sit with a cup of coffee and a bun while Molly chatted to Alyson.

IT TURNED out to be more than a while. Ian was halfway through his third cup of coffee and second slice of lemon cake, when Molly appeared clutching two large carrier bags. She sank into a chair next to him and he ordered her a coffee. 'Looks like a successful hour and a half,' he said.

'Was it really that long?' she asked, looking at her watch. 'Sorry, there's just so much stuff there.'

'You seem to have bought quite a lot of it.'

'Just a couple of dresses and some shoes. Oh, and a hat.' She opened one of the bags and took out a small, blue cloche hat, which she perched on her head. 'What do you think?'

'It suits you,' he said, meaning it.

'It was worth spending all that time in there. I got Alyson chatting and I've learnt quite a lot about coat bloke.'

He'd suspected as much. Molly was very good at getting people to chat. 'Did she tell you who he was?'

'Not exactly. She nearly let it slip and then clammed up. But what she did say was useful. I'd told her how much I liked the coat and said something about French designers, and she let slip that the coat owner was French. She called him *Monsieur*.'

'So you think it could have been Felicity's Julian?'

'I think so. We know there are very few coats like that one and also that he was supposed to be in Edinburgh.'

'Anything else?'

'Yes. I said I would really have liked to buy the coat for my boyfriend.'

'Boyfriend?'

'Just a hypothetical one. I was paying for all the stuff I'd bought by then and she said I was such a good customer that she'd let me have first refusal if and when she was able to sell it. Apparently, the owner told her that if he didn't return in a month, she should assume he wasn't coming back and that she could do what she liked with the coat.'

'Interesting,' said Ian.

'She also asked what my boyfriend looked like and how tall he was. I showed her a photo of him.'

'I thought you said he was just hypothetical.'

'It's just a picture I carry around. It's something I picked up in self-defence classes. If a man starts pestering you, saying you have a boyfriend can ward things off before they turn nasty.'

'So who is this guy you carry around on your phone?'

'Just some hunk I found on the Internet. I've no idea who he is. Male model, probably. I call him Josh. I think he looks like a Josh, don't you?' She got out her phone and showed him the photo. 'Anyway, Alyson said the coat would suit him because he was dark-haired like the owner, although *his* hair was longer. She asked if he was around six foot and nodded when I said he was. I assume she asked that because that was how tall the coat owner is.'

'Good work,' said Ian, wondering if, in the future, he could sit around drinking coffee and eating cake while Molly did all the work.

They walked back to his car and loaded Molly's shopping into the back. 'Are you okay for time?' he asked. 'I think we should call in at the station and ask if anyone remembers seeing a tall, dark man arriving in a red coat and leaving again without it.'

It was a short drive to the station and Ian slipped into a parking space outside the Station Hotel, a red and white brick building with an interesting selection of turrets. Scot Rail in its glory days, he supposed. If their guy had arrived on Sunday and not left to get himself murdered in Dundee that evening, he might have needed a bed for the night. They went into the hotel and asked at reception, but no one remembered seeing him. And they weren't prepared to check the register unless it was a police matter and they had a warrant. Something Ian thought he might suggest to Duncan.

From the hotel, they headed into the station and asked at an enquiry desk if anyone remembered seeing a man in a red coat on Sunday afternoon or evening, and were told that shifts changed from day to day and no one who was on duty that day would have been there at the weekend. And in any case, they were told, they only dealt with enquiries about trains, not the people who rode in them. Ian was about to give up and go home when he noticed the glass windows of Costa. Perhaps red coat man had called in there for a coffee before heading off to the shop.

There were a few people drinking coffee and staring dejectedly at their phones. A young girl was wiping tables. 'Were you working here on Sunday?' Ian asked. She shook her head. Ian looked over at the till. 'Do you know who would have been here then?'

'Not her,' she said, scowling at the woman behind the counter. Then she brightened up. 'I'm switching to the weekend shift soon,' she told him. 'My friend does Sundays and it'll get me away from her over there.' She scowled again at the woman, who was now handing over a couple of coffees and who looked up disapprovingly. 'Better go,' she said.

Ian handed her his card. 'Could you ask around and see if anyone saw a tall man with dark hair wearing a red coat?'

Molly nudged him. 'He wouldn't have been wearing it on Sunday evening,' she said.

'He'd have been wearing it on Sunday afternoon,' said Ian. 'And someone could have recognised him if he came back in the evening.'

'Are you police?' asked the girl, taking the card and reading it.

'As it says on the card, we're investigators.'

'We're helping the police,' said Molly.

'Cool,' she said, slipping the card into the back pocket of her jeans. 'I'll ask my friend and call you if she saw anything.'

12

Arriving back from Perth, Molly left to collect Ryan from school and Ian went next door to collect Lottie and take tea with Lainie.

'Did you have lunch in Perth?' she asked.

'No,' he said, not mentioning the two slices of lemon cake he'd had at the café while waiting for Molly, and wondering if he'd have room for any more cake.

An hour later he arrived home, having forced down a slice of Dundee cake. It would have been rude to refuse and Lainie was far too good a neighbour to upset by refusing what was a very kind offer. And after all, he'd not had any lunch. There were healthier diets than all-day cake but one day wouldn't hurt, and he could make it up tomorrow by eating, well, lettuce for all three meals.

Ian spent what was left of the afternoon uploading the notes he and Molly had made in Perth. Before shutting down his computer, he read them through and felt it had been a reasonably successful day. No major breakthroughs, but at least things were not standing still. They knew more about the coat and its whereabouts, and a little more about the coat's owner, although not *his* whereabouts. Ian was still in two minds about whether or not coat owner and murdered man were two different people. On the one hand, there was no reason to connect the dead man with Felicity's missing Julian. On the other, there was the matter of the envelope found in the dead man's pocket bearing the name Claude Lambert. The name everyone except Felicity attached to a man known as a regular drinker at L'Hotel Didier Pierre. A man Felicity knew as Julian but had failed to identify as the murdered man. Was the dead man Lambert? Had he been carrying a note addressed to himself but kept only the envelope?

He was confused. And tired. He tidied the office and made a to-do list for the next day. A good night's sleep and things would look clearer in the morning. Perhaps. There was paperwork to tidy up. He and Molly would spend the next morning on that and return to the red overcoat case in the afternoon, having given themselves time to mull it over and hopefully generate some ideas about where to go next. That evening Molly was going to watch Ryan in his first swimming gala in Dundee, and her mind would be fully occupied cheering him on and then possibly commiserating; Molly not having a lot of confidence in a team of small boys competing for the first time against other teams of rather bigger boys. It would be good for her to get away from work and concentrate on something else. He needed to do the same.

Lottie wouldn't complain about another walk and Ian felt he deserved an evening in the pub – an enjoyable spot of multi-tasking. Lottie liked spending time with Lainie, but Ian suspected she had spent the afternoon being offered, and enthusiastically accepting, unsuitable snacks. Rather like himself, he thought guiltily. After the two more than generous slices of cake he had eaten while waiting for Molly in the café and followed by a hearty slice of Dundee cake, he decided they both needed to offload some calories. If they didn't, it would be a diet of lettuce for several days. For both of them. A run in the park for Lottie and a brisk walk down to the pub would do them good. He would do his best to hold off on the crisps and limit himself to a single pint. A resolution he made frequently and rarely kept.

He had just put on his boots, wrapped himself in a warm coat and attached Lottie to her lead when there was a ring on the doorbell. It took him by surprise. Lottie jerked free of the lead and ran to the door, where she jumped up and down, barking furiously. Callers at this time of day were unusual. Unlikely to be a client since, if they did come to the office rather than emailing, they usually called first. He wasn't expecting a delivery or a social call. He scooped Lottie into his arms to stop her barking and opened the door. Then, feeling strangely breathless and making sure he had a firm grasp on the lead, he put Lottie down on the floor and gaped speechlessly at the visitor.

In front of him stood a tall, well-built man holding a large leather holdall in one hand and a laptop bag slung over his shoulder. His dark hair curled over the collar of a brand-new, navy blue, padded Gore-Tex hiking jacket. Ian only knew that the coat was new because it still had the tag dangling from the zip. However, it wasn't the coat that left him lost for words but its wearer. Ian was staring into the face of a man he had last seen lying on a mortuary slab. Admittedly this man had no bruises, but Ian was certain it was the man that Felicity had said categorically was not the person she had met in Paris and whom she knew as Julian. Felicity may have sworn that the murder victim was unknown to her, but there was no doubt at all that the man they had seen on the slab was dead. And yet here he was, standing on Ian's doorstep.

'Forgive me for intruding,' said the man, with a slight foreign accent. 'We've not met.' He put his holdall down on the doorstep and shook Ian's hand. Then he unzipped the coat and searched his pockets. Eventually finding what he was looking for he handed it to Ian. 'My card.'

Ian took the card and read it:

Claude Lambert

Détective Privé

'You'd better come in,' said Ian, leading him into the office and dragging a disappointed Lottie behind him.

Claude Lambert followed him. He looked around at the two desks, the board on the wall and the view from the window of

Dundee's lights across the estuary. Then he sat down in Molly's chair and spread his legs out in front of him as if he were a familiar visitor who felt entirely at ease. Something which, at this moment, was the exact opposite of what Ian was feeling. 'I can see I've taken you by surprise,' he said.

True enough. Claude Lambert ran an art gallery in Paris, not a detective agency. And the last time they'd met, he was dead. Now here he was, sitting in Molly's chair as if he owned it. 'Coffee?' Ian offered, not sure what else to say.

Claude smiled at him in a way that suggested he had the upper hand in the situation and had no intention of relinquishing it. 'I think perhaps we need something a little stronger,' he said.

He wasn't wrong. Ian pulled himself together and went to the kitchen to find a bottle of whisky and two glasses. He returned to the office and poured them both a generous measure.

'I'd better explain myself,' said Claude, uncrossing his legs and leaning towards Ian with the air of one about to explain what should have been obvious to anyone with a grain of intelligence.

'That's the least you can do,' said Ian, now warmed by the whisky and starting to feel intrigued rather than spooked. This clearly wasn't the same man. Similar in build and features certainly, but even allowing for the dead man's bruises, this was not the same face. 'I'd be interested to know what brings you to my office.'

Claude took a swig of his drink. 'An unexpected stroke of luck,' he said. 'I wasn't looking for you but when you, as it were, fell into my lap, I began to think that we could be useful to each other. Since we are in the same profession.'

'Luck?'

'I was hoping to lure someone else. A man I have been interested in for a while now but who is also putting me in some danger. I wanted to find a way to reveal him and observe him, unknown to himself if possible.'

'Your coat,' said Ian, with a sudden flash of inspiration.

'Precisely,' said Claude. 'Distinctive, isn't it?'

Ian nodded.

'I set a trap,' he continued. 'I knew I was being followed and I wanted, as I said, to lure this man into the open without allowing him to come face to face with me.'

'So you left your coat with Alyson, hoping this man had followed you there, with instructions to contact you when anyone enquired about it.'

'Which she did this afternoon, but not with the information I'd expected. I'd hoped to be given contact details in order to turn things around and start following this man instead of him following me. I'm still hoping that Alyson will contact me to say my quarry has been in touch.'

'I'm afraid that might not happen,' said Ian.

Now it was Claude's turn to look surprised. 'You know him?'

'Not exactly.'

'Then?'

'This man you are looking for, does he look like you?'

'It has been said that we are similar, yes.'

'Then I'm sorry to tell you this, but I think he died on Sunday night or early on Monday morning.'

Ian turned to his computer and clicked on an email Duncan had sent him earlier that day. Attached to the email was a photograph of the dead man, carefully doctored to remove the bruises. Ian compared it to the man sitting opposite him. They were alike. Same hair and build, similar features, but unmistakably different people. He turned the screen so that Claude could see it.

'This man was murdered?'

'My contact in the police has not seen the forensic report yet. The body was found on a rocky part of the Tay beach below the rail bridge. It's not clear how he got there. He may have jumped from the bridge, or he may have been pushed from a train. It's possible that he was travelling on the evening train from Perth, although it's unlikely that he could have jumped from a moving train into the water. There is a barrier on the bridge to stop people doing that.'

'Have the police named him?'

'The body has not yet been identified. This photograph has been produced for a press release. Perhaps you can now save the police the trouble and identify him yourself.'

Claude shook his head. 'This is the man I'm searching for. But if I go to the police, they might think I murdered him.'

'Why would they think that?'

'I'd better tell you the whole story. But first I need to know why you were in Perth. I assume it was not to buy a coat. Alyson told me you were looking for that actual coat, which suggests you had a reason for finding me.'

Ian switched on his phone and opened the photo Brett had taken at Waverley. 'That is you boarding the Inverness train?'

'Yes, that's me. But what is your interest in me?'

'A client asked me to find you. At least, she asked me to find someone fitting your description and who owned a red overcoat, but…'

'But?'

'She is under the impression that you are called Julian.'

'Ah,' he said, reaching for the bottle and topping up his glass. 'I think I know the lady you are referring to.'

'I can't tell you any more than that. Client confidentiality,' he said.

'Let me explain further. The lady's name is Felicity Bright. She no doubt told you we met in a bar in Paris. We have a shared interest in works of art and spent some time together. Then we arranged to meet in Edinburgh.'

'But why did she tell me you were called Julian? And why did you fail to meet her? And why are you posing as a private detective?'

'So many questions,' said Claude. 'I'm not posing. I am a private detective.'

Ian sighed. 'My enquiries tell me that the man Felicity met in a Paris bar was an art dealer called Claude Lambert.'

'I'm impressed. And you are correct. Let me explain further. The gallery I run was left to me by my great-uncle. At the time I was working with the French police, but the bequest came with the condition that I must run the gallery for a period of fifty years, which you can probably guess will keep me tied to it until I am in my nineties. I studied art when I was younger and know a lot about it, but when my studies ended, I decided not to make it my career. I wanted something more active, dangerous even, so I joined the police and trained as a homicide detective. My uncle's legacy allowed me to live in some comfort in Paris. Only a fool would turn that down. But I still craved excitement, so I employed a manager and opened my investigation office in a room above the gallery. So now I enjoy both worlds.'

'It sounds ideal,' said Ian. He'd been able to start his own business after inheriting from his grandfather. He at least had that much in common with his visitor, although it didn't explain what he was doing there. 'I still don't understand why Felicity thinks you are called Julian.'

'My current case brings my two lives together. My client is searching for the leaders of a cartel who steal works of art to order. These are sold to private collectors all over the world – some in America but most in the Middle East.'

'Isn't hunting down art thieves a role for the police?'

'The police, of course, are aware of it, but it's not high on their agenda of urgent cases.'

'And what is your client's interest?'

'He was a victim. Owner of a large estate with a number of valuable impressionist originals. He wants them found and returned.'

'That still doesn't explain why Felicity thinks you are called Julian.'

'And you are probably thinking I'm some kind of Don Juan who takes advantage of middle-aged, unattached ladies.'

Ian didn't disagree.

'I can see why you would think that. But you are wrong, although the trap I set for Felicity leads me to think that she was not the person she led me to believe she was.'

'You trapped her into meeting you? Why?'

'I was hoping she would lead me to an Englishman called Julian Grainger. You notice my trouble with the English pronunciation of the name. That is why Felicity had you searching for a Frenchman called Julian.'

Although it didn't explain why Felicity didn't want to find a man called Claude. 'This Julian Grainger was one of the cartel?'

'More of a middleman. And as you yourself noticed, similar to me in appearance. Grainger had been operating in Paris and I was on the verge of tracking him down when I was alerted to a Scottish connection. Have you heard of an artist called Hamish Gunn?'

Ian hadn't.

'Nineteenth century Scottish portrait painter. Can't say I care for him all that much, but he's sought after by Saudi oil magnates and arms dealers. I suppose portraits of dour-looking, kilt-wearing dudes with beards go down well in Saudi palaces. They become quite competitive by all accounts. Two portraits disappeared from Scottish collections last year and the rumour among my spies is that there will be more thefts. Security in some of these Scottish collections is lax and the thieves are clever. They bide their time and plan carefully. Interestingly, Gunn is not so popular in Scotland and the owners are only too happy to see them go and claim on their insurance. Of course, a couple of thefts alert dealers and the value increases alarmingly, much to the annoyance of insurance companies.'

'And Felicity works in insurance. So did you know who she was before you met her?'

'Never seen her before in my life.'

'So you started a relationship with her in order to find out more?'

'You make it sound unethical.'

Ian thought that was exactly what it was.

'I wouldn't say it was a relationship,' said Claude. 'We got talking and spent a day or two together.'

'But you picked her up in a bar.'

'That's what she told you? It was Felicity who made the first move,' he said. 'She picked *me* up in a bar where I am a regular. I knew Julian Grainger hung about in the bar occasionally and I suspected she was searching for him either to continue a deal or with something more sinister in mind.'

'You pretended to be him?'

'I was sitting at the bar when she came up to me and offered to buy me a drink. She had no reason to know who I was, but nevertheless I was suspicious. She asked my name and I said, "Does the name Julian mean anything to you?" She seemed to accept that I was Julian and it suited me to let her think I was him. I was still suspicious, and I didn't trust her. All the same, I made sure we spent time together. When she needed to return home, I was still unsure. I planned to be in Scotland so I told her we could meet. The date I gave her was easy to remember and I had every intention of being there.'

'But you didn't turn up.'

'No. By then I was sure that Grainger was following me and because I knew of his involvement in the fraud, it wasn't going to be a friendly meeting.'

'She told me you were in danger. How would she have known that?'

'I told her that my reason for not meeting again for a while was because I had unfinished business and it would be safer if we were no longer seen together.'

Ian was trying to get his head around all of this. He'd not trusted Felicity, although he couldn't quite say why. And now he didn't trust Claude either. 'What exactly was the nature of your relationship with Felicity?' he asked.

'I've shocked you?' Claude asked with a smirk.

Ian had to admit he was a little shocked. 'As far as I can see, you began a relationship with a blameless woman because you felt suspicious about her.'

'What makes you think she was blameless?' Claude asked.

'What makes you think she wasn't?' But, to be fair, Ian wasn't at all sure of Felicity's blamelessness. 'Okay,' he said. 'Set that aside for the moment and tell me why you are here in my office.'

'When Alyson gave me your card I was intrigued. We are in the same line of work, and I wanted to know more. Now I discover that you are involved in a similar search to myself, and it occurs to me that we could be useful to each other. Well, frankly, right now you are more useful to me than I am to you. You have fulfilled your contract to your client and have found me.'

'My deal with Felicity was to find out if you wanted any further contact with her. I have no intention of telling her I have found you unless it is what you want.' And to be honest, unless he had more proof that Felicity was somehow involved in the art fraud, it would probably be better for her if she knew nothing about his having discovered 'Julian'. But that was not his decision to make. Claude didn't know everything yet. Ian wasn't sure if he could trust him or not, but he needed to know about the body. 'The body that was found by the police had nothing to identify it other than an empty envelope with your name on it. Felicity heard about it and thought it could be you. I arranged with a friend in the police for her to view the body with a chance she might be able to name it. She assured us it wasn't you and claimed to have never met the man.'

'Do you think she was telling the truth?'

'She was very convincing,' said Ian. 'And obviously she was right. It wasn't you. But she gave us no hint that she knew it was this Julian Grainger, either, so it looks as if your suspicions are not justified and she'd not been involved with him or the fraudsters.'

'But it places me in a difficult position,' said Claude. 'I am able to identify Julian, but if I do, I could be arrested and charged with his murder. You say he was killed early on Monday morning?'

'The body was found on Monday, but the time of death hasn't been released yet. I think it's more likely he jumped or was pushed off the bridge late on Sunday night.'

'And I have no alibi.'

'Where did you spend Sunday night?'

'In an anonymous hotel on the outskirts of Perth.'

'They'll have a record of your booking.'

'But no proof that I was there all night.'

'How did you get to Dundee?'

'I caught a train from Perth earlier today and then a taxi to this address.'

Ian could see the problem. It was quite possible that Claude had killed Julian. He had a motive and the opportunity. But he didn't think Claude *had* done it. If he had, why was he still in the area and why make contact? 'You need to go to the police,' he said. 'If you don't, I will do so myself. I know who you are and I'm not risking everything by withholding evidence. If you go voluntarily, having spoken to me, and confirm his identity, you will be less likely to come under suspicion.'

'You think so?'

'I do,' said Ian. 'If you were guilty, you would have left the area, or at the very least not admitted to me that you knew the guy.'

'You could be right.' He downed another whisky and sat back in his chair. 'Okay. I'll make a deal with you. I will go to the police and if they arrest me, you will take over my case. Get to the bottom of the art thefts and find out who did kill Julian. And if they don't arrest me, we will work together to solve the case and share the profits. My client is paying me well. I can afford to split the fee.'

It was a tall order, but what else could he do? Even if Claude left right now, Ian couldn't unknow what he had been told. He could be accused of perverting the course of justice, a crime that carried a horrendously long sentence. 'Okay,' he said. 'It's a deal.' They shook hands. 'I suggest we call on DI Clyde, who is a friend of mine,' he said, picking up his car keys. 'If he doesn't arrest you immediately, he will be able to give us some very useful information.'

13

'The body is that of a man called Julian Grainger,' said Ian as Molly arrived for work the next morning. 'And Claude Lambert is found. We are going to work together.'

'You're joking,' said Molly, staring at Ian open-mouthed. 'Where did you find him?'

'He found me,' said Ian. 'But only after your excellent work searching for the coat.'

'And now he's working with us? Here?'

The sudden, and hopefully temporary, partnership had surprised Ian as well. It had, in fact, kept him awake for the greater part of the previous night. A visit to the police and the acquisition of an unexpected house guest were not conducive to a restful night. He'd fallen asleep eventually and had woken that morning realising he had to adjust to the inevitable and hope it didn't last too long. 'Reading between the lines,' he said, 'that's the only reason Duncan didn't arrest him there and then. He had to surrender his passport and agree not to leave the area. But we'd already agreed to work together.'

'How do we know if we can trust him?'

Lottie had missed her morning walk while he spent the time before Molly arrived on the Internet. 'I checked him out. He runs a legitimate detective agency in Paris. He's got all the correct certification.'

'French certification?' Molly looked at him sceptically. 'You don't speak French.'

'I know how to use Google Translate, but just to be sure, I sent Anna a quick email and asked her to check it as well.' To his relief, she had replied quickly and confirmed what he'd already worked out. Claude Lambert was a bona fide PI.

'So Anna's working with us too?'

'Only very part time. She's got plenty to do at Drumlychtoun, but she's agreed to help as a volunteer when we need a translator.'

They were interrupted by the sound of a door slamming and footsteps thumping along the passage outside the office. A tousled head appeared in the doorway. 'Okay if I take a shower before we start work?' Claude asked.

'Of course,' said Ian.

'*Bonjour,*' he said, smiling at Molly.

'This is my assistant, Molly Burrows,' said Ian.

'Charmed,' said Claude, stepping into the room, reaching for her hand and kissing it.

Molly nodded at him unenthusiastically.

'Have your shower,' said Ian. 'Then we'll have a catch-up meeting over coffee.'

Claude nodded and disappeared again. Molly and Ian listened to the sound of footsteps clumping up the stairs.

'He's sleeping here as well?' Molly asked.

'He is at the moment. By the time we left Duncan last night, it was too late to find him anywhere else. I said he could use the back office. At least we can keep an eye on him if he's here.'

'Duncan's idea?'

'He has to stay in the area.'

'Can't he check into a hotel?'

'The nearest hotel is in Dundee, and he doesn't have a car.'

'And what if Felicity decides to drop in?'

Ian had wondered that himself. But now 'Julian' was found, she would need to be told, and presumably they would have to confront each other. They could talk about how to do that, but for now it was probably best to keep them apart. Claude could lie low in the back office where he was currently sleeping on an ancient sofa bed that had moved with Ian from Edinburgh three years ago and hadn't been used since. And what were the chances that Felicity would drop in with no warning?

He explained it all to Molly, who sighed. 'I'll get the coffee on,' she said and disappeared into the kitchen.

BY THE TIME Claude appeared again, fragrantly showered, wearing a wool shirt with a scarf casually draped around his neck, his laptop bag dangling from one shoulder, Molly had made a pot of coffee and a plate of toast. Claude opened the bag and took out a laptop, which he perched on the edge of Ian's desk. He helped himself to coffee, two slices of toast and a spoonful of Lainie's raspberry jam.

'First things first,' said Ian, looking at the amount of space the laptop took up on his desk. 'You need a workspace.' He disappeared into an adjoining room and came back with a sturdy gateleg table. He opened it and lined it up between Molly's desk and his own. 'You can plug your laptop in down there,' he said, pointing to a row of sockets and handing him a card with the WiFi code. Then he walked over to the whiteboard that lined one wall of the office. 'I've jotted down what we discussed last night. Molly will transfer it to Fact Stuffer and set you up with a password that will access the relevant files.'

'Ian doesn't like Fact Stuffer very much,' said Molly. 'But it means we don't have to write everything up there.' She waved at the whiteboard. 'Where anyone can see it,' she added, giving him what Ian thought was a hostile glance.

'I prefer to see everything set out in front of me,' said Ian. 'I can think better like that. But Molly's right. It is a good way to keep our notes secure.'

Toast in hand, Claude walked over to the board and studied what they had written the previous evening. 'Impressive,' he said. 'But what if clients visit you? Isn't some of this confidential?'

'Exactly,' said Molly. 'But try convincing old Luddite over there.' She nodded in Ian's direction.

'That's not fair,' said Ian, laughing. 'Just because there's one bit of technology I don't like, doesn't mean I hate all of it. And as soon as Molly has created a Fact Stuffer folder, we can rub it off.'

'And use the board for brainstorming,' said Molly.

'I don't know of this, what is it called? Fact Stuffer?' said Claude. 'But if Molly can show it to me, I'll think about using it in my office in Paris.'

'It's useful,' said Molly, almost managing a smile. 'You have everything backed up, you can carry it around wherever you go and use it anywhere there is an Internet connection.'

Ian was starting to feel left out. Was Claude going to take over his business and his assistant? 'Can I suggest we stop this discussion before you both write me off as an out of touch old fogey, and concentrate on the case?' he said.

'You've given me a very good perspective on what you are doing here,' said Claude, in a manner that Ian found patronising. 'So let me bring you up to speed on the Paris side of things. May I?' he asked, picking up one of Molly's marker pens. 'First,' he said, not waiting for a reply, 'Julian Grainger.' He wrote the name and underlined it.

'Dead,' said Molly. 'Can we assume he didn't jump into the Tay voluntarily? And if not, who killed him?'

Julian drew a large question mark under his name. Then he turned to Ian. 'Your delightful inspector friend,' he said. 'He will keep you up to date?'

'As much as he is able,' said Ian. 'He can let me have a copy of the forensic report when he gets it. If he thinks we can help, he will contract me to work with him and that will give him greater freedom to disclose evidence.'

'And in return?'

'We agree to share all we know with him.'

'What about Kezia?' Molly asked.

'Who?' asked Claude.

'DCI Kezia Wallace is Duncan's boss,' said Molly. 'She doesn't like Ian.'

'It's mutual,' said Ian.

'She was friendly enough after the Dundas case,' Molly pointed out.

'Only because I disabled her suspect for her. And she was quite grudging about that.'

'Whatever,' said Molly. 'Duncan will still have to report to her.'

'Sounds like your cases are more interesting than mine,' said Claude, reaching for a third slice of toast. 'This Kezia, she is someone high up in the police?'

'Not as high as she likes to think,' said Ian, warming to him slightly with the thought that he and Molly had interesting cases on their books that perhaps Claude could only dream of. 'She still has to answer to the superintendent.'

'I will need to learn about police ranks in England,' said Claude.

'Scotland,' said Ian crossly. 'We're in Scotland. Police Scotland is separate from the rest of the UK.'

'I apologise,' said Claude. 'I forgot how touchy you Scots are.'

'Ignore him,' said Molly. 'It's just the Kezia effect. She used to work for the Met.'

'Ah, the force that got into trouble recently.'

'She was well out of the way by then,' said Ian. 'She made a very astute move coming up here.'

'I can't wait to meet her,' said Claude. 'But back to business. Do you have any suspects in mind? I have one or two contacts over here who might be able to suggest people. I will email them.'

'What about Felicity?' Molly asked. 'She had a motive.'

'Do we seriously suspect Felicity?' Ian asked. 'She's five foot two and slight. How could she have heaved a bulky six-footer over the barrier? And she denied knowing him.'

'She might have been lying and she could have been working with someone,' said Molly. She opened the Fact Stuffer file where they had noted her as a person of interest in Claude's case. 'It can't be a coincidence that she was in Paris at the same time Claude was working on his own art theft case.'

'Molly's right,' said Claude, writing Felicity's name on the board with a question mark and adding *accomplice* next to it.

Ian was starting to feel outnumbered. 'Claude is here because his sources tell him that Hamish Gunn is being targeted by the thieves. We need to think about where and when the next painting is likely to go missing. Do we know how many Hamish Gunns there are in Scotland?'

'I could work on that,' said Molly. 'If the thieves can find out where they are, I should be able to as well.'

14

Before lockdown Molly had worked at the Glasgow University library. She kept in touch with friends there, and this wouldn't be the first time she'd asked for their help accessing books and documents that were out of the ordinary and not what you would find in a public library. She enlisted their help now, and by the end of the morning she had screenshots from Gunn's biography sitting on her desktop, and a list of current owners of his paintings in Scotland. She was now planning to call them all and alert them to the threat of possible thefts.

'Don't be too specific,' Claude told her. 'No need to tell them how much the paintings are worth.'

'Why not?' she asked. 'Won't that mean they take better care of them?'

'Not necessarily. If they don't like them, they might rush off to the nearest auction house and raise some cash. Or they could make them more accessible to the thieves and claim off their insurance.'

'You don't trust Scottish owners of paintings?' said Ian.

'I don't trust any owners of paintings,' said Claude. 'Valuable paintings don't bring out the best in people. Believe me. I'm in the business.'

Ian looked at the list Molly had made of people she needed to call. It was going to take her a while. 'You okay to carry on with that?' he asked. 'Claude and I are going to see Duncan again. He's promised to let us see the forensic report on Julian Grainger.'

'Sure,' said Molly. 'I was wondering, Dad's taking Ryan bowling in Dundee this evening. Why don't the three of us go to the pub when you get back and unwind a bit?'

'Sounds like a plan,' said Ian. Having Claude as a house guest wasn't really any bother, although outside their interest in the case they didn't have a lot to talk about, so sharing him for the evening sounded like a good idea. Molly appeared to be warming to him. Not too much, Ian hoped. Just enough to ease the tension that had been obvious the first day they all worked together. It would also avoid the elephant in the room. The uncomfortable prospect of telling Felicity that he had found the man she believed to be Julian. He and Claude had skirted around it. Even Molly was reluctant to discuss it. But sooner or later it would have to be done.

Ian continued to worry about it as he drove Claude to Duncan's office in St Andrews. What if Felicity spotted them? She lived in the town, which was small enough to bump into people one knew. What on earth would he say? 'Oh, hi, Felicity. Look who I found!' Could he blag his way through and make out he'd been on his way to tell her about it? Would she believe him? Probably not. And where did that leave their enquiries about her? Claude still refused to believe she was a blameless loss adjuster who just happened to be in Paris at the very moment he was about to crack his case.

'You have something on your mind,' said Claude, as they headed out of town towards Duncan's office.

'Just worried we might run into Felicity. You know she lives in the town.'

Claude shrugged. 'She'll be at work, won't she?'

'Assuming she's who she says she is and not driving off somewhere in big black cars.'

'We need to know more about her first. I can't risk her knowing of my association with Julian.'

'She doesn't know Julian. She thought *you* were him.'

'Good point. But are you sure she was telling the truth?'

No, he wasn't sure. Claude was right. They needed to know more. An idea struck him. 'Can you contact the people who had paintings stolen and find out who they insured with? We know where Felicity works, so if any of them claimed through her company it would make her look suspicious.'

'There have only been two Gunns stolen in Scotland so far. I may be able to email the owners. Not much point in asking my French client. He won't have insured through a Scottish company. Is there any way we can we get information about how much was paid out? Would the Scottish police know?'

'I don't suppose they would. It would have been a matter for the owner and the insurance company. There'll be a lot of negotiation and I'd imagine they'll all be quite cagey about it.'

'And the police can't get the information from them?'

Ian thought Claude might be overestimating his status with the local police. 'Probably not,' he said. 'Not without a police warrant. And not unless they thought giving us the information would help their case.'

'Didn't Molly say Felicity had some young women working for her? Perhaps I could get to know one of them and see if she can hack into the system for me.'

'Absolutely not,' said Ian, thinking, not for the first time, that Claude was an unethical liability. 'First, it would be highly immoral. Second, it would be illegal. It could get me into big trouble.'

'Only if they could prove a connection between us.'

Ian stared at him, exasperated. 'As you are currently working in my office and sleeping in my house, I don't think that would be hard to prove.'

By now they were driving out of town towards Duncan's office. Claude sighed. 'If you say so. You English are very straight-laced.'

'Scottish,' said Ian. 'And yes. I care about my reputation. And by tomorrow morning we must have decided what to do about Felicity.'

Claude said no more until Ian pulled into the police car park.

Sulking, Ian thought. If he'd had to team up with a French counterpart, he would have preferred a less petulant one. He reached into the back of his car for his coat and, for the second time in as many days, headed to Duncan's office. Claude followed him warily. Did he think Ian had brought him here under false pretences and that he was going to be arrested? He tapped on the door, hoping Claude wasn't about to do a runner.

Ian was becoming used to the lack of heating in police offices. Everywhere was the same, he supposed because no one could afford gas since the war in Ukraine. Ian was lucky. His brother was testing a line of biofuels and a few months ago had visited him with a team who fitted a new boiler free of charge, which ran on gas produced from very large compost heaps. Ian now viewed the potato peelings he threw onto his own compost with great respect. One day he could be self-sufficient and produce his own gas, although he'd need to eat a lot more potatoes than he did now.

Ian huddled into his coat and edged his chair towards a window to take advantage of a small shaft of sunlight. Claude wound his scarf around his neck and pushed his hands into his pockets.

Duncan laughed. 'You get used to the cold,' he said. 'And come December they'll power up the boiler.'

'In France,' said Claude, with a look of superiority, 'we have state-owned gas. The price increase was minimal.'

For a moment Ian found himself wishing that Claude had been confined to a freezing cold prison cell. Why, he wondered, had Duncan not emailed the report to him to read in the warmth of his office? The answer was obvious. Duncan needed to know that Claude was under observation. Ian had become an unwitting jailer.

'Right,' said Duncan. 'The report on the body.' He opened a file on his computer. Then he turned the screen in their direction and let them read the document.

Ian put on his glasses and studied it. The cause of death had been drowning. 'So he was alive when he went into the water,' he said.

'Yes, but he was badly bruised and possibly unconscious before he hit the water,' said Duncan, pointing to some details in the report.

Ian read further. The report concluded that Julian Grainger had died where he was found, and the location suggested that he had fallen off or been thrown from the bridge close to the southern shore.

'The nine-thirty train from Leuchars on Sunday night was held up at the signal, waiting for another train coming in the opposite direction,' said Duncan. 'There would have been time for the perpetrator to leave the train, dragging the body. He could have tipped it over the barrier and climbed back onto the train as it began to move again.'

'Then it was definitely murder?'

'A defence lawyer would probably argue for manslaughter. The injuries suggest they were inflicted before he fell, rather than from landing on the rocks below the bridge, but they were not fatal. The man drowned, so he was alive when he went into the water. But he was almost certainly unconscious. It will depend on the prosecution service, but I'm guessing that when we catch whoever did it, we'll be going for a murder charge.'

'Any clues that suggest a suspect?' Claude asked.

'He was a large man,' said Duncan. 'His attacker would have been strong and well built.' He looked at Claude. 'Not unlike yourself.'

'It wasn't me,' said Claude.

'No,' said Duncan. 'I don't believe it was. There is some evidence, along with witness statements, that suggests we are looking for someone else. Unfortunately, I'm not at liberty to reveal any more.'

Ian suspected Kezia had a hand in that.

15

A trip to Drumlychtoun would do them good – both of them. Lottie hadn't had much attention recently beyond a daily walk in the park or a run along the waterfront if she was lucky. And to be honest, Ian was starting to find Claude's constant presence exhausting, not to say irritating. He couldn't say why. Claude was affable enough. A bit full of himself and inclined to harp on about how much better everything was in France, but he'd been more than generous in sharing all the information he had about art theft. He seemed to genuinely value what they had been able to contribute about the Scottish artist, Hamish Gunn. Although Molly had done a lot more work on that than Ian had.

So perhaps it was the fact of sharing his house that was getting to him. He'd lived alone since Grandad died three years ago and he supposed he'd become set in his ways. But he resented picking up damp towels in the shower, discovering he'd run out of milk or finding the washing machine running when he needed a clean shirt. He was being petty. He knew that. But he still needed a break. He could do with a couple of days of good food, excellent company and long walks by the sea. The excellent company not including Claude, although how he was going to break that to him Ian wasn't sure.

As it turned out, Claude appeared as relieved as Ian at the idea of time on his own. He'd have a relaxed weekend, he said. Maybe explore the village or catch up on some reading. Ian suspected that meant a lie in and an evening in the pub, his reading confined to the menu. But that was fine. As long as he didn't return home to an orgy, or a house burnt to the ground, he wasn't too worried about what Claude got up to.

Ian called Xander and suggested visiting the following weekend. A friend of Caroline's was over from the States, he told him, and would like to see a genuine Scottish castle. He expected a dismissive reply. Xander was still recovering from a stroke; a mild one, but still a stroke. And he wasn't sure how mobile Bridget was. The cast had been removed from her leg, but remembering his own recovery from a leg injury, he knew it could be a slow process back to any kind of fitness.

But Xander welcomed his suggestion of a visit. 'We'd be delighted to see you,' he said. 'It's been far too quiet here recently, even with Anna to cheer us up. And any friend of Caroline's is more than welcome. I'll never forget how she floored that thug the night of our party.'

That was an occasion Ian would never forget, either. The appearance of a man called Orlando Bryson, who claimed to be Xander's son and who had been hell-bent on murdering either him or Bridget. Ian and Caroline, not to mention Xander's sister, Ailish, had dealt with Bryson and his gang of thugs very satisfactorily. The only slight dampener in his memory was that it was the first time he had met Kezia Wallace. But nothing was perfect.

IAN ALWAYS ENJOYED the drive up the coast to Drumlychtoun. He'd picked Brett up early on Saturday morning, suggesting that as the castle was old and draughty, Brett might like to bring an extra jumper or two, and tactfully turning Caroline's thermostat down as they left. He still didn't know who was paying for the household expenses while she was away, and in the few months since she had left, heating costs had rocketed.

Brett was easy company, saying all the right things about the Scottish coastal scenery as Ian drove him to the castle. *Surprising,* Ian thought. *It must all seem a bit tame after the spectacular coast of California.* But perhaps Brett didn't get out much. Ian himself knew this part of Scotland well, but he could imagine himself being impressed should he ever be driven, for example, along the coast of Cornwall.

Arriving at the approach to the castle, Brett asked him to stop, as Anna had done on her first visit, to take photos. It was a glorious day, a frost still sparkling on the heather that grew on the banks of the lake in which the castle was reflected in its full glory.

'Wow,' said Brett. 'This is what I came to Scotland to see.'

They were greeted at the door by Xander, now, to Ian's relief, looking fit and healthy again, Bridget, who was walking with the aid of a stick, and Anna, who was clutching a slobbering bundle of brown fur. As Lottie bounded out of the car, Anna put the puppy down and watched, smiling, as the two dogs got to know each other.

'Who's this?' Ian asked, rumpling the puppy's fur as he introduced Brett, who stood back looking overwhelmed.

'This is Myrtle,' said Anna. 'A welcome to work present from Bridget and Xander.'

'We wanted to welcome Anna to the team in style,' said Bridget. 'But really Myrtle's a bribe to keep her here.' She rubbed her hands vigorously. 'Come in and get warm.'

'Maggie's made Scotch pancakes,' said Anna, leading them inside.

'Brett, you must make yourself at home,' said Bridget. 'Can't be the perfect hostess with this blasted leg but yell if there's anything you need.'

'I'll give you the full tour later,' said Xander. 'But come and have a cup of tea and a pancake by the fire.'

'How is your leg now?' Ian asked Bridget.

'Much better, thanks. I should be fully functional again in a week or two. Thank God we've got Anna here now.'

'I've appointed her as Alan's assistant manager in the estate office,' said Xander. 'And she's driving Bridget to physio a couple of times a week.'

'How did you manage to slip on the rocks? You must walk there every day.'

'It was so stupid,' said Bridget. 'I wasn't looking where I was going. Too busy collecting seaweed.'

'Why were you collecting seaweed?' Ian asked.

'It's the latest superfood,' said Bridget. 'A variety of kelp. We've a contract to supply a manufacturer of dietary supplements. Mostly it's harvested by machines along the coast, but I spotted some on our beach here and thought we could sell it as a special hand-gathered variety. Stupid idea, since it put me out of action for so long.'

'But it brought Anna back to us sooner than we expected,' said Xander.

'And I should be getting back to work,' said Anna, breaking a pancake in two and feeding the two drooling dogs. 'I'll see you all later.'

'Anna's joining us for a meal this evening,' Bridget explained. 'We don't want to crowd her and make her feel she has to care for two old fogies, but we thought since we have two special guests, we'd be a bit more sociable.'

'She doesn't live in the castle?' Brett asked.

'She has one of the flats in the west tower,' Xander explained. 'We have two other live-in employees. It's convenient for them and saves a commute from Montrose. And it's nice for us to know we aren't on our own here at night.'

Ian remembered wondering about that when he'd first visited. Xander and Bridget were not getting any younger, but he knew they'd soldier on here until the bitter end. He'd become very fond of them and had worried about their safety, particularly after the near tragic event with Orlando Bryson. The flat conversions had been a brainwave. Bridget's idea, he guessed.

'Right, Brett,' said Xander, pulling himself out of his chair. 'Ready for the tour?'

'Sure,' said Brett. 'But only if you feel up to it.'

Not tactful, Ian thought.

But Xander laughed. 'Oh, I can still totter around my own castle,' he said.

'I'd join you,' said Bridget. 'But I'd slow you down on the stairs.'

'You coming, Ian?' Xander asked.

'If it's okay with you, I'll take Lottie for a run. We've a few cobwebs to blow away.'

'I'll be in the kitchen with Maggie,' said Bridget. 'Come and join us when you get back. We can catch up on the gossip.'

Their gossip or mine? Ian wondered. Plenty had happened to him since he'd last been there, although Anna had probably updated them. She'd have been full of her trip to Paris as his 'assistant'. He needed to talk to her about that. Claude spoke near-perfect English, but Ian wasn't convinced that he'd share everything he found, and as their searches would involve French websites, it would be good to have Anna on hand as a translator. It needn't take time from her work at Drumlychtoun. He was sure Xander would insist on regular working hours and time off. She might be happy to have a distraction.

'Fascinating,' said Brett as he and Xander arrived in the kitchen, where Maggie was about to serve lunch. 'Such an awesome place.'

'Did Xander show you where the old castle used to be?' Bridget asked. 'I hope he didn't fill your head with nonsense about ghosts.'

'Brett was interested in our rogue's gallery,' said Xander.

'All those dreary people on the stairs?' Bridget asked. 'If they weren't family, I'd have got rid of them years ago. They're a dour-looking lot and all painted by second-rate artists no one has heard of these days. Pity we don't have a Rembrandt.'

'We'd never be able to insure it,' said Xander. 'We'd have to keep it locked up.'

'You do have a Hamish Gunn,' said Brett.

'Who?' asked Bridget, as Ian stopped towelling Lottie and listened.

'He painted one of the Roberts,' said Xander. 'All my forebears were called either Robert or Alexander,' he explained to Brett. 'It gets very confusing.'

'Which Robert?' asked Bridget.

'The great-grandson of the bishop. The one with the ruddy complexion, and the dead deer. Anyway, Brett tells me this Hamish Gunn fellow is quite sought after in America.'

'Can't think why,' said Bridget. 'He wasn't very good. Old Robert looks as if he was a heavy drinker. The deer is quite realistic though.'

'There was one stolen from a collection in San Francisco about a year and a half ago,' said Brett. 'Never been recovered.'

'I don't remember the painting,' said Ian. 'Can I take another look?'

Xander led him through the great hall to the stairs. 'That one,' he said, pointing to a painting of paunchy man with a red face, wearing a kilt and perched on a shooting stick. He was looking proudly at the deer he had just shot. A large specimen with a gory gunshot wound and, understandably considering the circumstances, a bad-tempered expression. *Bridget was right,* Ian thought. *Gunn should have stuck to animals.* The deer was skilfully painted. The man less so. It was all about money, Ian supposed. Dead animals didn't pay as well as land-owning gentry and poor old Gunn needed to make a living. He took out his phone and took a photo.

'Why the interest?' Xander asked.

'It's a case I'm involved with,' said Ian. 'I'm working with a French gallery owner turned investigator. He's looking into contract art thefts and possible insurance fraud. He mentioned Gunn as an artist that these thieves could be targeting right now.'

They returned to the kitchen, where Anna was gulping down a bowl of soup. 'Lunch break,' she explained. 'Can't resist Maggie's soup. And checking that Xander's looking after you properly.'

'Cheeky miss,' said Bridget, smiling at her affectionately.

'Anna's been helping me with some translation,' said Ian, explaining briefly about his recent teaming up with Claude.

'Do you think our painting is under threat?' asked Xander. 'Not sure I'd be all that sorry to lose it, although it would leave a gap on the wall.'

'Our only suspect was found dead in the Tay a few days ago, but we think he had associates, so yes, your painting could be in danger. Do many people know you have it?'

'Shouldn't think so. Just a few academics who might have studied Gunn. I can't see that'd there'd be much interest in Scotland. Far too many similar paintings.'

'But not by that artist,' said Brett.

'What's so special about Gunn?' asked Anna.

'I'm not sure,' said Ian. 'Someone must have thought he was worth having and that inflated the value.'

'I suppose having a work stolen for a private collector who probably paid way more than it was worth would give it a bit of notoriety and inflate the price,' said Bridget. 'Apart from that, he doesn't look special at all.'

'We could use it as a decoy,' said Anna. 'Put something on social media about the painting being here and catch the thief as he breaks in to steal it.'

'Absolutely not,' said Ian, hoping she wasn't serious. 'We shouldn't let anyone know it's here. In fact, I'd suggest storing it away until the thieves have been caught. Preferably somewhere miles away and very secure.'

'If you say so,' said Bridget. 'Our security here is pretty good, though. We had it all updated after that business with the ring. But if you really think it's necessary, I'll call our bank. We already have stuff in one of their vaults. I can arrange for someone to drive it there.'

Ian noticed that something had changed; infra-red sensors in most of the rooms, CCTV and double-locking doors, a new entry system at the gate to the courtyard. But to a professional thief probably nothing that couldn't be breached fairly easily. And it couldn't be locked up all the time. People had to come and go, things had to be delivered and people needed to get to work here. Maggie who cooked and one or two others who came in to clean. Then there was the estate office in the west tower. He'd no idea how many people worked there; four or five, he remembered from his previous visit. And there were three flats above the office. Residents needed key cards to get in, but it would be easy to leave doors open when, for example, unloading shopping. Someone could easily sneak in, and once in there were passages and dark corners to hide in. It would be easy to cut a painting out of its frame and leave with it rolled up inside a coat. Cars were parked along the shore of the lake all day with people fishing or walking on the beach. It would be a matter of a few seconds to cross the bridge and drive away. No, he'd consult with Claude and see if they could find a safe home for the painting until this was all cleared up. Not that he didn't trust Xander's bank, but did a bank have the space for anything larger than jewellery and cash? And how would they transport it safely?

But he could worry about that later. He was here for a relaxing weekend and he planned to enjoy it.

16

Claude had been out all day. He'd been asleep by the time Ian arrived back from Drumlychtoun the previous evening and had left early the following morning, leaving a note saying he needed to arrange a hire car in order to 'catch up with some contacts'. Who those contacts were, Ian had no idea. Claude been told to stay in the area. Duncan hadn't been specific about the exact distance he was allowed to travel. Ian thought it probably meant he shouldn't go anywhere that was too far to get to and return from within a day. Edinburgh would be okay and so would Glasgow. Even London, if he planned it properly, which Ian thought Claude was probably incapable of. But wherever he'd been, he returned late on Monday afternoon and parked his hire car in the road at the end of Ian's garden. At least he'd achieved the car hiring part of his day. He looked tired, Ian thought.

Molly looked up from her computer as he came in and sat down. He dropped his coat on the floor in front of him and scowled at them. 'Good day?' she asked.

'No,' said Claude grumpily. He kicked his coat further under the desk to make room for his feet. Ian was sure he wouldn't treat his red coat in that way and wondered if he had any plans for getting it back.

Now he had his hire car, he could easily drive to Perth to collect it, which would give him and Molly a couple of hours of peace and quiet to get on with some work.

Claude opened up his laptop and tapped crossly at some keys. 'I spent the whole day buying ruinously expensive whisky for various people I have worked with in the past,' he said. 'I was hoping to get some clues about the art thefts, or at least a hint of who might have had it in for poor old Julian. But there was nothing. I suppose you had a great time up in your Scottish castle.' He sounded as if he hoped Ian's whole weekend had been a washout.

'I did actually,' said Ian, trying his best not to look too smug. 'I found a Hamish Gunn.' He opened the photo he taken of the Gunn painting on his phone and showed it to them. 'Brett spotted it. I had no idea it was there.'

Claude looked at it in a way that suggested he had no interest in it whatsoever.

'It's great that he noticed it,' said Molly. 'Now we know about it we can make sure it's kept safe. I'll add it to my list.'

'That's what I thought,' said Ian. 'They are going to try to store it at the bank for a while.'

'How will they get it there?' Claude asked, suddenly looking more interested.

'Not sure they've worked it out yet,' said Ian. 'I'll probably get some of my security lads onto it. It's not a huge picture. They can drive it there in one of the estate vans.'

'Hmm,' said Claude. 'Mind if I make some toast?' He disappeared into the kitchen without waiting for an answer.

'Someone's had a bad day,' said Molly.

'Yeah,' said Ian, wondering if Claude, having cleaned him out of bread, would expect him to cook a meal this evening. 'Serves him right for knocking back the whisky.'

Molly laughed. 'And don't tell me you didn't sink a glass or two when you got back last night.'

'Maybe,' he said. 'But at least I didn't drive anywhere afterwards.'

'I was perfectly sober when I drove back here,' said Claude, reappearing from the kitchen and looking offended. 'What's the plan for tomorrow?' he asked.

Trying to change the subject, thought Ian. 'We need to decide what to do about Felicity,' he said. 'I have to let her know I've found you. It's what I was contracted to do, and I can't spin it out any longer.'

Claude smirked at them. 'Do you think I should take up where I left off and—'

'No,' said Ian and Molly firmly and at the same time.

'It could be the only way of finding out what her involvement is, if any,' said Claude.

'That would be entrapment,' said Ian. 'I don't think it's legal. Not in Scotland, anyway.'

'And it would be unkind,' said Molly. 'You should only get involved with someone if you like them. Not to get information.'

'Suppose I want to get involved with her because I find her attractive?'

Really? Ian tried to remember who had picked up whom in that Paris bar. Hadn't Claude said she was the one to make advances?

'Do you find her attractive?' Molly asked. 'I wouldn't have thought she was your type.'

Claude shrugged. 'She is quite attractive,' he said. 'And I don't really have a type.'

'Then you need to be honest with her,' said Molly. 'Tell her exactly who you are and what you do.'

'Molly's right,' said Ian. 'The only alternative would be for me to tell her I found you but that you don't want any more contact with her.'

'Or we could be honest with her and ask for her help. We know she's involved with Mr Craigie and his insurance claim. She might know more than we do about his burglary.' Molly stood up and grabbed a pen. She wrote Felicity's name at the top of the board and added arrows to the possible courses of action:

1.Tell her the truth and ask for her help

2.Tell her Julian is really Claude but that he wants nothing more to do with her

3.Let Claude contact her and carry on where they left off

'They all have pros and cons,' said Ian, fiddling with some paperclips on his desk. 'If we ask for her help and she's actually working for the thieves, we're going to make the situation much worse. She'd know what we're doing and be able to work around it. On the other hand, we will know where she is and can keep an eye on her.'

'And if we go for number two,' said Molly, 'she'll pay our bill and disappear. We might miss some valuable information.'

'And the third option is unethical,' said Ian.

They both looked at Claude, who was smiling enigmatically. 'Arrange a meeting,' he said. 'For all of us. We need to confront her.'

For once, Ian thought, he was probably right. 'How will you explain why you failed to meet her at Waverley?' he asked.

'Easy enough. Your country is in a mess. There are long queues everywhere.'

'I know that's a problem for people trying to get across the Channel from this side. Not sure it's as bad coming in the other direction.'

'Bound to be,' said Claude. 'If trains are delayed at Folkestone it messes up the whole schedule in both directions. Flights have been affected as well. Something to do with staff shortages at the airport.'

'Okay, I suppose that's believable. But perhaps you should move out of here and work somewhere else.'

'I have to stay in the area,' said Claude petulantly.

'Dundee Library is in the area,' said Ian. 'And we wouldn't have to explain to Felicity why we are working together.'

'I don't see why I should go there,' said Claude. 'I thought we were going to be honest with her. Tell her you found me and told me about the body under the bridge. The police have asked me to stick around while they continue their enquires, so we decided to work together on my client's art thefts.'

'It would be difficult if she started popping in here to visit you,' said Molly. 'We'd not get any work done.'

'It's not that I don't want you here,' Ian lied. 'But it would be better if you weren't here all the time.'

Claude appeared to be giving this some thought. 'I shall tell her that I have work to do in Edinburgh and will be in the area for a while. There's no need for her to come and find me here.'

It seemed like a reasonable compromise. Ian was still not sure that it was ethical, but far be it from him to keep them apart as long as they both knew the truth about their relationship, or friendship or whatever. And in a way, Claude was right. If there was any chance that Felicity's interest was any more than that of an insurer, they needed to know about it.

'That's settled, then,' said Claude. 'You tell her that I am found and arrange a meeting. Give her my phone number and she can contact me. And,' he added, looking pleased with himself, 'I have a plan.'

17

The news that the body Felicity had failed to identify was indeed a man by the name of Julian, to be precise Julian Grainger, and that the man she was looking for was actually called Claude Lambert, wasn't received with the excitement and gratitude Ian had expected. He and Molly had visited her at home that evening, having decided it would be better to leave Claude behind.

That was Molly's suggestion. 'She won't be poking around in the office or meeting Claude. And it would be friendlier, don't you think?'

Ian was not sure he agreed with it being friendlier.

Felicity also appeared to disagree. She stood on her doorstep, took the slip of paper on which he'd written Claude's telephone number and slipped it into her pocket without looking at it. 'How much do I owe you?' she asked, still standing on her doorstep, obviously not about to ask them in for a cup of tea and a friendly chat. Never mind a thank you for concluding her case so efficiently and quickly.

Ian handed her the envelope containing his invoice. She slipped that into her pocket as well. 'I shall pay this evening,' she told him. 'I assume you've included your bank details?'

He nodded. 'Claude asked me to let you know that he would be happy to talk to you.'

'He's in Scotland,' said Molly. 'Will you meet him?'

Felicity gave her a withering look. 'That, young lady, is none of your business. I merely asked you to discover his whereabouts.'

Ungrateful, Ian thought. But they had done what she'd asked and there was no reason why they should take any further interest. Felicity brushed an imaginary fleck of dust from her jacket and shut the door.

'That was weird,' said Molly, as they returned to his car.

'Worrying,' said Ian. 'You remember she told us that Claude was in danger? You don't suppose that we've just put him in more danger by telling her how to find him?'

'You think she's planning to harm him? For standing her up?' Molly asked.

'I've no idea,' said Ian. 'But I don't trust her.' It was one of the oddest cases he'd ever worked on. A middle-aged woman supposedly hunting for someone, possibly a lost lover. Although she hadn't actually said that, Ian couldn't think of any other reason for her wanting to find him. There were two men, one with the name of said lost lover, but not him. A dead body with nothing about his person except a scrap of paper with a name on it. The name of a private detective/art dealer and owner of a stylish overcoat, who was searching for a gang of thieves who were looking for the work of a second-rate, two-hundred-year-old portrait painter and who, coincidentally, was the very man who had apparently been carrying on an affair with the woman that the whole wretched business had started with. Ian felt breathless just thinking about it.

Molly was as puzzled as he was. 'Are we just going to let it go there?' she asked. 'Once Felicity has paid us, there's no reason to take it any further.'

'I'm not convinced she had nothing to do with the dead body. I think we need to keep an eye on her.' But as they would be doing it unpaid, it might not be the best use of their time.

'Shouldn't we tell Duncan?'

He thought about that. The last time he'd taken his suspicions to Duncan he'd been threatened with a charge of wasting police time. He didn't fancy that happening again. All the same, he was sure that they didn't know all there was to know about Felicity. 'You're still in touch with the girls that work in her office?' he asked.

'We said we'd meet up again soon. They're good company.'

'So you could well have chummed up with them some other way?'

'I suppose so. They were intrigued by me working as a PI. A couple of them were complaining about how boring it is working in an insurance office and are looking for something more exciting.'

'Did they know you were watching Felicity?'

'No, I told them I couldn't discuss cases and let them believe I was spying on a philandering husband. A couple of them were interested in Caroline's keep safe campaign so we're meeting again. But I really do want to keep in touch with them and not just use them for work.'

'Of course. It's great to make new friends.'

'But if they do let anything drop about Felicity…'

'Then there'd be no harm in letting me know.'

'So we're not actually spying on Felicity, just keeping an ear to the ground.'

'Exactly,' he said, smiling. 'And while we're doing that, we're still working with Claude and his search for the gang of art thieves.'

'Is someone paying him for that?'

'His client is paying him well and he offered to split the fee. We need to get that in writing. I'm not helping him for free.'

'It doesn't sound profitable if we're only getting half the fee. You don't think we should just tell him to forget it?'

Ian had been thinking exactly that. But he was still stuck with Claude as a house guest until Duncan was satisfied he had nothing to do with the murder and told him he could return home. And as he had to put up with him for a bit longer, it was just as well they had work to do together. In any case, after discovering there was a Hamish Gunn at Drumlychtoun, it was probably better to stay involved in Claude's case. He wasn't too worried about the painting, which no one seemed to like very much, but he'd never forgive himself if anything happened to Xander or Bridget. And now Anna was involved as well, it could be even more risky. Until they got to the bottom of Hamish Gunn's sudden popularity and hopefully uncovered who was responsible, he'd worry. Even if Xander's painting was safely locked up somewhere.

Molly pulled the list she had made of the Gunn paintings in Scotland from her bag and studied it. She'd discovered ten, either in galleries or private ownership, and now she added an eleventh, the one at Drumlychtoun. She'd contacted the owners, all of whom had been surprised that there should be any threat to them. 'Isn't it odd that this gang are focussed on an artist no one's ever really been interested in before?' she said.

Ian had thought the same. Why the sudden interest in second-rate Scottish portraits?

He put that aside for the moment. It would be something to come back to. Right now, he was more concerned with Claude's plan and how it would involve him and Molly. And where was Claude, anyway? For the last two days he'd been getting under his feet, eating all his food and generally making a nuisance of himself. But today there was no sign of him. If they were going to work together, he should really get a few things straight. They needed a contract, and agreement about hours and who was going to do what.

As they arrived back at the office, Ian's phone rang. It was a short call and when he ended it, he looked at Molly. 'It just got weirder,' he said. 'Felicity is coming here tomorrow. She has things to tell us, and she wants Claude to be here.'

∼

'SHALL I CLEAN THE BOARD?' Molly asked the next morning. 'Felicity will be here any minute.'

Ian looked at it. A few notes about Gunn, Claude's list of stolen paintings and one of Molly's brainstorms with circled names and coloured arrows. 'No,' he said. 'There's too much there that I want to keep. And don't tell me I should use Fact Stuffer.'

'Wouldn't dream of it,' said Molly. 'But do we really want Felicity to see everything we've written up there?'

'No,' he said. 'We'll use the living room.' Apart from anything else, he didn't want Felicity to know that he and Claude were working together. Not yet.

FELICITY ARRIVED PUNCTUALLY, looking as composed as ever and seemingly unfazed by the prospect of meeting Claude again. Claude himself was unusually quiet, merely nodding to Felicity as they gathered around a small table and made polite conversation over coffee and biscuits.

'Let's get down to work,' said Ian, taking out his phone. 'You have something to tell us?'

'I do,' said Felicity. 'But I would prefer you not to record it this time.'

'Okay,' said Ian, opening the home screen on his phone to show that he was not recording her, then placing the phone on the table in front of them.

'Thank you,' she said, icily. 'And you two.' She nodded at Molly and Claude, who stared at her blankly. 'Phones on the table,' she said.

Molly put her phone on the table. Claude looked as if he was about to object.

'Just do it,' Ian hissed at him.

'I'm afraid,' said Felicity, 'that I've not been entirely honest with you.'

Ian did his best to look surprised, while Claude appeared to choke on some biscuit crumbs. Only Molly looked unfazed. 'I'm sure you had your reasons,' she said.

'Although much of what I told you was the truth,' Felicity continued, 'there are a few details I omitted.'

'And why do you feel the need to tell us now?' Ian asked.

'Because I'm not stupid,' she said. 'If I don't tell you what I know, you will suspect me.'

'Suspect you of what?' Claude asked.

Felicity sighed and gave him a look that suggested he had just asked her a very stupid question. 'I think you know the answer perfectly well,' she said. 'But I shall start at the beginning.'

'I really would like to take some notes,' said Ian. 'You wouldn't be here unless you were about to tell us things we needed to remember.'

'You may write notes,' she said, 'and I will ask you to give me a copy of them.'

Fair enough, he thought, reaching for a notebook and pen.

'It began with a burglary a few weeks ago,' she said.

'Stonebridge House?' Ian asked.

Felicity looked at him in surprise. 'I'm impressed,' she said. 'How did you know that? It can't have been the only burglary around here recently.'

'You were picked up from your office in Dundee by a car that was owned by Douglas Craigie, who lives there,' said Ian. 'It was likely that you were working with him over a claim for goods stolen in the burglary. It wasn't difficult to find the details.'

'A refreshingly thorough investigator,' she said, with a disapproving scowl in Claude's direction.

'I too can be thorough,' said Claude, fidgeting in his seat and studying his fingernails.

Felicity ignored him. 'You worked out that Craigie insured through the company I work for. It was a straightforward claim at first. As is usual in these cases, we are delaying payment until we are sure that none of the stolen property has been recovered. In an urgent claim such as fire damage, we of course pay immediately. But you will appreciate that burglaries are different. I worked closely with Mr Craigie on his claim, and we became friends. But that is beside the point for now. You will see that it becomes relevant later on.'

'Was anything recovered?' Ian asked.

'You will know from your research that a few items of silverware, some jewellery and six paintings were stolen.'

Ian nodded.

'A sliver cream jug and some teaspoons were found at a shop in Dundee. Antique shops are alerted after a burglary and pictures distributed where possible. The owner of this shop contacted us within days of the claim and the goods have been returned. Unfortunately, none of the jewellery has yet been found, which is sad as it was of sentimental value to Mr Craigie.'

'What about the paintings?' Molly asked.

Felicity turned to her and smiled. 'That is very interesting,' she said. 'Five of the paintings were found at a street market in Forfar. The sixth is still missing, despite an extensive search of local markets and junk shops.'

Claude winced at the mention of junk shops. He slouched back in his chair, yawned and stretched his legs out in front of him.

'Let me guess,' said Ian. 'The sixth painting was a Hamish Gunn.'

'Once again, Mr Skair, you impress me. Yes, it was a Gunn. A portrait of a man believed to be a Mr Alistair Blair of Blairgovern House. He's holding a large fish. Mr Craigie was not unduly upset about the loss and told me it was a second-rate painting. I felt that the amount he claimed for its loss was an undervaluation, having studied the recent market for similar paintings. But it is not the job of insurance companies to point this out to clients.'

Suddenly Claude looked alert. 'Hamish Gunn,' he said. 'You didn't mention him when we met.'

'Why should I? We were merely looking at art together in Paris. But if you let me continue you will understand why.'

Claude sat back in his chair and sighed loudly.

'As I said, I did a little research into Gunn's paintings and was struck by the recent inflation in their value.'

'Prices fluctuate all the time,' said Claude, irritably. 'Gunn is currently popular in the Middle East.'

'Do you know why?' asked Ian.

'He wasn't a prolific painter,' said Claude. 'I assume the buyers are attracted by their rarity.'

Felicity gave him what Ian considered a withering look. 'I

wonder,' she asked, looking around at the three of them, 'have you heard of Dr Sebastian Trevelyan?'

None of them had.

'He lectures in art history at the University of Southern Texas. He wrote a book called *The Secrets behind the Canvas*. I'm surprised you have not read it, Jul... Claude.'

Claude shrugged.

'The book has some fascinating accounts of a phenomenon known as *impedimento*. It's when an artist—'

Claude interrupted her. 'Things hidden under the painting. Usually only discovered by X-ray. Normally something the artist has changed his mind about, or to hide controversial subject matter. Or simply just reusing a canvas for something they consider better quality.'

'So Hamish Gunn painted over his own paintings?' Molly asked.

'Not exactly. Have you read *The Da Vinci Code*?' Felicity asked them. 'It's by Dan Brown.'

'I don't read trashy thrillers,' said Claude. 'I prefer to spend my time on something with some literary merit.'

'A pity,' said Felicity. 'If you had read it, you might have realised why Gunn had suddenly become popular.'

Something began to stir in Ian's memory. He'd read the book while in hospital recovering from his leg injury. He'd enjoyed it, so it seemed he didn't share Claude's principles about improving literature. Although he didn't see why one couldn't enjoy both. 'There was a code in a painting,' he said. 'Something about the whereabouts of the Holy Grail.'

Felicity smiled at him approvingly. 'Nice to meet someone who has read widely,' she said.

Ian tried to look modest.

'Okay, so he's bloody Renaissance man,' said Claude. 'Can't see how that relates to Gunn.'

'If there are codes hidden in his paintings,' Molly asked, 'how would anyone know?'

'This is where it starts to get really interesting,' said Felicity.

'About time,' Claude muttered. Molly frowned at him.

'I've just remembered something,' said Molly. 'You remember the biography I was sent?'

'The Gunn biography from the university library?' Ian asked.

'My friend who works there,' Molly explained to Felicity, 'has access to a huge number of academic eBooks and she sent me some screenshots. I thought it would help to find out where some of his paintings were, but it also told me a bit about his life. He didn't start painting until he was in his forties. Before that he was an archaeologist and spent a lot of his time in the Middle East. Mainly in what was then Persia, now Iran. But he also went to India.'

'That's right,' said Felicity. 'I spent time in a museum in Edinburgh where they hold an archive of letters on microfilm that Gunn wrote to a fellow artist. I was able to print some for a small fee.' She opened her handbag and pulled out a sheet of paper. 'This is a copy I made of one of them. Gunn wrote it a few years after his final visit to Persia and he tells of a find he made during a dig on the Elburz mountains. It was a substantial find, but at the time Persia was going through one of many periods of violent unrest. They were unable to bring anything away with them – these days that wouldn't have happened anyway. Several members of the team had become ill, and all their efforts were concentrated on getting out of the country and safely home.'

Ian read the letter, which was written in a hand he recognised from letters he'd seen written by his own grandfather. Children must have been taught to write in a very particular style. Potential clerks, he supposed, needed to be able to produce uniform documents. 'He's telling his friend that he intends to return one day and retrieve the find. He mentions a very particular way he devised to map the site and to keep it concealed.'

'So you think he'd mapped it into his paintings?' asked Molly.

'It would explain the interest in them, don't you think?' Felicity asked.

'But how could they be decoded?' Ian asked.

'And how would anyone have discovered it?' asked Molly.

'We should ask our art historian,' said Felicity, turning to Claude.

'It's possible, I suppose,' he said. 'I might be able to tell by studying some of his paintings.'

'How many are there?' asked Ian.

Molly produced her list. 'I found eleven scattered around Scotland. Two are missing presumed to have been exported after they were stolen. There are very few in public galleries and most of those are not on view because as paintings they are not considered interesting enough.'

'I've one on my phone,' said Ian. 'The portrait at Drumlychtoun.'

'Can you enlarge it and make me a print?' said Claude. 'I'll get to work on it.'

'He wouldn't have painted maps into all his paintings, would he?' Molly asked. 'I don't know much about art, but wouldn't that make them all look the same?'

'Depends how he did it,' said Claude. 'I'm guessing he started with some kind of triangulation point and coordinates.'

Ian turned to Felicity. 'Did Mr Craigie take photos of his paintings?'

'We do have them on record, yes. I can let Claude have a copy of the Gunn.'

All very interesting, Ian thought. But where was it taking them? 'Why are you telling us all this?' he asked.

'I'll get to that,' said Felicity. 'There's a bit more to explain first. I was intrigued that five of the six paintings turned up in Forfar. They were good paintings and could have raised a tidy sum in the right market.'

'By right market, I assume you mean the black market,' said Ian. 'Perhaps they were offloaded in Forfar because time was running out, or the buyer wasn't as interested as expected.'

'Or because the thieves were not interested in them,' said Felicity. 'I wondered about that, so I went and talked to a dealer called Mike who runs the stall and asked how he had acquired them. Most of their stock comes from house clearances, but he told me these had been brought to him in a van by a lad called Jimmy. He'd been asked to collect them from a demolition site in the north of Dundee.'

'Did the police know about that?' Molly asked.

'I passed on the information, but by the time they got there the place had been flattened and cleared for new building. But to return to Jimmy. Mike was having a quiet day and offered Jimmy a cup of tea and they got chatting. Apparently, Jimmy had been contacted through a WhatsApp group where he advertised himself as a man with a van. Mike described him as a bright, observant and very chatty lad who showed him the original message he'd received, which had been sent by a user calling himself Julian. Jimmy'd been asked to call at a pub in Dundee to collect the money for the job and actually met Julian, who explained he was about to leave for Paris and could only pay him in cash.'

'So you set off for Paris hoping to find Julian?' said Claude. 'And met me instead. What did you hope to gain from that?'

'Couldn't it have been dangerous?' Molly asked, ignoring Claude's question.

'If I might interrupt,' said Ian. 'We need to know why Felicity thought she would find Julian that easily. Paris is a big place. All we know is that Jimmy was paid by a man called Julian who presumably knew what happened to the Gunn painting, and that he was on his way to Paris.'

'One at a time,' said Felicity, holding up her hand. 'As Mike told me, Jimmy is a very bright and resourceful lad. When he delivered the paintings, Mike told him that he knew they were stolen and showed him the list the police had given him. He suggested that Jimmy should go to the police before they suspected him of being involved in the burglary or as a member of the gang. Jimmy did this, and they were satisfied that he had no part in it. In fact, they thanked him for coming forward and told him they were sure that Mr Craigie would be grateful to him for the part he had played in the return of five of the six paintings. Jimmy had one more piece of information he thought would be useful. As Julian opened his wallet and pulled out the notes to pay him, a card fell onto the floor, unnoticed by Julian. Jimmy picked it up after he left. It was like this one.' Felicity opened her handbag and removed a card, the kind found in tourist offices and railway stations, anywhere that people are looking for holiday accommodation.

Ian took it from her and read it. *L'Hotel Didier Pierre. Close to L'Opera. Meeting place for all who are in the market for fine art.*

'Jimmy gave it to the police?' asked Ian.

'He did, but he had the impression that they were not interested. That police resources wouldn't stretch to trips to Paris to recover stolen property. It was lucky, therefore, that he'd taken a photo of it on his phone.'

'He contacted you?' Molly asked. 'How did he know who the insurer was?'

Felicity shook her head. 'No,' she said. 'He took it to Douglas Craigie.'

'Who handed it on to you?'

Felicity smiled coyly. Coy wasn't something Ian had attributed to Felicity, but it suited her. She could be quite attractive to someone. A widower, perhaps...

'Douglas and I had become friends,' she said. 'We had only met a couple of times, but he needed a partner to attend a charity dinner with and he invited me.'

'And you wore a turquoise evening dress,' said Molly. 'With a cream velvet jacket.'

'How on earth did you know that?' Felicity asked.

'You were seen by some of your employees in the bar of the Mal Maison.'

'You have been busy spying on me,' she said.

'Surveillance,' said Ian. 'You had employed us. We were just doing our job.'

'Above and beyond if you ask me,' Claude muttered.

'After that evening, we began to see a lot of each other. We got talking about the Gunn and the artist's sudden popularity and once I showed him my research, he became keen to find out what had happened to his painting. So I said I would go to Paris and make some enquiries.'

'I'm surprised he let you go on your own,' said Claude.

'Douglas was concerned for my safety, but I assured him I was perfectly capable of taking care of myself. And we both thought it best for *me* to approach Julian rather than him.'

'And you thought I was Julian, so why didn't you tell me why you were there?'

Felicity looked at him icily. 'I wanted to know where the painting was. If I'd told you that and you were actually Julian, not just someone pretending to be him, I'd have been in danger myself. I needed to find out more. I began to think the painting must still be in Scotland, which is why I agreed to meet you in Edinburgh.'

'All this is completely fascinating,' said Ian. 'But why come to us now?'

'Because we want to know what happened to Douglas' painting. I'm impressed by the work you and Molly have already done. And because Claude here is involved in ways I don't yet understand. But he is knowledgeable about art and will also be a link to whatever has been going on in Paris. I suspect he is working for someone else who has had paintings stolen and it could be a chance for all of us to work together. Douglas and I will put a sum of money at your disposal, and we will also continue to pay your hourly rate.'

'You're correct,' said Claude. 'I am working for a client who has had paintings stolen. Ian and I have already agreed to share the work and split the fee. So does your offer to him include me?'

'Assuming you can account for the hours you put in, yes, we will pay the same rate to you. We will expect weekly reports from both of you.'

'It's an interesting proposition,' said Ian. 'We need to discuss it among the three of us and draw up a contract. Can I get back to you later today?'

'Of course,' said Felicity. She pulled a phone from her bag. 'I'm sending you my mobile number,' she said. 'You may call me this evening.'

'I thought you didn't use a mobile,' said Molly.

'I said I preferred not to. I dislike being interrupted at all hours of the day or night. But I have been persuaded that it would be useful.'

Not too useful, Ian hoped. Would she now be sending them floods of emails, photographs and web links? There were none so fervent as the recently converted. Did she and Craigie send each other affectionate little messages with heart emojis and kisses? Which reminded him. 'We should meet Mr Craigie,' he said. 'Since he too will be a client.'

'Of course,' she said. 'Perhaps you would care to join us for a drink at Stonebridge House later this evening.'

The words rang in his head. *Join* us *at Stonebridge House.* He wondered if the ghost of the former Mrs Craigie was turning in her grave or whether she would be pleased that Douglas had found a companion. Even a scary one like Felicity.

18

Claude opened his eyes and looked blearily up at Ian. '*Merde,*' he said, shutting his eyes again and muttering something in French. Ian bent down to try to catch what he was saying. '*Les moutons*' was the only thing he could decipher. *Moutons? Sheep,* Ian thought, which in the current circumstances was irrelevant.

Ian had been against it from the start. Claude's plan was never going to work, but he was the only one of them who thought so. Even Molly came around to the idea once Douglas Craigie had exercised his charm on her. Ian was overruled.

They had been sitting in Craigie's living room at Stonebridge House. A stylish room, even with the gap on the wall where Hamish Gunn's painting had hung. Craigie was thoroughly enjoying his role as host and pouring them all generous glasses of 'a little something I've been keeping for the right occasion'. The little something turned out to be a dusty bottle of vintage Drambuie. The kind, Ian reflected, that sold at auction for around £200 a bottle.

'Such a relief,' said Craigie, 'that the burglars didn't take it.'

Ian took a sip and had to agree. Thankfully Molly was driving him and Claude back to Greyport. She expressed a dislike of strong liqueurs and was happy to be the nominated driver. Probably because she had been longing to drive Ian's car. He looked at Felicity, who seemed to be downing the liqueur with enthusiasm, and wondered how she would be getting home. The truth was that she probably wouldn't be going home. She was perfectly at home here. Ian wondered how long it would be before she changed the curtains and had the kitchen remodelled.

Craigie rubbed his hands. 'I say,' he said. 'This is so much fun. Never thought I'd get a shot at being a detective. And all thanks to you, Flickers.' He patted Felicity affectionately on the bottom.

Flickers? Our Felicity must be a fast worker. Did she have a similarly rakish nickname for Craigie?

'Dougie, dear,' she said. 'We're supporting this case financially. We don't want to interfere with the professionals, do we?'

'Of course not, my sweet. But you've got to admit, it's exciting. Really hotting up since your visit to Paris.'

What exactly was 'hotting up' was something Ian preferred not to explore too closely.

'Now, Monsieur Lambert, I understand you have a plan?' said Craigie.

Claude's plan was to use the Drumlychtoun Gunn painting as a decoy. Ian had already stamped on Anna's idea of doing this and Claude's plan was only slightly less hare-brained. But at least it didn't involve luring the thieves to Drumlychtoun. That was something Ian would never have allowed. The painting had now been removed for safekeeping in the cellar of Xander's solicitor in Montrose. It had been driven there in one of the estate vans along with case of organic veg. There was now a space on the wall halfway up the grand staircase and Bridget had promised to scour the attics and find something to replace it with. But she was unable to do this for a few more weeks. Xander forbade her and anyone else from climbing up the twisty stone stairs to the attic on the grounds that one broken leg at a time was enough to be going on with.

Claude's plan involved drawing attention to this space on the wall. Anna, he had discovered, was vlogging about her work at Drumlychtoun. She posted daily videos of people doing various things around the estate, uploading them to a YouTube channel. Ian assumed at first that this would only be of interest to her family and possibly to her estate management tutor in Perpignan. It surprised him to discover that after only a few days she had several thousand followers, and that the estate office was working hard to keep up with the demand for new orders from all over the world. Her next upload was going to feature the space on the wall, a photograph of the Hamish Gunn painting and the news that the following day it would be transported to Edinburgh for some restoration. A decoy parcel, a wooden box the same size as the painting but containing only a damaged frame, would be driven by a member of Ian's security team in one of the estate's delivery vans. Claude would follow behind in his hire car. They would be intercepted, Claude assured them, and the box stolen. He and the security men would then identify the thief or thieves, take down details of the car they were travelling in and report them to the police. If, by a stroke of good fortune, there was only one thief, they would detain him and transport him to the nearest police station.

What could possibly go wrong?

Quite a few things came into Ian's head. How would the thieves know the route they were taking and what time they were leaving? What if they were armed? What would they do when they discovered they had stolen an empty frame? All of these were dismissed by Claude as trivialities. Craigie and Felicity, particularly Felicity, thought it was an excellent idea and Ian found himself overruled. All he could do was give in and double the security watch at the castle.

THE WHOLE THING had been a disaster. Half an hour after they left Drumlychtoun a car had overtaken Claude and for a while blocked the view the van driver had of him. When the road was clear once more, he slowed down, assuming that Claude would catch him up. He waited ten minutes and then realised he'd lost him. The van driver turned back to look for him and discovered his car abandoned by the side of the road, the keys still in it, a few miles outside Forfar. It was a quiet stretch of road with no other cars in sight and no sign of pedestrians. He tried calling Claude's phone, but all he got was a garbled voice message in French. Fearing Claude might have been kidnapped, the driver returned to Drumlychtoun and unloaded the box there. He called Ian, who doubted the kidnap theory but agreed there was nothing they could do. Sooner or later Claude would turn up with an explanation, plausible or otherwise, of where he had been. He and Molly waited in the office for the rest of the morning, wondering if he'd returned to France and if that was the last they'd ever see of him. Then they had a call from the police. Claude had been found badly beaten and dumped in a field half a mile from the car. He'd been taken to hospital, suffering from concussion and a hazy memory of what had happened to him. One of the nursing staff had searched his jacket for some ID. She found Ian's card and called him. He left Molly in charge of the office and drove to the hospital.

IAN LOOKED DOWN at Claude's bruised face and wondered what the hell had happened. Had someone held him up, searched his car and, finding no painting, beaten him up? Had they meant to kill him? And if so, why? At least there had been no trouble at Drumlychtoun and Anna had immediately launched a new video reporting that the painting had safely reached its destination and showing a painting of some small children playing in a stream, which Bridget had chosen from one of the bedrooms to fill the gap it until it was returned. A return, Anna had added, that was not expected for several months.

Claude was now snoring loudly. Not a lot of point in waking him yet, the doctors said. He would most likely still be confused by the painkillers they'd given him and not remember very much about what had happened. Ian pulled up an uncomfortable hospital chair and prepared for a long wait. Molly had promised to bring him a flask of soup once she'd closed the office and arranged for Lainie to look after Lottie. They both agreed that even though there was a local constable seated outside Claude's room, it was best not to leave him on his own. Julian Grainger had Claude's name on an envelope in his pocket. Would the murderer have known about it? Ian tried to remember if that was a detail that had been released by the police and thought it probably wasn't. But could he take that chance? Who was to say Claude wouldn't be the next victim? He was lying in a hospital bed, drugged and vulnerable. Anyone could slip in and finish him off. Having done hospital duty himself in the past, Ian had no great faith in the constable's ability to stay awake or remain at his post.

Ian heard footsteps and turned, expecting to see Molly with a flask of soup. Instead he found himself staring into the face of Kezia Wallace.

'Why is it,' she said, pulling up another chair and sitting down next to him, 'that the moment one of my cases starts to get interesting, you beat me to it?'

Really? How could the case of a few missing paintings be of any interest to someone of her rank?

Kezia had come prepared. She opened her bag and pulled out a Marks and Spencer triple sandwich pack. She picked out an egg and tomato one, took a bite and then passed the pack to Ian. 'Want one?' she asked.

'Molly should be here soon with a flask of soup,' he said, helping himself to a prawn mayo sandwich. 'But I'm not sure how long she'll be.'

'We can share your soup when Molly gets here,' said Kezia.

Very matey. But one didn't argue with Kezia Wallace, and she had been generous with her sandwiches. It was a fair exchange. 'Why are you interested in this case?' he asked.

She nodded in Claude's direction. 'We were about to pull this guy in for more questioning over the Grainger murder,' she told him. 'Duncan's case really, but I was in the area, so I thought I'd ask a few preliminary questions before he leaves hospital. It seems he lied about where he spent the night of the murder. He told Duncan he was in Perth but was spotted at an Indian restaurant in Dundee late that evening. At about the right time should he have travelled into

Dundee on the train that was held up at the southern end of the bridge.'

'You think he killed the man and then tucked into an Indian meal?' Ian had no idea if murder gave one an appetite, but it seemed improbable. Wouldn't you want to get as far away from the crime scene as soon as possible?

Where had Claude told him he spent Sunday night? In an anonymous hotel on the outskirts of Perth, which confirmed what he had told Duncan. Was it likely that he'd innocently travelled to Dundee and back again that night? They had perfectly good Indian restaurants in Perth. There would have been no reason to go to Dundee. Unless he wanted to push someone off a train. But the body of Grainger had been found at the southern end of the bridge. Trains from Perth to Dundee ran along the north bank of the Tay. The murderer must have been approaching the city from the south, which seemed to let Claude off the hook. Claude was mildly irritating and arrogant, but Ian couldn't see him as a violent murderer. He found himself hoping very much that he was not one, particularly as they were currently sharing a house. He looked down at Claude's bruised face and bandaged arm. He looked more like a victim of violence than a perpetrator.

'The doctor said it could be a while before he's awake and coherent enough for an interview,' said Ian. Perhaps not the best thing to say as Claude promptly opened his eyes and sat up.

'Thirsty,' he said. Ian passed him a glass of water. 'Who are you?' Claude asked gruffly, staring at Kezia.

'DCI Kezia Wallace,' she said, showing him her ID. 'I have some questions to ask you.'

'It was those bloody sheep,' said Claude.

'I don't think DCI Wallace is here to talk about your attack,' said Ian, still wondering what sheep had to do with it.

'I'm only answering your questions if Ian can stay,' said Claude. 'I'm not well.'

'Fine,' said Kezia, biting into the remaining sandwich. 'I'd be interested to know what Ian's involvement is in this case, but tell me about the attack first.'

Ian explained briefly about the plan to lure the art thieves. 'It wasn't my idea,' he added. 'I did warn them not to do it.'

'You should have listened to him,' said Kezia, waving her sandwich in Claude's direction. 'It was a seriously dangerous and irresponsible plan. You were lucky you didn't end up like Mr Grainger.'

An odd thing to say, Ian thought. If Claude was now her main suspect.

'So,' Kezia continued. 'You were driving innocently through the Angus countryside, following a van containing a broken picture frame. And then what? The attackers drove between you and the van in front? Why didn't the other driver stop to help you?'

'I told you,' said Claude. 'It was the sheep. A car pulled between me and the van. It was driving slowly, and we were on a twisting road so I couldn't overtake it. Then there was a clear stretch and the driver put his foot down and sped off. And before I could speed up myself the road was full of sheep. Something must have alarmed them, and they were hurtling through a gate that had been left open. I had to stop and as soon as I did, this thug dragged me out of the car, beat me up and left me in the field. My head hurt like hell and then I blacked out and the next thing I knew I was in an ambulance.'

'Did he say anything?'

'Not a word,' he said.

'Can you describe him?'

'Two blokes wearing black.'

'There were two of them? You just said it was a thug who dragged you from the car.'

'The driver of the car must have doubled back. The other one watched while the big bloke beat me up.'

'The second one was smaller? Would you recognise them again?'

'Not sure. Maybe.'

'What about the car?' Kezia asked. 'Did you see the number plate?'

Claude shook his head. 'If I'd known I was about to be beaten up I'd have written it down,' he said sarcastically.

She turned to Ian. 'Did you know the driver of the van?' she asked.

'He's part of the Drumlychtoun security squad,' he said. 'It's a team I set up for the laird and I know them all well.'

'So you trust them?'

'Absolutely. They're all ex-coppers with impeccable backgrounds. They would have had no part in the attack.'

'Did the driver say anything about the car that drove between him and Monsieur Lambert?'

'It kept its distance and then disappeared. He thought it had turned off the road, but it could have been doubling back to where Claude was. He thought it was a silver-grey Prius. He didn't note the registration, but there was no reason for him to think he needed it.'

'Right,' she said. 'I'll get a local team onto that. It could have gone through an ANPR camera somewhere, although they're a bit few and far between around there. Let's move on to the other matter.'

'I'm tired now,' said Claude, sinking back into his pillows with the expression of an irascible, bed-ridden octogenarian.

'Just one more question,' said Kezia. 'Why did you lie to my colleague about where you spent Sunday night?'

'I didn't lie,' said Claude, adopting a look of injured innocence.

'You were seen in the Golden Lotus restaurant in the centre of Dundee at ten forty-five on Sunday night and yet you said you'd stayed at a hotel on the outskirts of Perth.'

'I took a taxi,' he said.

'Why?'

'I was hungry.'

'It's a twenty-mile drive. Why not eat in Perth?'

Claude shrugged. 'I felt like eating in Dundee.'

'We'll need the name of the hotel and the taxi company you used. I suggest that once you are discharged from the hospital you arrange with DI Clyde to make a statement.' She scrunched up her sandwich wrapper and threw it into a bin.

Molly arrived with a flask of soup, which Claude greeted with enthusiasm. Just as well he'd had one of Kezia's sandwiches, Ian thought. It didn't look like there'd be any soup left for him.

Kezia turned to Ian. 'Molly can sit with Claude,' she said. 'Walk with me to the entrance.' It was an order, not an invitation.

Ian stood up. 'I'll be back in a minute,' he said to Molly.

Hospitals are all the same. After spending three months in one himself, Ian recognised everything; the waft of disinfectant, the squeak of shoes on the linoleum floors, the hurried, tired expressions of the medical staff. There were too many reminders of the pain he'd been in. He'd be glad to get out into the fresh air again.

'What do you think?' she asked Ian as they walked down the stairs.

She was asking him? She must have more faith in him than he'd thought. 'He's hiding something,' said Ian. 'But I don't think he killed Grainger. He was looking for him but that was because he hoped he'd lead him to the art thieves. There's no motive for killing him.'

'I'm inclined to agree,' she said. 'There's not enough to charge him with. In any case, he seems far too incompetent. This killer planned carefully. He knew the trains stopped at the southern end of the bridge and timed it perfectly.'

'Someone with local knowledge?' Ian asked.

'Possibly,' she said. 'Or someone who knows about trains. But we should watch our M. Lambert for a while yet. He might not be the murderer, but I have a feeling he might know who it is.'

'What about the men who attacked him? If that was connected to the murder, why didn't they kill him?'

'My guess would be that Claude Lambert is still useful to them. Maybe the attack was a warning.'

'I don't understand why they stopped him and not the van. Anna mentioned an estate van in her vlog and they're all covered in Drumlychtoun logos, which would be easy to spot. She didn't say anything about another car. It must have been planned knowing there would be a second vehicle; the car pulling between him and the van, the sheep in the road. It was an ambush. It's almost as if they knew the details of the plan.'

'Could Claude have told anyone about it?'

'I suppose he might have reported to his client in France to show what progress he was making, but I can't imagine a French art collector employing thugs to attack the man who is doing his best to find his missing paintings. I don't know who he would have told locally. He's barely been out of the house.'

'Keep an eye on him,' said Kezia. 'Are you able to do that?'

Easily, he thought. Claude was under his feet pretty much permanently. 'Sure,' he said. 'We're still trying to get to the bottom of Hamish Gunn's sudden popularity.'

'Keep in touch,' she said, patting his arm. 'And take care.' She climbed into her car and drove off.

Ian retraced his steps back to Claude's bedside.

An affectionate gesture from Kezia Wallace. That was a first. Perhaps she was beginning to take him and his work more seriously at last.

19

'I have to get back and collect Ryan from school,' said Molly as Ian returned to Claude's bedside.

'Fine,' he said. 'You get off and I'll see you in the morning.'

She picked up her bag and the empty soup flask and left.

A very young doctor in a white coat appeared. Ian watched as she lifted a chart from its hook at the end of the bed and studied it. She strode towards Claude and pointed a thermometer at his forehead while taking his pulse. Then she peered into his eyes with a small torch and scribbled something on a piece of paper, which she pushed into the bulldog clip at the top of the chart, using it to hook it back into place on the bed rail.

'How are we feeling?' she asked.

'I need to get out of here,' said Claude, sitting up in bed.

'I agree,' she said. 'We have no reason to keep you. Your tests have come back clear. All you have are a few bruises and a sprained wrist. You were very lucky.'

Claude flapped at his hospital gown. 'So where have you put my clothes?' he asked.

'In a bag in there,' she said, pointing to a locker at the side of the bed. 'I assure you we have no desire to keep you here a moment longer than necessary. However, you have been suffering from mild concussion. From what you tell us, you don't live locally and are unable to return home. Is that correct?'

Claude scowled at her. 'Through no fault of my own. I live in France and the police are holding my passport.'

The doctor looked alarmed. 'Are you under arrest?' she asked.

'He's not,' said Ian. 'He's merely helping the local police with an enquiry. They have asked him not to leave the area. He is free to come and go as he pleases as long as he doesn't leave the country.'

Claude swung his legs over the side of the bed and stood up unsteadily, reaching for the bag of clothes. A bright green plastic bag with the name of the hospital stencilled in black letters. Claude opened it with a look of disgust. 'In France,' he said. 'We use these bags for trash.' He removed a shirt and some trousers, shook them as if he suspected them of being infested with lice, and spread them out on the bed. Then he winced and sat down breathlessly, clutching his wrist.

The doctor handed him a glass of water. 'It would be best if you were not alone. You are still in shock. Do you have somewhere to stay?' she asked.

'I'm staying with him,' said Claude, with a nod in Ian's direction.

The doctor looked at Ian for confirmation.

'He is,' said Ian, wishing he wasn't. If the doctor thought Claude had nowhere to go, she might have been persuaded to keep him a bit longer.

The doctor looked relieved. 'In that case I will arrange your discharge notes. You may get dressed and collect them from reception on your way out. I will write you up a prescription for some painkillers and a wrist support.'

'I FEEL LIKE A GERIATRIC,' Claude complained as he climbed into Ian's car, clutching a handful of paperwork and the white paper bag containing his medication that they had collected from the hospital pharmacy.

Ian drove them back towards Greyport. It was the evening rush hour and traffic was slow. He tried to remember what food he had in the house and decided to stop at Tesco in Dundee to stock up. Claude could wait in the car.

It was an idea that didn't appeal to Claude. 'What if he's still watching me?'

'Who?'

'The man that attacked me.'

'I thought you said there were two of them.'

'I did, but...'

'You lied to Kezia. Why?'

Claude stared out of the car windows, looking round anxiously. 'I can explain when we get to your house. We should go straight there.'

'But we'll need to eat.'

'I suppose... but I'll come into the store with you. Just in case I am being watched.'

'Why would they watch you? How would they even know where you are?'

'I don't know. How did they know where to attack me?'

It was a good point and one he'd already been through with Kezia, but he didn't want to alarm Claude any further by telling him they thought someone knew about his plan. 'Anna's vlog was quite specific about the time the painting would leave Drumlychtoun,' he pointed out. 'And the route from there to Edinburgh is an obvious one.'

'And how did they know where the sheep would be?'

Ian had no idea. 'They probably had a good look at the route the day before,' he said. He supposed Claude was still suffering from shock and he should try to calm him down. 'Look,' he said. 'They will have checked your car and will know that the painting wasn't with you. Anna has uploaded a post saying that it is now safely in Edinburgh. Why would they come after you again?'

Claude looked unconvinced, but said no more until they reached the Tesco car park. Ian helped him out of the car and led him into the store, grabbing a trolley on the way. It was going to be slow progress.

Claude was still not steady on his feet and the shop was crowded with people stocking up for the weekend. It was going to take forever if he had to drag Claude around with him, so he installed him on a sofa in Costa, which was at the side of the store with a good view of the car park. He bought him a cup of coffee. 'Give me your phone,' he said, checking that it had enough battery. 'You have my number. Call me if you see anything that worries you. I won't be far away.'

He returned fifteen minutes later with a full trolley. Claude had finished his coffee and was flirting with a woman sitting at a table close by. *Not as scared and injured as he had made out, then.* 'Come on,' said Ian, nodding in what he hoped was a friendly way at the woman. 'Let's get you home.'

It had been a long day. Far longer than he'd expected. He'd taken the call from Duncan at midday, driven to the Montrose hospital fearing the worst, survived an unexpected meeting with Kezia Wallace and was now stuck with his not-totally-welcome house guest for goodness knew how much longer.

He collected Lottie from Lainie and received his usual rapturous greeting when he picked her up. 'Long day?' Lainie asked.

'Way longer than I expected. I'm so sorry.'

'Don't worry. You know I love having Lottie.'

Just as well, he thought. Lottie wouldn't have been welcome at the hospital. And her dislike of Kezia Wallace equalled his own.

He cooked a couple of steaks for supper and opened a bottle of red wine. 'You've not been banned from alcohol, have you?' he asked Claude.

'No,' said Claude.

Ian wasn't sure this was the truth, but Claude was an adult. If he chose to ignore a doctor's advice it was not Ian's problem. What was the worst that could happen? He'd occasionally ignored advice himself about mixing medication and alcohol when he first left hospital. It led to a longer than usual night's sleep and if it did that to Claude, well, it meant a few more hours of peace and quiet for Ian himself. A risk he was happy to take.

'When you've had a good night's sleep,' said Ian, as they finished their meal. 'We need to go over the case and decide what to do next.'

'There are one or two things I need to tell you,' said Claude. 'I have not been entirely honest with you.'

Why did that not surprise him? 'About the painting? About the attack?'

'And about Julian Grainger,' said Claude.

'Oh, for God's sake,' said Ian. 'You weren't the one who killed him, were you?'

Claude shook his head. 'No. I didn't kill him. I wasn't lying about that.'

'But you were lying about just about everything else?'

'Not everything. I'd better start at the beginning.'

Ian reached for a bottle of Glenlivet and prepared himself for a long night.

Claude took a swig of whisky and stretched out on Ian's sofa. Ian sat in an old armchair that had belonged to his grandfather and which now had threadbare covers and sagging springs.

'I knew Julian Grainger better than I let on,' said Claude. 'We studied art history together in London for a year and we shared a flat in Herne Hill.'

'That's why you speak such excellent English,' said Ian.

'I spoke it quite well before that. I learnt at school and my family travelled a lot. But you are correct. During that year I became fluent and picked up your, what are they called? Idioms.'

'Tell me more about Julian Grainger,' said Ian.

'He was what I think you call a hustler. He was a natural salesman and into dodgy dealings even as a student. I'm not sure that at the time what he was doing was illegal, but it probably came close.'

'And when you finished your course?'

'I returned to Paris and joined the police. We kept in touch because I think as far as Julian was concerned, I was a useful contact.

He expected inside information from me, the lowdown on art thefts, that kind of thing.'

'And did you give it to him?'

'Occasionally.'

Ian frowned at him.

'Don't look at me like that. We exchanged information, much of which helped to clear up our own investigations.'

No worse than the British police paying informers, he supposed.

'After I left the police, we saw less of each other. He occasionally offered to sell me paintings he thought would be of interest for my gallery. I usually refused them because I suspected he had come by them dishonestly. I wouldn't risk putting them on display. I would only be able to sell them on. And finding buyers of that kind means working the black market. Anyway, I heard from him again a few weeks ago. He had a painting he wanted my advice about. He had obtained it for a client but needed me to look at it before he sold it on.'

'Do you know why?'

'My first thought was that he suspected it was a fake. But now I think it was something quite different. We arranged to meet at the Didier Pierre. He told me he had a photo of the painting and if I was interested, he would arrange to bring it to the gallery for closer inspection. I waited in the bar for an hour and had decided he must have changed his mind when Felicity came in.'

'Do you think he sent her in his place?'

'That was my first thought. But as you noticed, Julian and I were similar to look at. I think Felicity was telling us the truth about that. She was there to find him but had not met him before. She may have been given a description or seen a photograph. She mistook me for him, and I let her believe I was Julian in order to discover more. She began to call me *Julien* – you notice the difference in pronunciation? She didn't seem surprised that the Julian she met at Didier Pierre was French, so she obviously hadn't known him well.'

'You told me she made the first advance – "picked you up" is what you said. Are you sure she wasn't just a woman on her own looking for company?'

Claude shook his head. 'She's not the type,' he said, and Ian assumed he was something of an expert in the etiquette of meeting women in bars. 'No, she was there to meet a specific person, I'm sure of it.'

'So you were both expecting to meet Julian?'

'You remember what she told us when we were at Craigie's? She'd seen a flyer for the Didier Pierre and the lad who told her about the painting also told her about a man called Julian. I'm pretty sure he wasn't expecting her.'

'How many times did you meet in Paris?'

'Just twice. That first evening she told me she was from Scotland and had an interest in Scottish portraits. It was as if she expected me to show the same interest. One which I've never had, but it intrigued me. We arranged to meet the next day to discuss things further and I went home and did some research. Which is when I discovered Hamish Gunn and the fact that he had become popular among art thieves who had apparently discovered a market in America and the Middle East.'

'And you thought Felicity had something to do with that?'

'I didn't know, but I wanted to find out more. I told you about my current client?'

'The one who had some impressionists stolen?'

'Yes, I looked again at his list of stolen artworks and what do you think I discovered?'

'A Hamish Gunn?'

'That's right. A bearded dude with a gun in one hand and a dead bird in the other. A second-rate painting that I'd ignored. His impressionists were far more valuable, so I'd concentrated on finding them. I'd assumed the Gunn was taken in error. But when I dug a bit deeper, I found that there had been a number of thefts of Gunn's paintings recently and I began to wonder why. So I decided to visit Scotland to find out more and maybe to meet up with Julian again.'

'You arranged to meet Felicity, thinking she would reveal more of her connection to Julian?'

'I was worried about him. He'd not turned up in person. I didn't know if Felicity was on his side or out to get him. But she was the only link I had to him.'

'And why didn't you turn up to meet her?'

'Because I had the feeling I was being followed. I was at the station but kept myself hidden. Felicity was there under the dome, and I wanted to see if anyone was with her or maybe watching her.'

'And were they?'

'She waited about half an hour and then a man came and they left together.'

'Not Julian, I assume.'

'No. I know now that it was Douglas Craigie.'

'Interesting,' said Ian. 'And he, too, had a Gunn painting stolen.'

'I didn't know that then, of course. Or that Felicity had insured it for him. But I was certain that Julian was mixed up in it somehow. That is why I set a trap for him with my coat.'

'He knew about your coat?'

'We used to joke about it. I bought it at a market in Greenwich when we were students. At one of those stalls full of old army uniforms and ancient ballgowns. Julian used to tease me about wearing it all the time, even in the summer. It's very unusual and I knew that if Julian caught a glimpse of it, he would know at once that it was me.' Claude drained his whisky glass and Ian poured him another. 'I must get it back,' he said. 'It has much sentimental value for me.'

'I'll get Molly onto it first thing tomorrow. But first you need to tell me about who attacked you. Why did you lie about there being two of them?'

'There were two of them there,' said Claude. 'But one beat me up while the other one stood and watched.'

'Did either of them say anything to you?'

Claude didn't answer.

'So one of them dragged you out of the car and beat you up while the other one watched. And all of this took place in complete silence?'

'I shouted,' he said. 'I shouted quite a lot but then got punched in the mouth. It's lucky I've got any teeth left.'

'And they said nothing to you?'

'Well… yes, the big guy kept kicking me and hissing "where's he hidden it?" I assumed he meant the painting from the castle. But that didn't make any sense because as far as anyone knew it was in the van ahead of me. They were supposed to stop that, not my car, but they deliberately came between us so they could stop me. I didn't understand it. Still don't.'

Nor did Ian. The two thugs deliberately ambushed Claude, even though Anna had made it clear in her vlog that the painting was travelling in an estate van. Why? And who were they? 'You told Kezia they were two big blokes dressed in black. Was there anything you noticed that might distinguish one from the other?'

'They were both wearing hats and had their faces covered. But while I was lying in that hospital bed I did wonder if the one that didn't do the beating might have been a woman.'

Now they might be getting somewhere. Why hadn't he told Kezia that? 'What made you think so?'

'Something about the eyes, perhaps, and women move differently.'

Ian didn't like stereotypes, but he couldn't stop himself thinking that only a Frenchman would have noticed the way a woman moved while he was being beaten up. 'It couldn't have been Felicity, could it?' After all the five of them had planned it together. She knew all about where and when the so-called painting was going to be moved. So did Craigie. But what possible motive could Felicity, or Craigie, have for attacking Claude?

Claude was shaking his head. 'No, if this was a woman, she was a lot taller than Felicity. Almost as tall as me.'

Around five ten or eleven. And Felicity was much shorter.

'And,' Claude continued, 'she had very unusual eyes.'

'Unusual in shape, colour?'

'They were green and one of them had a dark mark on it.'

'You noticed that while this other guy was beating you up? How close was she?'

'After I was dragged into the field, she came up quite close. Checking to see if I was still conscious, I suppose.'

'And when he'd finished kicking you, they just left?'

'I heard them drive away and that must have been when I blacked out. After that, I don't remember much until some woman was shouting at me in the ambulance.'

Okay, he'd left out some details, but apart from not mentioning that one of the attackers might have been a woman, this was basically the account he'd given Kezia. More important was his lack of a believable alibi for the night of the murder. 'Can you explain your trip to Dundee for a curry?'

Claude sighed. 'I felt like a curry and took a taxi to Dundee. It was an exceptionally good curry.'

'It would need to be,' said Ian, trying to work out the cost of a taxi from Perth and back. 'You realise the police will check this out?'

'Of course. And they will find that I am telling them the truth.'

'But why? There are perfectly good curry places in Perth. Your little junket to Dundee and back must have cost you around a hundred quid.'

'My client will pay.'

'So this was to do with your work?'

'If you must know, yes. I received a text.' He sighed, took out his phone and clicked open the messages app. He held it up for Ian to read. *Golden Lotus Dundee 10.30 tonight.*

Ian looked at the time the message was sent – 18.30. There were no details of the sender so probably someone using an anonymous app. Not Claude's client, then. 'Have you any idea who sent it?'

'At the time I was certain it was Julian. He'd already tried to contact me in Paris and failed to turn up. I was expecting him to try again.'

'He seems to make a habit of not turning up.' But it did give them some helpful clues about the timing. If it was indeed Julian Grainger, he had been alive at 6.30. He'd planned to be at the Golden Lotus at 10.30, which tied in nicely with the train that was held up at the south end of the bridge at 9.45. And it gave Claude an alibi. As long as the taxi records showed that he was telling the truth and the staff at the Golden Lotus could vouch for him, he was in the clear. Ian felt strangely relieved. Claude could be a pain in the backside, but Ian had never seen him as capable of murder.

Ian wrote all of this down and then looked up and saw that Claude was asleep. The poor guy had had a hell of a day and it was surprising he'd stayed awake as long as he had. Ian wasn't going to wake him just to get him into bed, so he found a couple of blankets and a pillow and made him as comfortable as he could without disturbing him. He turned out the light and took Lottie for a walk round the garden, trying to work out where today's attack had left them. He yawned. It had been a long day. The best thing he could do was get a good night's sleep. They'd regroup in the morning and try to make a plan. A sensible plan this time. How they would do it, he wasn't sure. Right now, there were too many questions spinning around in his head.

20

Ian was awake early the next morning and was in the kitchen making coffee when Claude appeared, looking a lot better than he had the night before. He was still walking a little stiffly, and Ian remembered something he had been told during his spell in hospital. Claude had only been in hospital for one day, but Ian supposed the principle was the same. *Keep moving.* It had infuriated him at the time when all he wanted was to curl up in bed, pull the covers over his head and shut out the world. But they had been right. Forcing himself to get out of bed and walk, even if it was just to the end of the ward and back, made him feel better.

He relayed this bit of wisdom to Claude and it was not well received. 'I think I'll just take it easy today,' he told Ian. 'I'll have a shower and get to bed.' He headed to the door.

'No,' said Ian. 'We're walking down to the village to buy breakfast. You can have a shower when we get back.'

Claude groaned. 'You did a massive shop yesterday. Surely that included breakfast.'

'A walk will do you the world of good,' said Ian. 'Trust me. And the pastries from the shop are wonderful. If you stay here, it will be a bowl of stale cereal and you'll have to watch me and Molly eating our croissants. I'm not buying you any unless you walk to the shop with me.'

'Medical expert, are you?'

'I spent three months in hospital with a gunshot wound and believe me, every day I refused to exercise added at least an extra two days to my recovery.'

'Oh, very well,' said Claude. 'If it stops you nagging, we'll go.'

Claude moaned and groaned at him while they walked down the hill, but once they reached the harbour wall he was distracted by the view of the estuary, which he grudgingly admitted was looking its best that morning in the bright sunshine, a train making its way over the bridge and a few small boats bobbing up and down on the water. He cheered up even more when he caught the scent of baking wafting from the shop.

Ian tied Lottie's lead to a railing that the shop owner had thoughtfully provided for dogs. Although this was most likely to encourage customers to leave their dogs outside rather than for the comfort of the dogs themselves. Ian was a regular there and the lad behind the counter had already picked up Ian's usual two croissants with tongs and put them into a brown paper bag as he and Claude approached the counter. 'What do you fancy?' Ian asked. 'I can recommend the almond croissants, although the pastries are delicious as well.'

'An apricot Danish. And one of those,' said Claude, reaching for his wallet and pointing to a raisin swirl.

'My treat,' said Ian. 'It's the least I can do after dragging you down that hill.' He tapped his card onto the machine and picked up the two bags. They left the shop and untied Lottie, who looked hopefully at the bags in Ian's hand. 'It's easier going uphill,' he said, noticing Claude's heavy sigh as he looked back the way they had come, at Ian's house at the top of the hill. 'Take my word for it.' He'd never worked out why walking downhill when injured was much harder work than walking up again. But after living there for three years, he had ample proof that it was.

Arriving back again, Claude hung his coat up and bent down to rub his calves, although he grudgingly admitted that Ian was right. 'Glad you made me do that,' he said. 'It feels a bit less sore now. But I'm ready for a coffee.'

'The nice thing about living here,' said Ian, removing Lottie's lead and hanging up his own coat. 'Is that the walk down to the village and back takes exactly the same time as it takes the machine to brew the coffee.' He'd switched it on just before they left and as they came through the door, they could smell the coffee and hear it bubbling away in the kitchen.

Molly had arrived and was bustling around tidying the office. 'How are you today?' she asked, eyeing Claude's bruised face.

Claude gave her his best 'soldiering on while badly injured' smile and she pulled up a chair for him and poured him a cup of coffee. 'Thank you, my dear,' he said, taking a large bite of his apricot pastry.

'Any calls while we were out?' Ian asked, carrying his own coffee to his desk.

'Just the security driver at Drumlychtoun. He has the keys to Claude's car and wants to know what to do with them. He and one of the others can collect the car but they need to know where to drop it off.'

'That's good,' said Ian. 'I don't suppose hire companies are too happy about their cars being abandoned.'

'So what should they do with it? Do you want to keep it, Claude, or should they return it to the hire company?'

'We're not done yet,' said Claude. 'I'll hang on to it for a bit.'

'He'd better bring it here,' said Ian. 'It's going to be a day or two until Claude can drive.'

Claude scowled at him. 'I suppose I can make myself useful around here,' he said.

'What's the plan for today?' Molly asked.

'Claude wants to get his coat back,' said Ian. 'He's stuffed full of painkillers and probably hungover from last night so, like I said, I don't think he should drive yet.'

'That's fine,' said Molly. 'If there's nothing urgent to get done, I can drive him to Perth this morning.'

And no doubt take a quick look at Alyson's latest stock, Ian thought. But after a twenty-mile drive with Claude she'd deserve a bit of retail therapy. 'I'll go and update Craigie,' he said. 'He won't know about Claude being attacked.' He reminded Claude that Duncan was expecting him to make a statement and that he'd need details of his taxi rides. Receipts from the restaurant and the hotel would be useful as well.

'All on my phone,' said Claude.

'I'll call Duncan,' said Molly. 'If he's at Bell Street this morning we could drop in there on the way back from Perth.'

'Good,' said Ian. 'I don't know about you, but there's so much conflicting stuff swirling around in my brain I need to get it all together and take a long hard look at what we've got. Let me know if meeting Duncan this morning works and then we'll meet back here this afternoon.'

'Do I get a say in any of this?' Claude asked. 'If Molly's happy to go to Perth to get my coat, I could stay here and catch up on some sleep.' He yawned to emphasise the point that he'd been severely injured. 'I had to sleep on the sofa last night.'

'You crashed out there,' said Ian. 'Dead to the world on whisky and painkillers.'

'You're just trying to get out of seeing Duncan,' said Molly. 'Into the car and let's get this done.'

Thank goodness for Molly. She handled Claude far better than Ian did. It amused him to see her wrapping his scarf around his neck and coaxing him into his coat. Plenty of practice with Ryan, he supposed. In some ways Claude behaved in much the same way as a stubborn eight-year-old so Molly was used to it. He smiled as he watched Claude limping stiffly down the path one more time. Probably grumbling every step of the way.

The office now quiet, Ian called Craigie, who told him he would be working from home this morning and would be happy to see him around coffee time. As far as Ian was concerned all day was coffee time, but he took this to mean mid-morning. Before leaving, he called the driver at Drumlychtoun and said he could pick up Claude's car any time that was convenient. Assuming he would bring someone to drive him back to Drumlychtoun, Ian told him to park it in the road outside his house and drop the keys through the letterbox. But he also said there was no rush. It would be doing the drivers of Fife a favour if Claude could be kept off the road for at least a couple of days. Having sorted that, he rounded up Lottie and loaded her into the back of his car. There was plenty of time for a walk on the way to Stonebridge House.

IAN GAVE Lottie a quick run along the coastal path and then headed to Anstruther. Stonebridge House seemed too large for a man living on his own and it was no surprise that Craigie had sought female company, although Felicity Bright wouldn't have been Ian's first choice. But then, with his reputation for messing up relationships, he was hardly one to criticise. He hoped Felicity was a keen gardener because there was plenty of scope for one here. Ian turned his car off the road into a gravel drive surrounded with what estate agents would probably describe as mature bushes, which Craigie was attacking with hedge clippers from the top of a wobbly stepladder. *Was that wise?* Ian wondered. What would happen if he fell? He already knew that the neighbours around here minded their own business. An injured man could lie on the ground for a while before anyone noticed him. Ian was relieved to see that Craigie had a phone tucked into the back pocket of his trousers, which probably meant he was aware of the danger.

Craigie waved as Ian parked in the drive. 'Ah,' he said, jumping down from the ladder. 'You've timed it well. I'm ready for a break and some coffee.' He leant his shears against the stepladder and led Ian inside into the kitchen, where he ground coffee beans and spooned them into the top of a machine. 'It's bit slow,' said Craigie. 'But worth the wait. Are you here to report some progress on the missing painting?'

'Not exactly good news,' said Ian, giving him an account of Claude's failed plan and his resulting injuries.

h dear,' said Craigie. 'I'm so sorry. How is poor Claude this morning?'

'He's okay,' said Ian. 'A bit bruised and stiff, but he'll be fine in a day or two.'

They sat listening to the burbling coffee machine for a few minutes. Then Craigie poured them a cup each and pulled up a chair.

'You say they separated Claude from the van driver?' Craigie asked, pushing a tin of biscuits in Ian's direction.

'It was a clever ambush,' said Ian, helping himself to a digestive biscuit and breaking off a piece for Lottie. 'They must have known the road very well. At that point it's just a narrow, twisting lane. No chance of overtaking so Claude was some way behind the other driver when he was stopped.

'A flock of sheep, you say?'

'That's right. My guess is that one of the attackers was driving while the other waited in the field to let the sheep out. He had probably been dropped off there. The car pulled out of a farm entrance just in front of Claude, slowing him down and separating him from the van.'

'It sounds very well planned,' said Craigie.

Ian agreed.

'And yet they let the van go,' Craigie continued. 'The one with the decoy painting. Sounds a bit incompetent, doesn't it?'

'Put like that it does. I don't know what made them assume the painting was in Claude's car,' said Ian. 'Anna had made it clear that it was going in the estate van. She even mentioned how it would be stacked in a crate that was normally used for vegetables. She couldn't have made it clearer if she'd drawn a plan of the inside of the van.'

Craigie took a thoughtful sip of his coffee. 'I'm having trouble with the idea that these people were so well organised that they came between the two cars, separated them by quite a big distance, timed the letting out of a flock of sheep to perfection, and still stopped the wrong vehicle.'

He was right. 'You think they knew it was a set-up?'

Craigie looked puzzled. 'Then why bother?'

'They had it in for Claude?' Ian suggested. He didn't reveal what Claude had told him the man had hissed in his ear: *Where's he hidden it?*

'Warning him off, perhaps,' said Craigie. 'But maybe more than that. I think perhaps they knew the Drumlychtoun painting was not the one they were looking for. Which suggests there is one particular painting they are after. And that means they could still be looking for it.'

'Precisely,' said Ian. 'I've been thinking over Felicity's theory. In some ways it's a very good one, but does she really think that all these black market art buyers or whoever they are will decode a hidden map and then start digging up bits of desert all over the Middle East?'

'There must be something else about the paintings,' Craigie mused.

'I agree with you,' said Ian. 'I think there must be one particular painting they are after.'

'Any theories about which one or why?'

'Not yet,' said Ian. 'But if the attack was a warning to Claude rather than an attempt to steal the painting, it looks as if we may be able to rule out the Drumlychtoun one and the two that have turned up in American collections. Which leaves yours and the one belonging to Claude's client in France.'

'And any that haven't been stolen yet. Does that change the way you tackle this case?'

'Bound to,' said Ian. 'But right now, I'm not sure how. Do you have any ideas?'

'I suppose comparing photos of the paintings might help,' said Craigie. 'But you're the experts – you and Claude. I'm sure you can come up with some ideas.'

'Right,' said Ian, draining his coffee cup. 'I'd better get back to the office and do some thinking. Thanks for the coffee. I'll leave you to your hedge cutting.'

'I think I'll take a break from it,' said Craigie, walking with him to the door. 'I have work to get on with. I might just pay someone to do the hedge for me.'

Ian thought that was an excellent idea. He waved as he got into his car. He had some puzzling out to do, but at least he wasn't going to be kept awake with the thought of an injured Craigie lying in his drive with a broken leg and hypothermia. And Craigie had seemed as surprised as Ian about the attack, so although he had known about Claude's plan, he probably hadn't been the one to alert the attackers.

THE CONVERSATION with Craigie had given Ian a lot to think about. He explained Craigie's theory to Molly and Claude as they sat in the office that afternoon.

'I can't get my head around this,' said Molly. 'Craigie's saying there's only one painting that has a map coded into it?'

'He thinks the whole map idea is wrong.'

'So what is it about this one painting that makes it more valuable to art thieves than the others? And what does Julian Grainger have to do with it?' she asked.

'Julian wasn't an art thief,' said Claude. 'He may have been involved in some dubious deals, but he negotiated with the thieves. He didn't steal paintings himself.'

'Like a middleman?' Molly asked.

'Yes. He was a go-between. Private collectors approached him about a painting they wanted, and he dealt with the thieves who actually stole them. And he had experience as a journalist. He knew how to spread facts about artists that inflated the price of their work. Gunn is a good example. No one bothered about him until a couple of his paintings were stolen. Then every private collector in the world wanted one.'

'Could Julian have arranged for a couple of thefts just for that reason?' Ian asked.

'Quite possibly,' said Claude. 'But my theory is that someone inadvertently came across this thing about the codes in his paintings and discovered there was something in one of them that was way more valuable than the others. The trouble is that no one knows which one it is.'

'Is there any record of how many of his paintings still exist?' Ian asked. 'Where they all are and how many have been stolen so far?'

'He didn't have a large output,' said Molly, opening a file on her computer. 'Remember, he didn't really start painting until he retired from archaeology. I'm not saying my list is complete, but so far I've found eleven in Scotland. Two of those were stolen last year.'

'Word on the grapevine is that those two are in private collections in Saudi and America,' said Claude.

'Two more were stolen from private ownership but have since been returned. There have been no more thefts recently. Craigie's was the last one to be reported.'

'We'll keep an eye on that,' said Ian. 'I think Julian Grainger is the key. We know he was in Scotland at the time of the Craigie burglary and was responsible for the return of all but the Gunn.'

'But he didn't return them,' said Molly. 'He sold them to a dealer.'

'Yes, but not an art dealer. This was Forfar flea market. They were going to be found sooner or later and I think Julian knew that. Forget the paintings for a moment and think about the timeline.' He picked up a pen and made a list on the board.

Julian contacts Claude and arranges to meet him in Paris. He's worked out that there is something valuable in Craigie's Gunn painting but needs Claude's expertise to decipher it.

But Grainger didn't get to the meeting. Possibly because Felicity got there first. Claude thinks she may be connected to Julian but is not sure, so he arranges to meet her in Edinburgh in order to watch her.

'Remind me why you were in Edinburgh, Claude,' said Molly. 'You didn't come just to watch Felicity, did you?'

'I was looking for paintings stolen from my client, one of which was a Gunn. I thought this was too much of a coincidence. Julian was trying to contact me and I suspected he could be connected to both thefts. Scotland was the most likely place to find him, and I hoped Felicity might be able to lead me to him.'

Ian continued writing:

Julian texts Claude a message to meet him in Dundee but is murdered on his way there.

He is found in the Tay with an envelope addressed to Claude in his pocket.

'Did you see the envelope?' Molly asked. 'Was it still unsealed, or had it been torn open?'

'That's an excellent question,' said Ian. 'It was unsealed.'

'I don't suppose there's any way we can tell if it was written by Julian himself?'

'Let's assume it was,' said Ian. 'Let's say he was on his way to find Claude, but since he'd failed to make contact with him so far, he was working on a plan B. He wrote a letter to Claude while he was on the train. He had the envelope in his pocket ready to post if Claude didn't turn up, but he was dragged off the train while still holding the letter. The murderer takes the letter but fails to check Julian's pockets.'

'Neat,' said Claude. 'All we need to know is what the letter said and who has it now.'

Molly was looking thoughtful. 'He must have had a phone, or he couldn't have sent Claude a text. He probably had a wallet as well. What happened to those?'

'The murderer took them? Trying to make it look like a robbery?'

'If he searched Julian's pockets to find them, wouldn't he have found the envelope as well?'

'Perhaps he did and left it there to implicate Claude in the murder.'

'Is there any way the police can trace the text he sent?'

'I can ask Duncan, but as far as I know if the sender used an app like TextMe it will have been sent from a different number and will be untraceable.'

Molly tapped her pen on the desk. 'What we need to do is find out why the painting is so special.'

'That sounds like a job for Claude.' Ian turned to Claude, who was gazing out of the window. 'If you compared photos of Gunn paintings, would you be able to pick out why one of them is different, and special?'

'Not sure.'

Not helpful either. 'Molly,' said Ian. 'Print out photos of all the paintings you can find. Spread them out in the back office and shut Claude in with them until he comes up with some ideas.'

'Okay,' said Molly, laughing. 'Am I allowed to give him food and drink?'

'I suppose so,' said Ian. 'While he's doing that we'll try to work out where Julian was coming from. Can you check all the trains that arrive in Dundee from the south on a Sunday evening?'

'What will you do while I'm shut in and Molly's surrounded by train timetables?' Claude asked.

'I'm going to check out the woman with the weird eyes.'

'How?' Molly asked.

'Well, I could wander around Scotland gazing into women's eyes. But it would probably be quicker to get Duncan to check the Scottish database for a description of a tall woman with green eyes, one of which has a dark-coloured mark.'

BY EARLY EVENING Molly had mapped all the train routes into Dundee on Sunday evenings. She printed out a Scotrail map and pinned it to the board. Assuming he didn't start further south than Edinburgh, he could have boarded a train to Dundee at one of fourteen stops. She narrowed it down to trains that arrived in Dundee between nine-thirty and ten-thirty – two local and one that stopped only at Leuchars.

Ian studied the map. 'We could visit the stations with a photo and ask if anyone saw him boarding a train.'

'Won't the police have done that?'

Ian hoped they would. It was another question for Duncan. He'd arranged to meet him that evening at the Pigeon, where he planned to ask him to search police records for women with green eyes. Duncan would probably laugh at him, but there could be a chance that he would think it was an interesting line of enquiry.

It was time to release Claude, who Ian acknowledged had worked hard all afternoon with a magnifying glass, an online biography of Gunn and some pages Molly had printed from the archive at Glasgow University. He emerged from the back office yawning and rubbing his eyes.

'Any luck?' Ian asked.

'I think Craigie was right to knock Felicity's theory on the head,' he said. 'I made detailed measurements of all the paintings from various angles and checked out the subject matter, wondering if that could be some kind of code. I ran a check on all the places Gunn had visited to paint and tried to link them on a map of Scotland and compare them to dig sites. The only thing that really stands out is the enormous fish in Craigie's painting. It's the only one painted indoors. The others are all outdoor scenes with dead animals and birds.'

'Any idea where the indoor one was painted?'

'Didn't Mr Craigie tell us it was place called Blairgovern House?'

Ian tapped the name of the house into Google. It was a grey sandstone building with turrets, in a village on the banks of the River Dee where it descended from the Cairngorms. It was currently a care home. *Not much point in visiting the house,* he thought, looking at the décor in the painting, which was hardly conducive to patients in care. These days it would all be pastel colours and tasteful pictures of flowers. He studied the background in Craigie's fish painting. A library with couple of portraits and something that looked like an illuminated scroll alongside shelves of books. Who stood indoors to be painted while holding up a fish as if he had just hauled it out of the water? Gunn's strength, arguably his only strength, was scenery; Scottish heather moors, gloomy glens and snow-covered mountains. He made passable attempts at stags and game birds, but the only people he painted were dour-looking Scots wearing kilts. What had induced him to set himself up as a portrait painter? More money, Ian supposed. People paid to have themselves portrayed for posterity and were probably less keen to shell out for the kind of countryside they could see every day from their windows.

'I'm tired,' said Claude, yawning.

Ian took pity on him. 'I'm meeting Duncan in the pub later. Fancy joining us?'

'The police inspector? No thanks. He'd probably arrest me.'

'Hardly,' said Ian. 'He'll have checked your alibi, might even be ready to give your passport back. And he's a really nice guy.'

'All the same,' said Claude. 'I think I'll stay here and get an early night.'

21

Duncan bought two pints of beer and a packet of bacon flavoured crisps. He carried them to a table near the window, where Ian had installed himself with Lottie. 'Not brought your house guest?' he asked as he placed the beers on the table and handed Ian the crisp packet.

'He's still feeling a bit bashed about,' said Ian, taking a gulp of his beer. He opened the crisps and fed a handful to Lottie, who was drooling at his side. He wasn't sorry Claude had decided not to join them. Ian was becoming increasingly aware of the advantages of living alone. 'Any chance of letting him have his passport back soon?' he asked hopefully.

Duncan laughed. 'I thought you'd be best buddies by now. Same line of work and all that.'

'Let's see,' said Ian, draining his beer glass. 'Since he arrived, he's been suspected of murder, got himself beaten up, failed to come up with any helpful ideas about stolen paintings. He keeps me awake with his snoring and leaves damp towels on the floor. He doesn't even volunteer to walk Lottie or help with the washing up.'

Duncan patted him sympathetically on the shoulder. 'I'll get you another pint,' he said. 'You look as if you need it. How about something to eat?'

'In a bit,' said Ian.

Duncan checked his watch. 'Don't leave it too long and I'll join you,' he said. 'But there's plenty of time before Jeanie gets here.'

'Still being force fed greens?' Ian asked when Duncan returned from the bar.

'Not exactly,' said Duncan. 'I just get disapproving looks if I stray into anything that actually tastes good.'

'How's the murder enquiry going?'

'We're still making enquiries about Julian Grainger's background. Once those are completed, and assuming they don't reveal anything suspicious about Claude, he should be free to go.'

'How long will that take?'

'Can't say. Julian Grainger was a slippery character. No apparent next of kin. Mixed up with some shady types who all have reasons for wanting to dispose of him. Right now, your friend Claude looks like the least probable of our suspects.'

'We think Grainger was involved with the Craigie burglary,' said Ian, wondering if that would complicate the case.

'Interesting,' said Duncan. 'But most of the stolen goods from that have been recovered, haven't they? We're assuming it was local lads getting their hands on whatever they could grab while Craigie was out. We've not closed the case, but it's not a priority. Let me know if you find anything else that might connect it to the murder.'

'I'm guessing Claude hasn't told you everything about Sunday night when he made his statement?'

'To be honest, once we'd checked the taxi receipts and questioned the staff at the hotel he told us he was staying in, we were not that interested in how he chose to spend his time and money. It's an alibi and until there's evidence to the contrary, there's no further need to think that he could be a suspect. Don't worry. He won't be with you for much longer.'

Ian sipped his pint and wondered whether he should tell Duncan about the text message. Claude had told him in confidence, but this could be evidence and he'd be breaking the law if he didn't keep Duncan informed. 'He didn't tell you about the text he had on the Sunday afternoon of the murder?'

'No, he didn't mention that. Who was it from?'

'Claude thinks it was from Grainger. They're old friends, apparently. The text asked Claude to meet him at the Golden Lotus at ten-thirty.'

'Damn,' said Duncan. 'That could be important. Why the hell didn't he tell us?'

'It was anonymous. Claude only assumed it was from Grainger because he'd failed to turn up at the meeting they'd arranged in Paris a week or so back. I suppose he thought it would be meaningless as evidence if it couldn't be traced.'

'A bit of a flimsy excuse for not telling us,' said Duncan. 'It would have added weight to his alibi.'

'Do you want me to bring him in again?'

Duncan considered for a moment. 'Not right now,' he said. 'But I think we should keep in him the area for a while longer. Sorry. You'll just have to be stricter about the damp towels and the washing up. Get Molly to nag him.'

Did Duncan think he was incapable of doing his own nagging? Well, he wasn't a born nagger. He'd been on the receiving end too often, so Duncan could well be right. 'We're thinking that Grainger might have been about to pass on information about the missing Gunn.'

'Whose missing gun?' Duncan asked frowning. 'Was it reported?'

'Gunn the painter, not the firearm.'

'Never heard of him,' said Duncan.

'Not many people had until recently, when his paintings started getting stolen.'

'And you think Grainger could have been involved? From what we've found out about him I'd say it was quite likely.'

'He'd tried to make contact with Claude a few days after the burglary,' said Ian. 'They'd kept in touch since way back when they both lived in London. Claude thinks Grainger might have been after his expertise as an art historian.'

Duncan drained his pint and started on the second one. 'And Grainger had an envelope in his pocket addressed to Claude in Paris,' he said thoughtfully. 'Any theories about that?'

'We think it's possible that Grainger knew he was in danger and was writing Claude a letter as a backup in case he didn't make it to their meeting.'

'So you think Grainger took a train with the intention of meeting Claude for a curry but wrote to him in case he didn't get there? Then what happened to the letter?'

'It's either at the bottom of the Tay or the murderer took it.' That wasn't the only thing that was missing. Ian remembered Molly's comment. 'Did you find Grainger's phone or a wallet?' Ian asked.

Duncan shook his head. 'We assumed they were stolen by the murderer. We have found a number for him but the phone hasn't been traced through any GPS masts so it must have been turned off.'

'Do you know where Grainger boarded the train?'

'He took the seven-fifteen from Waverley. Picked up by the CCTV in Edinburgh,' said Duncan. 'Grainger and your friend look similar so for a while we wondered if the murder was a case of mistaken identity. But there didn't seem to be any motive for murdering Claude, so we dropped that idea, or we did until he was attacked. The attack and the murder may be connected, I suppose.'

'I have descriptions of Claude's attackers,' said Ian. 'They were wearing hats and had covered their faces, but he thinks the one who stood by and watched might have been a woman. Tall and slender with unusually vivid green eyes.'

'Interesting,' said Duncan. 'He didn't mention that to Kezia, or me.'

'He was probably still shaken up by the attack.' Not really an excuse but Ian was getting used to Claude's gradually emerging truths, while Duncan wasn't.

'I'll check the records,' said Duncan. 'She doesn't sound like your everyday villain. I can go through the database and see if there are any very tall women with green eyes.'

'I'm not really expecting you to find her, but it would be a good place to start.'

'I'll get on to it tomorrow,' said Duncan as a young man arrived to take their food order. 'But right now, it's time to stop talking shop and order something to eat. What do you fancy?'

Ian looked at the chalkboard on the wall of the pub. It was not an easy decision. Should he have the lamb shank or the steak and mushroom pie? He glanced down at Lottie, who was gazing up at him with a rapt expression. She knew all about menus. He decided to go for the lamb shank. It would be easier to pass her surreptitious morsels. He placed his order and turned to Duncan. 'What are you having?' he asked.

'I'll have the seafood salad.'

Ian looked at him in surprise. Salads were not his style at all. 'Watching the pounds?' he asked.

'I told you. Jeanie's the one doing the watching,' he said. 'And she'll be here in a minute. Mind you, she's right. Some of my clothes are getting quite tight around the middle, if you know what I mean.'

'You should get a dog,' said Ian. 'I've lost pounds since I got Lottie.'

WALKING HOME AT CLOSING TIME, Ian had a sudden thought. Grainger had been seen on CCTV boarding the 19.15 train at Waverley. He had been thrown from a train on the south side of the bridge. A train had been held up at the signal on the approach to the bridge at ten minutes past ten, which meant the train arrived at Dundee station five minutes late at ten twenty-three. Trains from Waverley to Dundee took between an hour and an hour and a half depending on how many stations they stopped at on the way. Even if the 19.15 was a slow train it would have arrived at the bridge long before ten past ten. And that meant that the train he had caught from Waverley was not the one he'd been thrown off. And that, in turn, meant that Grainger had got off the train somewhere between Edinburgh and Dundee and then got back on again a couple of hours later. Why? Ian could think of only one reason. He had something to leave, perhaps hide, at one of the towns on the way.

THE NEXT MORNING Ian clicked open an email from Duncan and downloaded the attached screenshot from the CCTV that showed Grainger boarding the seven-fifteen train at Waverley. 'A wee job for us,' he said, printing out the picture and handing it to Molly. 'Thanks to Duncan, we now know that Grainger left Edinburgh at seven-fifteen on Sunday evening. But that's unlikely to be the train he was thrown off. The only train to be held up at the signal was the nine o'clock from Edinburgh, much later. He must have stopped somewhere along the way.'

'This is Julian Grainger?' Molly asked, studying the picture of a man carrying a suitcase. 'It's recognisably the man in the picture they mocked up from the body, but it's odd to see him alive.'

'And much more recognisable when we start asking people if they saw him between seven-fifteen and ten on Sunday evening.'

'Is that what we're going to do?'

'In a bit, but first I need you to check the seven-fifteen and nine o'clock trains from Edinburgh to Dundee and make a list of stations where they both stop.' He looked at the photo again. 'I'm interested in the suitcase.'

'It's not unusual for train passengers to carry suitcases.'

'It's not, but there was no suitcase left on the train when it arrived in Dundee and nothing found near the body.'

'The murderer stole it, perhaps?'

'Possibly, but I think it's more likely that Grainger broke his journey so that he could leave it somewhere. We need to visit the stations and see if anyone remembers seeing him.'

'Are we taking Claude with us?'

'No, he's gone over to Stonebridge House to see if Craigie can spot anything helpful in the paintings.' *Which was just as well,* Ian thought. Dragging Claude round stations would probably slow them down.

'Right,' said Molly, turning from her computer screen half an hour later. 'There are seven stations where both trains stop. We can probably rule out Haymarket. It's right in the middle of Edinburgh and he could have walked to where he wanted to go.'

Six stations to visit didn't seem too bad. They could strike lucky at the first one they chose, but even if they had to visit all of them, they could do it easily by the end of the day.

'There is about an hour and a half between the two trains,' she said. 'So unless he just sat in the station waiting, he must have either walked or taken a taxi somewhere. That would be about a half-hour trip in each direction assuming he caught the next train at the same station.'

'You're right,' said Ian. 'We'll assume he got off the train to leave the suitcase somewhere, and then back on again at the same stop. I can't see why he would travel to a different station on the same line. And at some point, he must have been spotted by the murderer. Do you suppose he was seen at the station he got out at? I can't imagine the murderer followed him from Waverley and sat patiently waiting for him between trains.'

Molly was tapping her teeth with her pen. 'How would the murderer know which station he was going to if he wasn't following him?'

'Perhaps he didn't leave the train until it started moving again and it was too late for the bloke tailing to get off. He had to double back from the next station. Or maybe Grainger was able to leave the station without being spotted and the guy waited there until he returned.'

'Are we assuming that Grainger had the painting in the suitcase?'

'It's possible. Anyway, it could be what the murderer thought.'

'Then there wouldn't be any reason to follow him to Dundee. He could have just killed him and taken the suitcase as soon as he got off the train.'

'That's a good point.' Was his theory about to be blown out of the water?

'What if he'd arranged to meet someone to hand over the painting in Edinburgh but something went wrong? Plan B was to meet Claude in Dundee, so the murderer had to follow him onto the train to try and steal it from him.'

'Doesn't explain why he broke his journey, though, does it?'

'He noticed he was being followed and thought it would be a way of hiding for a bit?'

Ian shrugged. This was all guesswork and wasn't getting them anywhere. 'Come on,' he said, pulling on his jacket and picking up his car keys. 'Let's go to all these stations and see if anyone spotted him. Then we can try and work out where he was going and why.'

They started at the stations closest to Dundee and moved south. Ian had been hopeful about Leuchars. It was the right distance from St Andrews, where there must be a number of arty contacts. It would be twenty minutes in a taxi, twenty minutes talking to someone in the town and twenty minutes back to catch a later train. But the station itself was a busy one, even on a Sunday evening, and no one remembered seeing Claude. It did, however, have CCTV. 'We won't rule it out,' said Ian. 'If we draw a blank at the other stations, I can ask Duncan to get the footage for us.'

They drew similar blanks at the next three stations but then struck lucky at Kirkcaldy. None of the staff they spoke to were on duty on Sunday night. There were a few taxis waiting in the forecourt but none of the drivers recognised the photo. Ian handed out his card, hoping they would ask around. Perhaps one of their colleagues had seen Grainger.

Then they spoke to a woman called Ruth, who worked in a small kiosk selling coffee in cardboard cups. Ian had almost not bothered to talk to her, doubting her kiosk was open on a Sunday evening. But they were here now and also badly in need of coffee. He ordered two cappuccinos and showed Ruth the photo. 'Oh, aye,' she said. 'I ber him. He was catching the nine-thirty to Dundee and trouble with the ticket barrier. He had one of those e-tickets on his phone and had to call for help. He probably broke his journey here. Those e-tickets don't always work if you change trains.'

'Was he carrying a suitcase?' Ian asked.

'I don't think so.' She thought for a moment. 'No, I'm sure he wasn't. But I did see him on his way into the station. He posted a letter in that box over there.' She pointed to a postbox across the road.

'Did you see him arrive an hour or so earlier? On a train from Edinburgh?'

'That would be the eight o'clock?'

Ian nodded.

'I don't think so,' she said.

Ian gave her his card. 'If you remember anything else, could you call me?' he said.

'Oh, aye. My daughter Jan was here on Sunday. I'll ask her.'

Ian wasn't hopeful, but who knew? Jan might just be the type who noticed everything from illicit meetings to strange packages left under seats. But as Molly had pointed out, it wasn't unusual for people to carry suitcases on trains. It was the kind of thing that could easily go unnoticed.

'What now?' Molly asked as she finished her coffee and tossed the paper cup into a bin.

'Back to the office. We'll look at maps and work out where Grainger could have gone after he left the station.'

'And then what?' she said, sighing. 'Call at all the houses along the route?'

'Got a better idea?'

She laughed. 'We could get Claude onto it. Having him do house-to-house calls would keep him out of the office.'

Not such a stupid idea, Ian thought.

'Download the voter roll for Kirkcaldy,' he said. 'We'll get him to go through it and look for names he recognises. You never know, there might be art history type people there. And as you said, it will keep him out of our hair for a bit.'

By the time they arrived back in Greyport there was no need for them to do that. As they walked through the door, Ian's phone rang with a number he didn't recognise. The caller introduced himself as Stu of Stu's Taxis. 'You were asking about a man wi' a suitcase,' he said. 'Could be a fare I picked up on Sunday evening. I remember it because it was a return trip. That's unusual from the station. Most people just want to be taken home. But it looked like he was delivering something.'

'Why do you say that?' Ian asked.

'Because he didnae have the suitcase when he left the house.'

'Thank you,' said Ian. 'That's extremely helpful. Just to confirm, you picked him up at around eight o'clock on Sunday evening?'

'Aye, off the train from Edinburgh.'

'Where did you take him?'

'To a house in Parker Rise, number 27.' Ian, his hands full with his phone and car keys, repeated the address for Molly to make a note of.

'And after that you took him back again to catch the nine-thirty to Dundee?'

'That's right. I waited about ten minutes then drove him back to the station.'

'Was he alone?'

'Aye, he came out of the station alone.'

Ian could sense a *but* and held his breath.

'After I dropped him back, I parked up on the rank outside the station, hoping there'd be another fare off the next train. I noticed that he didn't go straight into the station. He'd crossed the road to post a letter and then I saw him talking to someone. Looked like they were having an argument.'

'Can you describe the man he was arguing with?'

Stu chuckled. 'Aye, but it wasnae a man.'

'He was arguing with a woman? Did they get on the train together?'

'Well, I can't see the platform from my cab. But your man went into the station on his own. She looked like she was talking to someone on her phone. Then she headed off towards the town.'

'Can you describe her?'

'I was too far away to see much, but I'd say she was tall and quite skinny.'

'Could you see what she was wearing?'

'Oh, aye. Black jeans and bomber jacket, cowboy boots I think.'

'What colour hair? Or was she wearing a hat?'

'No hat. Hard to say about her hair, it was getting dark. But it was short, I can tell you that much.'

'It's okay. Never mind. You've been really helpful. Thanks.'

'No problem. And any time you're needing a cab you've got my number?'

He had indeed. Was that why the guy called? Touting for trade? Well, never mind. It had given him plenty to work on.

Ian ended the call and they went into the office. 'What do you make of all that?' he asked Molly.

'Very interesting,' she said. 'We need to tell Duncan, don't we?'

She was right. They had information that could very well help with the murder enquiry. 'I'll call him now,' said Ian, reaching for his phone.

Duncan answered immediately and Ian could hear that he was noting down everything he was telling him. 'I take it you're continuing your own search for the paintings,' he said.

'Unless you tell me why I shouldn't,' Ian said, defensively.

'No reason at all,' said Duncan. 'But don't be visiting that house.'

Ian understood why that would be a bad idea. All the same, it would have been useful to know who lived there and what was in the suitcase.

Duncan must have sensed this. 'Look,' he said. 'Unless it looks like impeding our enquiry, I can share the details with you. If we find the suitcase, I don't see any reason why I can't disclose the contents.'

'That's great,' said Ian. 'Thanks.'

'No problem. You've moved our murder enquiry along. It's only fair that I help you in return.'

It was a relief that he hadn't been accused of wasting police time as he had once before. A rebuke that still made him feel uncomfortable. This time, however, Duncan had acknowledged that what Ian told him was both relevant and helpful.

As Ian ended the call, Claude arrived back carrying a bag of sandwiches he'd picked up in the shop. Probably the first useful thing he'd done since he arrived. Ian was warming to him. Molly made a pot of tea, and they sat down in the office for an update.

'Molly and I are piecing things together,' he explained. He picked up a pen and started writing on the board. 'This is what we think might have happened on the day of the murder.'

Grainger had kept Craigie's painting after the burglary. He knew something was inflating the black-market price of Gunn's paintings and wanted to get to the bottom of what it was. He planned to ask Claude's advice and texted him to arrange the meeting in Dundee. He realised it wasn't safe to carry the painting around with him because he suspected he was being followed. So he took the train from Waverley getting out at Kirkcaldy to leave the painting with whoever lives at 27 Parker Rise.

'We will know who that is once Duncan gets back to me,' he said.

After leaving the painting he returned to the station where he had a heated discussion with a woman in a leather bomber jacket.

'Do you think it's the woman who watched while Claude was attacked?' Molly asked.

'I think it's more than likely. The description matches.' He continued writing.

As soon as she knew Grainger was headed for the train she called the murderer – possibly the man who beat Claude up – who boarded the train at one of the stations further up the line. He attacked Grainger and tried to extract information from him about where he'd left the painting, and then killed him.

'There's no way we can know if Grainger told him anything. And he can't have known the train would be held up at the signal,' said Molly.

'No, he probably planned to leave him on the train. There weren't many passengers that night. The police questioned the few who came forward and none of them saw anything. But they were all travelling in the front carriages, so we can assume Grainger and his attacker were at the back.'

'So where do we go from here?' asked Claude. 'Do we just leave it all to the police now?'

Ian shook his head. 'No. Anything to do with finding the murderer we must leave to the police. But we are free to continue our enquiries about the paintings. And if the two cases overlap, well, I've not been told I can't continue.'

'I think there are some obvious leads we can follow,' said Molly, taking the pen from him. She wrote:

Find the woman in the leather jacket.

'I think she was the one following Grainger,' Molly continued. 'She didn't expect him to leave the train in Kirkcaldy. She probably saw him on the platform when the train started to move again. She could have either have jumped off at the last minute but missed him getting into the taxi, or she travelled on to the next stop and had to double back, which is why she didn't know where he'd gone.'

'What is the next station?' Ian asked.

Molly looked at her list. 'Markinch. It's only ten minutes away.'

'We'll go and ask if anyone there saw her. Do they have CCTV?'

'I think all stations do,' she said.

Ian looked at his watch. 'We'll go there tomorrow,' he said. 'If no one saw her, we'll need to get back to Duncan for the footage.'

'I've not finished,' said Molly, picking up the pen again and writing:

What did Julian post?

'Not sure how we can find that out,' she said.

Ian and Claude both shook their heads. 'We'll shelve that for now,' said Ian. 'Anything else?'

'I can't think of anything. Sorry.'

Ian turned to Claude. 'Anything helpful from Craigie?'

'Not really. There's nothing obvious in the paintings themselves. The only thing he suggested was computer analysis of them. I've heard of it being done when checking for fraud, but I'm not sure how it could be used in this case.'

A germ of an idea was forming in Ian's brain. 'Do you know anyone who does that kind of analysis?'

'Some of the auction houses use them, but only for very high-profile cases.'

'And the people who do it, are they IT specialists or art historians?'

'I think they need to know about coding and that sort of thing.'

'I might know just the person,' said Ian.

One of Ian's earlier cases had been the solving of a historic murder case of a rich hotel owner. He'd only recently set up in business and had no full-time assistant. He'd been helped by the daughter of a friend; a singing student from New Zealand spending the summer in Edinburgh. Her father had arranged singing lessons for her, but she confided in Ian that her real love was IT – in this case hacking into computer systems. She was now working as a forensic hacker in Auckland. Ian was sure she'd be happy to help them, and the moment Claude had sent him the images he emailed them off to her, asking her to analyse them for possible hidden codes.

22

Duncan called later the next morning. 'No luck with your green-eyed woman,' he said. 'But we checked out 27 Parker Rise. My sergeant called in and discovered it's an Airbnb. The current tenant just arrived that morning and had no idea who was there before him. We traced the owner, who lives in Glasgow, and he was able to give us a list of recent lettings. The last tenant booked in for two weeks ending on Monday morning. He signed into the Airbnb site six months ago using the name Jack Henderson. He gave a Gmail address, a mobile phone number – which is currently switched off or out of signal – and a home address in Lancaster. He was staying in the house with a wife and two children. We are still trying to contact him. Lancs police will let me know when they talk to him.'

Ian turned to Molly, who was scrolling through voter rolls. 'It's Airbnb,' he said. 'Not much point in doing that. But see if you can find anything on Jack Henderson in Lancaster.' He passed her the note he had made of Henderson's address.

'Jack Henderson?' Claude asked, looking up from his screen.

'You know him?' Ian asked.

'Don't think so. But I'll email my gallery manager and see if he's on our system.'

'If he and his family were on holiday in Kirkcaldy,' said Molly, 'perhaps he visited galleries in Scotland. He might have met Julian Grainger at one of them.'

'Or perhaps he was poking around flea markets and bumped into Grainger.'

'That's likely,' said Claude. 'Julian was a friendly type. They might have got chatting about Gunn and exchanged phone numbers.'

'That makes sense,' said Ian. 'Grainger is scared. He calls Henderson and arranges to leave his suitcase with him while he goes to Dundee to meet Claude.'

'Would Grainger have had any worries about putting the Hendersons in danger?' Molly asked.

'He was a slippery character,' said Claude. 'But I think he'd cover his tracks. He might not have cared too much about the Hendersons, but he would definitely have tried to make sure that he wasn't leading anyone to the painting.'

'Do we even know that the painting was in the suitcase?' said Molly. 'Perhaps it was a decoy.'

'None of which we'll know until we hear from Duncan again,' said Ian. 'Either of you fancy a drive to Markinch while we're waiting?'

Claude yawned. 'Still puzzling over these pictures,' he said. 'Think I'll get back to them.' He shambled off into the back office and shut the door.

'I'll go,' said Molly.

'You've not had enough of stations?' Ian asked.

'I can manage one more,' she said, laughing. 'Do you want to come?'

'I'd probably get more done here,' said Ian. 'I don't think there's much to be gained from both of us going.' And Molly was always better at getting information from people than he was. She could smile sweetly at whoever was in charge and persuade them to let her look at CCTV footage. One look at him and they started demanding warrants. Perhaps he still had a whiff of police about him.

'You're probably right,' said Molly. 'I'll only be gone about an hour.' She looked out of the window at the black clouds gathering over the estuary. 'I'll call in at the shop on my way back and pick up something for lunch. We won't want to be going out if it's stormy later.'

'A desk lunch suits me,' said Ian, watching as Molly stuffed a notebook into her bag and set off down the path to her car.

SHE RETURNED an hour and a half later, loaded with brown paper bags and looking pleased with herself. She put the bags down on Ian's desk. 'They had your favourite,' she said. 'Hot beef and mustard granary rolls.'

A real treat. Those flew off the shelf almost before they had time to land and always before they had a chance to cool down. Their arrival was unpredictable. A matter of chance whether or not they were in the shop at the right moment. Molly had struck lucky today.

'They only had two left,' she said. 'I had to get a cheese roll for Claude.'

'I thought you looked pleased with yourself,' said Ian.

She grinned at him. 'The rolls are just the icing on the cake.' She opened her bag and handed Ian a sheet of paper on which Ian could make out an image of a woman jumping from a train. A tall woman dressed in a leather jacket. 'I talked to the station manager and asked if he remembered a woman arriving on the five past eight train on Sunday evening. It was lucky for us that he was working on Sunday evening. He'd been called in at the last minute because of a staff shortage that day.'

'And he remembered her?'

'He remembered her very well because he'd ticked her off for pushing ahead of a wheelchair user he was trying to help off the train.'

'A woman in a hurry then. Interesting. Did he notice where she was going?'

'That was even more interesting. She pushed him out of her way and rushed across the bridge just in time to get the train coming in the opposite direction.'

'So you were right. She could have arrived back in Kirkcaldy about fifteen minutes after Grainger.'

'And waited for him to return to the station.'

'But how did she know he was going to come back?'

'I don't know,' said Molly, looking disappointed.

'Don't look like that,' said Ian kindly. 'You did really well. How did you manage to get the photo?'

'Oh, that was really easy,' she said. 'I just asked nicely.'

'What did you ask nicely for?' said Claude, appearing at the door looking as if he'd just woken up.

'This,' said Molly, handing him the CCTV printout.

'Could this be the woman who attacked you?' asked Ian.

'She didn't attack me. She watched while a very large man did it.' He took the picture and studied it. 'Yes, it looks like the same woman. Can I smell food?'

'Molly picked up lunch,' said Ian, handing him a bag containing a cheese roll. He took a bite of his own roll and turned to his computer as an email pinged in.

'This is interesting,' he said, clicking it open. 'It's a reply from Nick in New Zealand.' He read it out:

Great to hear from you again and happy to help, although I'm not sure how helpful you will find the following. I ran the photos through a few apps. They're very thorough – used by the military here to look at ground formations, but they work just as well with other images. I'm certain that there are no hidden codes in the pictures but there are a couple of things that could be of interest. First, Gunn always painted on the same size canvas except for the one with the fish, which is bigger by about six inches in each direction. The other thing I did was to run the fish painting through a text reader. The text on the scroll in the background is blurred and almost impossible to decipher. Once enlarged and sharpened up, it turned out to be a rather dreary family history; a long list of names and various bits of land they owned. I've attached a readable transcript. But here's the interesting bit. I ran it through a code breaker and it picked out the following:

Things are not always what they seem

the first appearance deceives many

the intelligence of a few perceives what has been carefully hidden.

I checked it out. It's a quote from Plato's Phaedrus. *Does that mean anything to you?*

Ian typed a reply.

Thanks Nick. Could be really helpful.

Could it? he wondered. It obviously meant something. It couldn't be a coincidence because the hidden text was too long for it to have been random. Had it been put there by Gunn? Or by the commissioner of the painting? Blair of Blairgovern House, he remembered. They needed to find out more about its background. 'Right,' he said. 'Molly, get back to all the stuff you downloaded from the university and see if you've missed anything about this particular painting. I'm going to look into the Blair family and in particular the bloke in the portrait.'

'We should probably go to Glasgow,' said Molly. 'There's a load of family records in the archive and we might be able to have a chat with their art history people.'

'Do you know who they are?' he asked. 'Will they chat to just anyone?'

'We'll go through my friend who still works in the library. She knows everyone.'

'Okay,' said Ian. 'Claude, you need to go back to Stonebridge House. Check out Craigie's paperwork about the painting – see if we missed anything. Molly and I will go to Glasgow. Let's meet back here later this afternoon and compare notes.'

Claude muttered crossly about having to return to where he had just come from. *Tough,* thought Ian. He and Molly had an hour's drive to Glasgow, and then another hour back again. All Claude had to do was drive a few miles down the coast to sit in a comfortable house enjoying Craigie's hospitality and chatting about art. He watched Claude put on his recently reclaimed coat, brushing some flecks of dust from the collar. The coat gave him a distinguished air and Ian could understand why he was so attached to it. He put on his own coat, which had seen better days, and wished *he* had something that would give him the same air of confidence. But perhaps it was being French that did that. Something Ian could never be.

As they drove, Molly called her friend in the university library and was given the name of a research student who, the friend explained, would be more prepared to spend time chatting and would probably know more than she did. She was good friends with this guy, she said and would arrange for him to be at the library when they arrived. Ian could drop Molly off there and spend time on his own in the archive. He had been there before when working on a different case. It was a quiet place, and the staff were usually more than happy to spend time helping him with his searches. The last time he was there, Ian reflected, was the day he'd met Elsa. It reminded him that he really should, as Mickey had put it, *do something about his idiocy*. Talk to Elsa. Not on this occasion, though. When he met her, she'd been living in Bearsden, which was close to Glasgow. Now she lived up in the Trossachs and it would need a separate trip. But that was probably a good thing. Fond as he was of her, he couldn't imagine carrying on any meaningful conversation with Elsa if Molly was there playing gooseberry.

BY THE TIME the three of them met back again in the office, Molly and Claude both looked despondent. Molly had been very quiet on the drive back, saying she'd not discovered very much and might as well keep the notes she'd made until she'd heard what Claude and Ian had discovered.

'Right,' said Ian. 'You both look tired and fed up. Let's make a few notes about what we've found out and come back to it tomorrow morning. Claude first?'

'Okay, not much to add, really. Craigie bought the painting at an auction fifteen years ago as a present for his wife on her fortieth birthday, along with some salmon fishing equipment. It was something she'd wanted to do for a while, and they arranged a holiday at a place called Kingussie on the River Spey.'

'I know it,' said Ian. 'It's famous for its river fishing.'

'The painting came with a certificate of provenance. That's a certificate that proves it's authentic and a well-maintained one will show who has owned the painting since it left the studio of the artist. In this case it was very straightforward. As we already know, the painting was commissioned by Alistair Blair of Blairgovern House in 1885. It's listed as *portrait of the owner with fish* so we can probably assume that the man in the painting was Alistair himself. It remained in the house until the death of Blair's great-grandson in 2005, when Blairgovern was sold along with its contents at auction.'

'That's helpful,' said Ian, writing it all on the board. 'I'll go next because I picked up a bit more about Alistair Blair. He built Blairgovern House in 1880, retiring there at the age of sixty after a lifetime spent travelling. He had a wife and son and I'm not clear whether they travelled with him or if they stayed behind in Scotland, perhaps with her family. It probably doesn't matter much. What does matter is that on his travels he made a fortune. I found details of his will and he left enough money for his heirs to live on at the house in style. He was a typical Victorian adventurer who had no qualms about plundering treasure from abroad. He was probably praised for it. His son grew up as a well-off landowner, adding to the Blairgovern estate and letting it out to tenant farmers. The grandson suffered financially in the first world war and had to sell of a lot of land during the nineteen-twenties. *His* son struggled to keep the place running and died in debt in 2005 when, as Claude has already discovered, the house was sold. At no stage did it occur to anyone that the Gunn painting was worth anything and it remained in the family until then. So over to Molly.'

'Not much to add, I'm afraid. I talked to my friend's art history graduate. He said he couldn't see anything remarkable about the painting and that Gunn is not generally considered to be of any value either artistically or socially. The only thing he did remark on was the frame, which he said was probably the original one and is different in style from other Gunn frames. There was just one more thing that could be important.' She hesitated. 'Might be nothing.'

'Go on,' said Ian.

'Well, my friend has to keep a record of people outside the university who visit the library and she told me there had been someone else asking about the Gunn documents.'

'Did she say when?'

'She had to check her log and the microfilm was accessed a few days after the burglary at Stonebridge House.'

'Did she give you the name of this person?'

'She's not supposed to, but she had to go to the toilet and kind of accidentally on purpose left the details up on her computer screen.' Molly smiled at them.

'And,' said Claude, 'you just happened to read them. Well done, Molly.'

Ian agreed, although it would never be admissible as evidence. But should it be needed there were ways around that. A suggestion to Duncan that it might be worth his while getting a warrant. But they were not ready for that yet. There was nothing to suggest that this person didn't have a perfectly legitimate reason for checking out Gunn. All the same... 'The name?' he asked.

Molly flicked through her notebook until she found the page she needed. 'Martina Waterperry,' she said. 'Should I check her out?'

'Definitely,' said Ian. 'But it can wait until tomorrow.' He looked at his watch. 'It's been a long day and Ryan will have missed you. Get off home and we'll see you in the morning.'

Ian and Claude watched as she made her way down the garden. 'You're lucky to have her,' said Claude. 'When I start picking up more work, I shall get an assistant. I don't suppose Molly fancies moving to Paris, does she?'

'Don't even think about it,' said Ian. 'She's way too valuable here. You'll just have to look for a French version of Molly.'

They were both tired and Ian was about to go into the kitchen and open a bottle of wine when there was a ring on the doorbell. Lottie started her usual frenzied yapping and skidding along the floorboards. Ian picked her up and opened the door. For the second time in a few days, he stared open-mouthed. But this time it wasn't a French art historian detective that looked like a recently viewed corpse. It was Elsa.

She reached out a hand and patted Lottie on the head. 'I was in Dundee this afternoon,' said Elsa. 'So I thought I'd drop in. You don't mind, do you?' she asked.

Ian shook his head dumbly as Claude appeared from the kitchen with an opened bottle of wine in his hand.

'Not interrupting anything, am I?' asked Elsa.

'No,' said Ian, managing to recover the power of speech, although in a very limited way.

'I'm Claude Lambert,' said Claude, stepping in front of Ian and holding the door open for her. 'I'm a colleague of Ian's over from Paris. We're working on a case together.'

'Elsa Curran.' She smiled at him. 'Delighted to meet any colleague of Ian's.'

What did she mean by that? Ian wondered, remembering that the last time they'd met he had been sitting on a straw bale far too close to Caroline, who he remembered explaining to Mickey was a colleague.

Claude put the bottle down. '*Enchanté*,' he said, reaching for her hand and kissing it. 'Come in. Ian's just about to drink this.' He reached for the bottle and waved it at her. He handed it to Ian, patted him on the shoulder and winked at him. 'Think I'll take a walk down to the pub,' he said, putting his coat on.

'That's a lovely coat,' said Elsa, stepping into the hall.

Not fair. Claude had this wonderful breezy confidence and a coat that attracted the notice of beautiful women. Ian wasn't sure which he envied the most.

'It was lovely to meet you,' said Claude, kissing Elsa on both cheeks and setting off down the path.

'Nice man,' said Elsa. 'Has he been here long?'

'A few days,' said Ian, holding the bottle of wine awkwardly. 'I'll get some glasses. That's if you would like a drink, or do you need to be getting back? I wouldn't want to keep you. Not if you've got things to do.'

'Ian,' she said. 'Just shut up and pour me a glass of wine. And later you'd better make me a strong coffee. I do have to drive home.'

'But not yet?'

'But not yet. I wanted to see where you live. Why don't you show me around?'

He gave her a tour of the living rooms leaving the back office, where Claude was camping on a sofa bed, because he was certain it would be in a mess.

'So this is where it all happens,' Elsa said, looking around the main office and out of the window towards the estuary, where lights were beginning to twinkle in the dusk. 'Lovely view.'

He wanted to say the view was even better from upstairs but thought he had better not.

Elsa wandered over to the board. 'Is this the latest case?' She studied the photos of the Gunn paintings. 'Are they all Scottish?' she asked.

'Yes, and all by the same painter. All stolen recently.'

'Really? Why would someone want to steal them? They're not very good, are they?'

'That's why this case is so fascinating. People are going to great and sometimes violent lengths to get their hands on them. We're trying to work out why.'

'And your French colleague, is he working on that as well?'

'His client in France had several paintings stolen. One of them was a Gunn. It was Claude's idea for us to work together.'

Elsa moved over to Molly's lists and scanned them. 'I know that name,' she said, pointing to *Martina Waterperry*. 'I can't remember why, but I'm sure I've heard it recently. Who is she?'

'Probably not involved at all, but she was making enquiries similar to our own at the university library. Her name's up there to remind Molly to check her out tomorrow.' He stood at his desk fiddling with some paperclips. Should he bring up their last meeting, try to explain? He didn't know where to start. 'I'm sorry,' he said. 'I need to apologise. Mickey said you were upset and...'

She moved closer to him and put her fingers on his lips. 'There's no need,' she said. 'You were in the middle of a case. It was just a missed drink.'

'But Caroline...'

Elsa shrugged. 'You have friends who happen to be attractive women. So what? I don't have any claim over you. Like I said, just a missed drink. Don't beat yourself up over it. I bet your friend Claude would think nothing of missing a drink with friends if he was called away to something more urgent.'

Too right. Claude probably had a history of broken dates. He doubted that Felicity had been the first. But Mickey had told Ian he was an idiot and he'd taken it to heart. And he really was an idiot because he'd been dithering over what to do about it for three months. 'I'm not like Claude,' he said, wondering if she'd think that was good or bad.

'No, you're not. Claude's a charming smoothie and rather full of himself. You, Mr Skair, are a caring, attractive man who needs to have a bit more confidence.' She looked him in the eyes and grinned. 'Now, why don't you show me the contents of your fridge. I'm starving.'

Lottie recognised the word *fridge* and nudged Ian in the leg. 'Looks like you're not the only one,' he said, reaching down to pat her.

'I hope you are not about to offer me a bowl of dog food,' said Elsa, laughing.

'I was going to suggest mushroom omelettes,' he said. 'But if you'd prefer dog food, I'm sure Lottie could spare you a little.'

A WHILE later there was a tap on the living room door. Claude opened it cautiously and peered in at them. 'Not interrupting anything, am I?' he asked.

'Not at all,' said Ian. 'I've just made Elsa some coffee before she leaves. Why don't you join us?'

Claude came in, poured himself a coffee and sat in an arm stretching his legs out in front of him. He grinned at them. 'Look you've had a good evening,' he said, watching as Elsa sat up and u her fingers to smooth her hair.

'Lovely,' she said. 'Ian made omelettes.'

Claude laughed. 'You've been sitting here all evening eating omelettes?'

'He showed me round the house as well,' said Elsa.

'Did he now?' said Claude with a smirk.

'How was the pub?' Ian asked, feeling fairly sure that Claude's evening would have been nowhere near as enjoyable as his own.

'Interesting,' said Claude. 'You know that weird sensation of someone walking over your grave? Well, hearing an unusual name twice on the same day has a similar effect.'

'Unusual name?'

'I was talking to a bloke at the bar, an antiquarian book dealer. Who'd have expected that in a place like this? Somehow the subject of botany came up, can't remember why. Anyway, he mentioned the name of a botanist who used to live around here, name of Waterperry. Joseph Waterperry. He published some illustrated books about exotic flowers.'

'That's it,' said Elsa. 'I remember where I've heard that name. Martina Waterperry sold Mickey some engravings. Really beautiful plants grown in Lebanon, in the style of some manuscript that went missing.'

Ian, who had been feeling pleasantly drowsy, was suddenly alert. 'These engravings,' he said, 'can you remember who made them?'

'I wasn't really paying attention,' she said. 'I can ask Mickey, though, and let you know.'

'And this Joseph Waterperry,' he said, turning to Claude. 'When did he publish his book?'

'Late nineteenth century, I think.'

'There has to be a connection,' said Ian. 'It's an unusual name. And both of them interested in flower illustrations. Then Martina checking out Gunn round about the time the fish painting was stolen. We'll get onto that first thing tomorrow.'

'Have I helped with your case?' Elsa asked.

Ian kissed her on the cheek. 'I think you just might have,' he said.

Ian found a torch and he and Elsa walked down his steep garden path to her car. It had been a mild day, but now Elsa shivered in the evening air. 'I have something for you,' he said. He'd wondered all evening whether or not to give it to her. It was too long since he'd bought it, too expensive, inappropriate. He'd decided against it until he saw Elsa shivering. He clicked his own car open and reached into the back for the box that had been there ever since the end of the opera camp and his upsetting visit to Inverbank, where he'd had an earful from Mickey and learnt that Elsa had been so upset by *his* behaviour that she'd had to take time off and visit friends by the sea. 'For you,' he said, handing Elsa the box.

She stood under a streetlamp, balancing the box on the bonnet of his car and untying the ribbon. She pulled the soft alpaca wool jumper out of its box and held it against her cheek. 'Oh, Ian,' she said. 'It's perfect.'

23

Ian picked up his phone and carried it out of the office and into the garden before answering it, leaving Claude and Molly to speculate on why he was suddenly being secretive about his phone calls.

'Good morning, my love,' he said, blushing at his own term of endearment. Were they ready for that? Was he about to ruin everything again?

'Hi,' said Elsa. 'Did you sleep well?'

'Oh, yes,' he said. 'You?'

'Yes, and I meant what I said last night.'

Ian couldn't remember word for word what she had said, but knew that it went a long way to dispelling his image of himself as a prize idiot.

'Anyway,' Elsa continued. 'Martina Waterperry. I'm just writing an email with everything Mickey and I remember about her. Also photos of the two prints he bought from her. It will be with you soon, but I just wanted to say good morning to you before I start work.'

'Lovely,' he said. 'And we'll talk again soon?'

'I was hoping we might do more than talk. Once you've sorted your painting mystery, you and Lottie could come up here for a weekend.'

'I'd love that,' said Ian. 'And thank Mickey for his help.'

He ended the call reluctantly and returned to the office, where Claude and Molly suddenly stopped talking. What had they been saying about him? Ian ignored them and opened his email.

Mickey bought the engravings a few months ago, Elsa wrote, *just after I'd started to work here. He answered a box number advert in an arty magazine. They're illustrations of a fragraria or Himalayan strawberry, and a Mysore trumpet vine. He thought they'd look nice hanging over the reception desk. They were sold and delivered in person by Martina Waterperry, who found them in an attic in her father's house after he died. Her great-grandfather had made the engravings for one of his books. The two Mickey bought came from the first print run but many copies were made later so they are not particularly valuable.*

Mickey checked them out online and discovered that Waterperry had based the series of engravings on a manuscript that had been plundered from the palace of Tipu Sahib in the late eighteenth century during a skirmish with the East India Company army. No one knows where the manuscript is now but if it was ever found it would be extremely valuable.

Martina Waterperry was a rather severe woman who arrived on a motorbike with the engravings strapped to the back. Mickey paid her in cash and she didn't leave an address or any other contact details.

Ian clicked on the two attachments. Then he printed everything and pinned it to the board. 'Come and give us an art historian's opinion,' he said to Claude.

Claude stared at them. 'Hard to tell from a photo,' he said. 'But yes, I'd say the style is a throwback to something much earlier. Copying them from an ancient manuscript makes sense.'

'It's not much of a description of Martina,' said Molly.

'Why do we need one?' asked Claude.

Molly sighed. 'Two reasons. We know she was looking at the Gunn letters at the library and if she's interested in Gunn, I'm wondering if she's the woman who had an argument with Grainger the night he died. The taxi driver said she was tall and wearing a black leather jacket. The kind you'd wear to ride a motorbike. And Elsa's description of her could fit the woman on the CCTV printout'

'You could be right,' said Ian. 'I'll scan the photo and see if Elsa thinks it could be the same woman while you google Martina Waterperry and find out who she is.'

While he was waiting for Elsa's reply, an email arrived from Duncan.

Henderson's out of the picture. He'd been on a walking holiday with his family and met up with a man fitting Grainger's description while sheltering from the rain in a hotel bar near Kinghorn. They got chatting about Airbnbs and he gave Grainger his address. Suggested meeting for a drink. A couple of days later Grainger was standing on his doorstep saying he needed a favour. He wanted to leave his suitcase for a few hours. He had a call to make and didn't want to be weighed down with luggage. He said he'd be back the next morning but if anyone called asking about it, he was to hand it over. Henderson thought it was a strange request but couldn't see any harm in it. Nobody came to collect the case and Grainger didn't return. Henderson was checking out later on the Monday. He thought perhaps he should drop the case off at the nearest police station, but decided to open it first and see if Julian had left an address inside. All he found in the case was a pile of old magazines. His wife was getting impatient to leave so he left the case at the house with a note to the next tenant to say that it might be picked up. We collected it ourselves and handed it over to forensics but don't expect there to be anything useful.

'Like we thought,' said Ian. 'A decoy.'

'I suppose he assumed that whoever was following him would eventually track down where the taxi had taken him and take the suitcase,' said Claude. 'I suppose a heap of magazines would weigh about the same as a painting and by the time whoever took it discovered otherwise, Julian would be well out of the way.'

'That's possible,' said Ian. 'But then he was seen by the woman near the taxi rank who stopped him, and they had an argument before he went into the station.'

'That makes sense,' said Molly. 'She was trying to get Grainger to tell her where the painting was. He refused and when he left, she called up her hitman to waylay him on the train.'

'Was the argument before or after he posted the letter?' Claude asked.

Ian checked the notes he had made after talking to Stu the taxi driver. 'He crossed the road to post the letter and that's when he was seen talking to the woman.'

'And we still don't know where the painting is,' said Claude. 'If only we knew what it was he posted.'

Ian sighed. It felt as if for every step they took forward, they took another one backwards. While he was trying to work it out, an email arrived from Elsa, which he read out.

Tall and skinny, wearing a black leather biker jacket and trousers, short darkish hair. Weird green eyes and yes it could be the woman in your picture.

'That sounds like the woman who attacked me,' said Claude. 'We're making progress. We know she's called Martina Waterperry and she's been spotted on three occasions all relevant to the thefts and the murder.' He made a list and pinned it to the board.

Sightings of Martina Waterperry:
Delivering prints to Inverbank
At the attack near Forfar
Arguing with Julian outside Kirkcaldy station

'And I've found her,' said Molly, looking up from her computer screen. 'She doesn't have much of an online presence, but she turned up when I did an image search for her name.' She turned her screen so that they could both see. 'She's a director of an offshore investment management company based in Edinburgh.'

'What exactly does offshore investment management involve?' Ian asked.

Molly clicked into the website. 'It all looks very exclusive,' she said. 'It's not the sort of company you can approach if you only have a few quid to invest.'

'Sounds like tax avoidance,' said Claude. 'Legal, but possibly not very ethical.'

Molly scrolled down the page. 'This is interesting,' she said. 'It talks about converting non-cash assets into fungible tokens.'

'What the hell does that mean?' Ian asked.

'To me it sounds like a way of converting stolen goods into cryptocurrencies,' said Claude.

'Not sure that's much clearer,' said Ian.

'Imagine you have come by a priceless work of art by dubious means,' Claude explained. 'You are in possession of something that is worth a fortune but there's no way you can raise the cash on it should you need to. But you can exchange it for cryptocurrency – something that's fungible. So your artwork becomes the property of someone else, you are richer by millions but there is no way the transaction can be traced.'

Ian was having trouble getting his head around this, but to be fair he found it hard enough understanding online banking. 'Is it legal?' he asked.

'*Mon cher*,' said Claude. 'This is global finance. The concept of legality doesn't arise.'

'Like Russian oligarchs,' said Molly. 'When the government tried to seize all their yachts.'

'You're right,' said Claude. 'The ownership of things like that is highly complex.'

'So this company sits in an office in Edinburgh shuffling people's assets around with no actual money ever changing hands?'

Claude laughed. 'Pretty much. The days of grubby bank notes are well and truly over.'

'Except in flea markets and antiques stalls, which is where Craigie's paintings turned up.'

'This company would only be interested in high-value items. Anything else just gets offloaded to markets.'

'But Gunn paintings aren't that valuable,' said Ian.

'Not the paintings themselves,' said Claude. 'But there *is* something about them that interests buyers.'

'We're going round in circles,' said Ian. He looked across the desk at Molly, who was drawing a mind map. 'Do you have an idea?' he asked. 'Or are you just feeling artistic?'

'I'm joining the dots,' said Molly. 'Look.' She held up her mind map.

She'd written *Gunn's Fish* in the middle and circled it. Then she'd drawn arrows pointing to more circles which she labelled: coded text; missing manuscript; size of painting; Waterperry the botanist; original frame; Gunn as archaeologist; Blair's travels. 'What we need to do now is work out the narrative.'

'Go on,' said Ian.

'It needs a chronology,' said Molly. 'It probably starts well before Gunn, but this is what I think. I'll write it on the board and you can chip in with ideas.'

'1790 or thereabouts, Tipu Sahib's palace is plundered and among the things stolen was a manuscript. This probably remained in the possession of someone in the East India Company for several years. At some point Gunn is in India on a dig, at the same time Waterperry is sketching flowers in the Himalayas and Mysore and Blair is travelling around doing whatever he did. The three of them meet up and between them they buy, or perhaps steal, the manuscript and bring it back to Scotland. Blair commissions a portrait, which Gunn paints using a larger canvas than usual because they are going to conceal the manuscript behind it. Then he leaves a coded message in the painting.'

Ian turned to Claude. 'Is that possible?'

'With the right kind of frame, yes.'

'Can you tell if it's the right kind of frame from the photograph?'

'No, it would depend on the back. But hidden compartments are not uncommon.'

'What about preserving a manuscript? What would it have been painted on?'

'I assume it was on vellum. Lambskin usually, but in India it could have been goatskin. Properly looked after, it can last for centuries. Vellum is susceptible to damp and sudden changes in temperature. It needs to be wrapped in acid-free paper. Assuming they knew that, they would have been able to get hold of rag paper. It could have been hidden behind the canvas and the frame backed with wood rather than paper.'

'So Molly's theory could be correct,' said Ian. 'But why leave it there for so long? And how would Martina know about it?'

'Martina's father died recently and left her with prints that her great-grandfather had made. Maybe she found other documents that had belonged to him. Letters, perhaps.'

'Why do you suppose she sold the prints?' Molly asked. 'It doesn't sound like she's short of money.'

'She sold them before Gunn's paintings started to interest collectors. Perhaps she hadn't realised the connection.'

'Then someone contacts her about exchanging a Gunn painting that they'd had stolen, and she starts to put two and two together.'

'The whole thing started when someone read Trevelyan's book and Gunn paintings began to go missing.'

'Are we suspecting Martina of murdering Grainger?' Ian asked.

'She'd have a motive if she was the one to commission Grainger to steal the painting,' said Molly. 'He'd get suspicious when he was told to offload everything that had been stolen from Craigie except the Gunn painting. He'd want to know why, so he planned to talk to Claude before handing it over.'

'We should pass that on to the police,' said Ian. 'Although it's all speculation. They probably won't take it seriously.'

∼

'YOU CAN'T BE SERIOUS.' Duncan took a swig of his pint and laughed. 'You really want me to bring this woman in for an interview?'

Ian nodded.

'A perfectly blameless woman, who just happens to have the same colour eyes as someone who may or may not have attacked your colleague. A man, I would hasten to add, who has been a singularly unreliable witness so far.'

Put like that, Duncan did have a point and Ian wasn't really surprised by the way he'd reacted. Thank God he hadn't taken it to Kezia Wallace. She'd probably have him banged up by now for wasting police time.

Duncan hadn't finished. 'And all this speculation about the murder victim just possibly being the man who got off a train in Kirkcaldy to leave a suitcase with an acquaintance. A suitcase that turned out to contain nothing more incriminating than a few magazines.'

'Both the taxi driver and the woman at the coffee kiosk identified him from a photograph of the murdered man.'

'Who also bears a striking resemblance to Claude Lambert.'

'Who was in a hotel in Perth that night.'

'Anyway, we checked out suitcase man. Just an innocent holiday maker in an Airbnb. Lancs police aren't going to let us forget that in a hurry.'

'Then I don't suppose it's any good asking you to check what went through the Kirkcaldy sorting office last Monday morning?'

Duncan gave him a look that suggested he might phone Kezia and have him carted off in handcuffs.

'Didn't really think you would,' said Ian, downing the remains of his pint. 'Another?' he asked, pointing to Duncan's glass.

'Don't mind if I do,' said Duncan. 'And one of their cheese rolls.'

By the time Ian got back from the bar with two pints of beer and two cheese rolls, Jeanie had joined them. She was flushed from dancing, wearing an orange and purple checked shirt with tight jeans and what looked like brand new cowboy boots in an interesting shade somewhere between flamingo pink and mahogany brown.

'Can I get you a drink?' Ian asked.

'You can get me a weak shandy. I can see the two of you are several pints in and I have to drive home.'

'Cheese roll?' Ian asked.

'No thanks, love. I'll share Duncan's. He's supposed to be dieting.'

'Nice boots,' said Ian, returning with her shandy and pulling up a chair next to her. 'Thanks,' she said. 'They're the real thing. Caroline sent them after a weekend in Arizona. The colour is called Scotch

Goat. She thought that would appeal to me. She's travelling most weekends.'

'That's right,' said Ian. 'She says she wants to see as much of America as she can while she's there.'

'You must miss her.'

'Yeah,' said Ian.

Duncan muttered something into his beer and Ian felt his cheeks redden.

'Well, she'll be back at Christmas,' said Jeanie. 'You can plan something nice to celebrate.'

That could be awkward. He hoped Jeanie wasn't about to invite them to cosy up in her spare bedroom for the festivities. No one would be more pleased than he would to see Caroline safely home, but their friendship wasn't like that. The problem was that no one could get that across to Jeanie.

'I hope you've been behaving yourself while she's away.'

Now it was Ian's turn to mutter into his beer. 'Actually,' he said. 'I've been spending time with her exchange partner. A nice young man called Brett.'

'It was Brett who drew attention to the Gunn painting at Drumlychtoun,' said Duncan. 'Ian's latest case,' he added.

Jeanie looked puzzled. 'I don't think I've heard of Gunn,' she said. 'Is he famous?'

'Right now,' said Ian, 'his only claim to fame is being stolen.'

'Why is he being stolen if no one's heard of him?'

'That's what makes this case so fascinating,' said Ian.

'There's some half-arsed idea that he painted codes into his painting. Some kind of treasure hunt for the super-rich,' said Duncan. 'It's already been the cause of an attack and a possible murder motive for which we have no suspects.'

Hadn't Ian himself just suggested a suspect? And been told he was wasting their time.

'So how is Ian involved?' Jeanie asked.

'He and his smart-arse French colleague with the fancy coat were looking for missing paintings. They seem to think there is a link with that and our murder case.'

'There is a link,' said Ian. 'The dead man had Claude's address in his pocket.'

'Which made him our number one suspect,' said Duncan.

'So why not arrest him?' Jeanie asked.

'Watertight alibi,' said Duncan. 'Otherwise he'd be under lock and key by now.'

'Why would the murderer leave his name and address in his victim's pocket?' asked Ian, feeling a sudden need to spring to Claude's defence.

Duncan shrugged. 'Murderers don't always think clearly.'

'Aren't psychopaths known for their clear thinking?' asked Jeanie.

'Only fictional ones. And I shouldn't be discussing the case,' said Duncan, surreptitiously biting into Jeanie's half of the cheese roll.

'Tell me about the flashy coat,' she said.

'It's a dark red Jean de Saul Chesterfield,' said Ian. 'With a velvet collar and purple lining. Claude's had it for years. It's a kind of trademark for him.'

'Nice,' said Jeanie, eyeing Ian's scruffy parka. 'Private detectives should have good quality coats.'

She'd probably pass that on to Caroline and the next thing Ian knew there would be some posh American coat arriving in the post. Perhaps he should invest in an Inverness cape type coat, or a Columbo-style trench coat. Or perhaps he should get a black overcoat and turn the collar up the way detectives on the covers of crime novels did. And what about Molly? Was there a recognisable style for women detectives? All he could think of was a Sarah Lund jumper.

As he and Lottie walked home, he thought about jumpers. He'd checked Sarah Lund's – couldn't remember why – and remembered that they were made from alpaca wool. And that thought took him in quite another direction. A direction he was more than happy to go in.

24

'You have to go to Stonebridge House,' said Molly as Ian arrived back from his morning walk with Lottie.

'When?' he asked, filling Lottie's water bowl and hanging up her lead.

'Right now,' said Molly. 'They said it was urgent.'

'They?'

'Felicity's there as well. Mr Craigie said she'd had a letter.'

Felicity probably received a lot of letters in her line of work. What was so special about this one that she needed to call him out urgently? 'She can't drop in here to talk about it?'

'Mr Craigie sounded quite worried. You'd better go over there. They are paying us, after all.'

'Okay. Do they want Claude as well?' As far as he knew Claude was still fast asleep.

'No, he said you should go alone.'

Strange, he thought. Felicity and Craigie were employing both of them. 'Well, if it's urgent, I'd better get over there now. You can tell Claude where I am when he's awake. I'll call you when I know what's going on.'

Much to her disappointment, he decided to leave Lottie behind.

She watched him soulfully from the window as he descended the path towards his car. He didn't imagine he would be long. He'd take Lottie for a nice long run on the beach at lunchtime.

It was an easy drive to Stonebridge House. Even with the morning rush the roads were quiet. Ian arrived fifteen minutes later and parked in the driveway. Craigie must have heard his tyres on the gravel drive and was standing at the open front door when Ian stepped out of his car. He looked relieved to see him and led him into the house. 'We're in the kitchen,' he said, 'having breakfast. Coffee? Toast?'

Ian accepted both readily. He usually had breakfast after he'd walked Lottie but Molly had made him feel he shouldn't delay and he hadn't had time for either. 'What's all this about?' he asked.

Felicity handed him a cup of coffee and sat down next to him. She passed him a brown jiffy bag, which he took cautiously.

'It's okay,' said Craigie. 'We've already opened it. There's nothing sinister or dangerous in it.'

'So why...?'

'Read the letter and you'll understand,' said Felicity.

Ian carefully removed the letter and noticed there was something else. He upended the jiffy bag and a small key fell out, jangling against his coffee cup. He picked it up carefully and edged it back into the bag. 'In case of fingerprints,' he explained in answer to Craigie's questioning look.

'Ah, we didn't think of that. I hope we haven't destroyed any evidence. We've both handled the key and the letter.'

Ian opened out a single sheet of paper and placed it on the table in front of him.

Dear Ms Bright

I am sending you this because from what I've heard during my recent enquiries, you are trustworthy and will take care of this key discreetly until I am able to call on you to collect it.

This is my insurance and I know that you will understand since that is the business you yourself are in. I expect you to receive this on Tuesday morning and will endeavour to contact you by Tuesday evening. If I fail to do that it is because my worst fears have been realised.

No doubt I deserve the fate that may or may not be about to befall me. I trust you to ensure that the object I have concealed falls into the right hands and is returned to where it belongs.

Take the key to the Grangeworthy Health and Fitness Centre close to the northern approach road to the new Forth bridge. I have the use of a secure locker there and have gone to great lengths to ensure that no one knows about what I have placed in it. All the same, you should take care. There are those who would go to any lengths to obtain it. As will have been proved by my non-appearance to collect the key. Go in daylight and take with you someone you can trust. Try to ensure you are not followed but when leaving keep to the main roads for as far as is practical. When you reach your destination, you must remove the contents of the locker and take them somewhere safe. Examine the contents of the package – there is a clue in the wall hanging. Once you have verified that all is there you will know where it must go.

Yours respectfully
JG

IAN SAT BACK in his chair, not sure what to say. 'When did you get this?'

'This morning.'

'But today is Friday.'

'Postal strike,' said Felicity.

Of course, there would have been no collection or deliveries early in the week.

'It has to be the painting, doesn't it?' asked Craigie.

'I suppose so,' said Ian. 'JG could be Julian Grainger. The man we suspect was behind the thefts. But how would he know about Felicity?'

'He must have seen me with Claude in Paris and later with Douglas. It wouldn't be difficult to find my connection to the insurance company. You and Molly did.'

'We should go to the police,' said Ian.

'And what are they going to do?' Felicity asked impatiently. 'All I've got is a key. Nothing incriminating about that.'

'Except that the man who sent it to you was murdered.'

'There's no evidence that it's the same man, is there?' said Craigie.

A good point. Duncan had already dismissed Ian's latest theory.

'And they could connect me to the murder,' said Felicity. 'If they knew I was trying to contact Julian Grainger.'

Ian looked at her. All five foot two of her. All the same, could she be a suspect? What would the police make of her getting letters from someone who had been murdered within hours of sending it? Something didn't feel right. Had Julian Grainger, sensing his own demise, decided to do the right thing and return the painting to its rightful owner? If so, why not just write to Craigie? 'So what do we do about it?' he asked.

'We do what the letter suggests,' said Craigie. 'Felicity trusts me and I assume she also trusts you. The three of us will go and collect this, whatever it is, and bring it back here to examine. If it's my painting, then I can prove I'm the rightful owner and hang it back on my wall.'

'And if it isn't?'

'Then we go to the police.'

'And if it is your painting and has something valuable hidden in it?'

'Then I'll need to take legal advice. I've no wish to own something I have no right to.'

'When are you planning to do it?' Ian asked.

'Right now,' said Craigie. 'I can't think of any reason to delay it.'

'Do we include Claude?'

'No,' said Felicity. 'I don't trust him.'

This was all very sudden. It felt like a trap, but he couldn't work out who was trapping whom, or why. Ian would have preferred to take time to think about what they were going to do. Perhaps arrange some backup in case they were followed. On the other hand, that could attract attention. And maybe Craigie was right. The sooner this was done, the better.

'We can't go in my car,' said Felicity. 'It's too small.'

How did she know that? The letter hadn't mentioned what they were to collect or how big it was. Was Felicity just assuming it was the painting, or did she know more than she was letting on?

'We can take mine,' said Ian. 'Or yours, Douglas.'

'If it is the painting, your car would be better. It's big and heavy. A hatchback makes sense.'

'What if Claude is part of this?' Felicity asked. 'He knows Ian's car.'

Why was she so determined to implicate Claude? He was a proven liar, but that could also be said of Felicity herself. Claude wasn't high on Ian's list of trusted colleagues, but he no longer suspected him of any evil intent. For one thing, he was far too lazy. 'He was still sound asleep when I left,' he said. 'But if it makes you feel happier, I'll call Molly and make sure she keeps an eye on him. She needs to know that I won't be back in the office for a while anyway.'

'I suppose we don't have much choice,' said Felicity. 'I'm sure I wasn't followed driving here this morning and the sooner we go the better.'

'Sit in the back,' Ian told her. 'If there's even a hint of anyone following us, I'll head off in a different direction until we're sure we've lost them.'

'Who exactly are we on the lookout for?' Craigie asked.

That was a very good question. 'Anyone on a motorbike,' he said. 'Or a silver-grey Prius.'

'Should I take my shotgun?' asked Craigie, not entirely seriously. Or at least Ian hoped he wasn't.

'Absolutely not,' said Ian, as visions of Craigie taking pot shots at random motorcyclists passed through his head.

'Sounds like a good idea to me,' said Felicity.

'No.' Ian was determined to be firm over this. 'It's broad daylight. We'll be driving on busy roads. We can be arrested and jailed for carrying a firearm. At worst we'll be held up and robbed. If that happens, we give them what they want, no question.'

'Absolutely,' said Craigie. 'No painting is worth putting our lives in danger. Think of poor old Julian Grainger.'

Felicity sighed, clearly labelling them both as a couple of snowflakes.

∼

GRANGEWORTHY HEALTH AND FITNESS CENTRE had the air of an out-of-town hypermarket of the type visited by white transit vans on the outskirts of Calais. *Were they still there?* Ian wondered. Or had Brexit done for that kind of thing? In any case, instead of people stocking up with crates of cheap beer and wine, Grangeworthy was full of people working out on torturous-looking machines and lifting weights. Developing muscle and losing weight in equal quantities.

It was a stark building on the top of a hill overlooking the approach road to the Forth road bridge, approached from the main road by a long drive across treeless expanses of running tracks and football pitches. Their drive there had been uneventful with no sign of anyone following them. Ian parked near the entrance, and they made their way inside. It reminded him of a recent trip to Ikea. On the ground floor they passed a play area where children bounced on trampolines and hid amongst a mass of coloured balls. It looked like fun, although looking back on his childhood with his brother when they had roamed free in the local countryside, climbing haystacks and damming up streams, he thought this was probably a more sanitised kind of fun.

They ascended an escalator, which took them up to a cafeteria with a nice view of the car park, the road they had just left and beyond it the Firth of Forth. They found the lockers close to a series of doors with electronic signs saying things like *Nifty Fifties, Body Pump* and *Queenax*. The days of turnstiles and ticket offices were clearly over. If you wanted one of these sessions you booked using an app and then signed in with a code, which magically opened the door to admit you.

The lockers had numbered keys, which seemed strangely low tech compared to everything else around them, but which made finding the locker they wanted a lot easier. Ian was not sure how they'd have managed if they'd needed an app to open it. JG had chosen one of the larger lockers. The kind that those doing a pre-work gym session might use to hang their city suits in. Getting up at six in the morning, working out for an hour and then working for eight hours or so in a suit was not a way of life Ian had ever experienced. He'd never regretted it. But looking at the number of lockers, it was obviously something a lot of people did on a daily basis.

Felicity unlocked the door and Craigie reached inside for a package that was almost as big as the locker itself. It was wrapped in bubble wrap and fastened with webbing strips. Craigie grabbed one of the straps and heaved it out. 'It's the right size for the painting,' he said, 'allowing for all this wrapping.' He pulled it out of the locker and leant it against the door. It was bigger than Ian had expected – much larger than the Drumlychtoun portrait. It took all three of them to manoeuvre it back to the entrance and out to the car. One or two people looked puzzled as they made their way out of the building, but no one stopped them or tried to wrestle the package away from them. They loaded it into the back of the car and drove off. That was the easy bit. If anyone was waiting to tackle them it would be on the way back once they had the painting. He had no worries about the first part of their journey, which was on the motorway. And once they turned off onto the A90 to Dundee there would still be plenty of traffic – moving traffic, so no danger of theft while held up in a jam. In any case, all the doors were locked from the inside. Once off the main road and in the lanes near Stonebridge House they would need to be more careful. This was where, should they be tackled, he decided it would be best just to give the thieves what they wanted. It would be frustrating, but Craigie had agreed that they shouldn't put up a fight. Ian wasn't so sure that Felicity would be of the same mind. But he needn't have worried. They turned safely into the drive at

Stonebridge, unfollowed and unmolested. Ian sent Molly a text to say he was at Stonebridge but hoped to be back in the office soon.

∼

THEY CARRIED the package into the living room and laid it on the leather top of a mahogany desk. Craigie reached for a pair of scissors and carefully cut through the webbing. Then he unrolled the yards of bubble wrap that had encased it and laid it flat on the desk. The three of them stood and looked at it. As Ian had learnt, Gunn had been far more skilled painting animals and scenery than people. Alistair Blair stood to one side of the painting wearing what Ian assumed was typical nineteenth century gentleman angler attire: a brown single-breasted jacket, waders and a wide-brimmed hat. He had a beard and a bored expression, and was holding the fish out in front of him with both hands. The fish was very large and Ian wondered if Gunn had been persuaded to exaggerate its size. Blair would hardly want to be portrayed for posterity holding up something the size of a minnow. But, exaggerated or not, the huge salmon that Blair was holding was authentic down to the last detail. Every scale and marking was immaculate and Gunn had captured the sheen on the fish's underside to perfection. It had its mouth open as if gasping for air, which it probably was, and an expression of anxiety – quite understandable in the circumstances – in its eyes.

But something about the picture was not quite right. A fish drawing its final breath and a man in waders. Surely an outdoor scene was Gunn's usual style. Ian was no expert, but every painting he'd seen by Gunn had captured scenery typical of Scotland: grouse moors; heather-clad hills; lochs and flowing rivers. He was a natural landscape painter. That was his strength. His people were wooden – caricature Scots with no life to them. This man, with his waders and wet fish, was standing in what looked like a library. There were sketchily painted books on shelves and a couple of paintings in which Gunn had shown little interest in the subject matter. Ian bent closer to look at what was the real subject of the picture. The illuminated scroll hanging close to Blair's right shoulder. He'd seen one of these at Drumlychtoun, presented to whichever Lyton it was that had restored the family title and fortunes. At the top, the family crest, then lists of properties and titles, the whole thing finished off with the king's seal. The Blair document was similar. Although, unlike Xander's, this one was not in a frame or under glass. Gunn had not wasted time on irrelevancies like book titles, even though this was clearly a library. But he had copied this document in painstaking detail. And this was where Nick had worked out the code.

Things are not always what they seem; the first appearance deceives many; the intelligence of a few perceives what has been carefully hidden.

Given more time he should probably check it and find the hidden code for himself, but right now he was prepared to take Nick's word for it. He heaved the painting over and studied the back. The frame was a plain one, and fixed to the back of it was a sheet of wood held on with four thin batons. That would account for its weight. 'Can you take this off?' Ian asked Craigie, not wanting to set about possibly destroying what had been in place for more than a hundred years.

Craigie opened a drawer of the desk and took out a thin but sharp paperknife. He slid it under one of the batons and prised it off. It came away easily. He repeated the same with the other three batons and then lifted off the sheet of wood. Underneath they should have seen the back of the canvas. Instead, there was what looked like a linen cloth. Craigie stared at it for a moment then carefully lifted a corner, revealing the edge of a flower painted in gold leaf. 'We should leave it,' he said. 'Wrap it all up again and take it to an expert. If that's what I think it is, it's very delicate. It's been covered like that for many years, exposing it to light and air could damage it. I'll lock it in the safe tonight and take it to a man I know in Edinburgh first thing tomorrow.'

Ian and Craigie had been completely engrossed in the painting and the secret it held. Felicity appeared less interested and started wandering around the room, fidgeting and staring through the window. Suddenly she stood still and smiled in a way Ian found sinister. He became aware of a prickling at the back of his neck and a draught from an open door. He turned around and found himself face to face with the barrel of a gun.

'Wondered when you'd notice we were here,' said a woman dressed all in black who gazed at them with the greenest eyes Ian had ever seen, and who was pointing a gun straight at his face. Standing in the doorway, a few feet behind her, was a large man with an armful of tattoos, who appeared to be unarmed although probably capable of flooring all of them with a single flick of the wrist.

'Over there,' said the woman, gesturing to the wall with the gun. 'You too.' She pointed the gun at Craigie, who shuffled over to stand next to Ian, fidgeting nervously with the sleeve of his jacket. Ian looked around. They were standing against the one wall of the room that was bare and out of reach of anything that might help them escape. He looked across to the other side of the room, to a fireplace that had a handy selection of fire irons hanging from a brass stand. But any move in that direction and one of them would be shot. As they would if they made a sudden dive for the door, which in any case was blocked by fourteen stone or so of the kind of man one hoped never to meet in a dark alleyway at night. He looked at Felicity, trying to catch her eye, but she had sidled over to stand next to the woman with the gun. 'Felicity,' she said. 'You had better introduce me to these two gentlemen. They clearly don't know who I am.'

'I know who you are,' said Ian. 'You're Martina Waterperry. Great-granddaughter of one of the men who stole Tipu Sahib's manuscript.'

'You were right, Felicity,' said Martina. 'He's more intelligent than he looks.'

'You know Felicity?' Craigie asked.

'Of course,' said Martina. 'Felicity is my sister. We're here to reclaim what is rightfully ours.'

'How can you be sisters?' Craigie looked more shaken by this than by having a gun pointed at him, or for that matter, having his recently returned painting snatched from under his nose. 'You lied to me.'

Felicity shrugged. 'Not really,' she said. 'I just didn't mention that I had a sister.'

'Half-sisters would be more accurate,' said Martina. 'Felicity's mother was married to my father until they divorced and he married my mother.'

Looking at the two of them standing next to each other, Ian could see a likeness. Similar features and colouring. Even in their build, although Martina was a good eight inches taller than Felicity, they were both slim, almost boyish. Presumably the second Mrs Waterperry was a tall lady.

'My mother was always bitter about the divorce,' said Felicity. 'When she remarried, she insisted I changed name as well. She did allow me to visit my father once a year, which is how I got to know my little sister.' The idea of Martina as a little sister made her giggle.

Martina reached into her pocket and pulled out a bunch of cable ties. 'I'm afraid we shall have to tie you up until we are well away from here. Jock,' she said, gesturing to the man in the doorway who looked at her blankly. 'Grab a couple of chairs and immobilise them,' she said impatiently. 'Felicity, remove the manuscript and wrap it up. We don't need to deprive Mr Craigie of his painting. In fact, we owe him for helping you back with it. You'd never have been able to carry it on your own.'

Felicity carefully removed the manuscript and placed it between two cushions, which she strapped together with parcel tape.

'You'll never get away with it,' said Craigie.

'You think?' said Martina. 'I already have a buyer for the manuscript. By this evening it will be on its way to Texas, hidden in a special consignment of Scottish leather goods. Mr Craigie has his painting back. No one will ever know we were here.'

'Except that someone left the two of us tied to chairs,' said Ian.

'I'm sure a detective of your experience will find a way out of that,' she said. 'In time. But once the manuscript has left the country an anonymous text will be sent to our friend with the red coat who will be able to come and rescue you.'

'Your friend?' Ian asked.

'I use the term loosely,' said Martina. 'Claude Lambert was no more than an irritation. Jock may have been a little over-enthusiastic with his message. I should have had him seen to before he left Paris. But hey, no real harm done.'

'And was Jock also over-enthusiastic with Julian Grainger?'

'Julian threw himself over the Tay Bridge and drowned,' said Martina. 'If he'd done as he was told from the start that would have been unnecessary.'

'So his job was to have the paintings stolen and hand them over to you?'

'There was only one I was interested in. At first I didn't know which one, but Julian worked it out and decided to double cross me. Then he had his most fortunate fit of conscience. He must have decided to return the painting rather than let me get my hands on it. He didn't, of course, know that Felicity and I are sisters. But he did know of her association with Mr Craigie. Without his very helpful letter, we'd have been searching for much longer.'

Ian looked at Jock, who was having trouble disentangling the cable ties. Ian had experienced problems like that with paperclips as well as other bits of office stationery that liked to get itself into knots.

'Hurry up, Jock,' said Martina, shifting her attention from Ian and waving the gun in Jock's direction.

'I'm doing ma' best,' Jock muttered, not noticing a shadow in the doorway he had just vacated.

Jock eventually freed a handful of cable ties and pushed a chair across to where Ian was standing. Craigie took advantage of this. As Jock was occupied with the chair and a handful of cable ties and Martina was tutting impatiently, Craigie lunged forward, grabbed Felicity around the neck and pointed the letter opener at her throat. He dragged her over to the fireplace, where he picked up an iron poker and slid it across the floor in Ian's direction. Ian's past rushed through his head as Martina swung round and pointed the gun directly at him. He could only pray that her aim was bad and that she would get him in the leg or shoulder. He was about to close his eyes when he spotted the flash of red in the doorway and Claude leapt across the room, grabbed the poker and, incompetent as ever, hit Jock over the head with it. *For God's sake,* Ian thought. *Go for the woman with the gun.* Working with Claude had taught him one thing. You need a job doing, don't expect Claude to do it. The one good thing about Claude's action was that it had distracted Martina. In the split second that she moved the gun away from him, Ian lunged towards her and knocked it out of her hand, kicking it under Craigie's desk.

Realising she was now at a disadvantage, Martina punched Craigie in the face, grabbed Felicity by the wrist and tugged her away from him. 'Run,' she said, both of them disappearing through the door.

'Let them go,' said Claude. 'Molly's called the police. They won't get far.'

Jock was lying on the floor, moaning. Ian and Claude dragged him to a sitting position and tied his wrists and ankles with the cable ties.

'Well done, sir,' said Craigie, slapping Claude on the back.

Yes, he deserved their thanks. 'Just a couple of things,' said Ian. 'What brought you over here? How did you know anything was wrong?'

'That's all thanks to Molly,' said Claude. 'She was trawling through images on Facebook like she does. I always thought it was a bit of a waste of time, but it paid off on this occasion. She found a photo from way back of Felicity and Martina together. It had been tagged by someone on a shooting party who captioned it *Waterperry's two daughters*. We'd just got your text saying you were back here with the painting so we thought I should drive over and check that everything was okay. When I saw the motorbike parked outside, I texted Molly and she called the police. What was the other one?'

'Sorry?'

'You said a couple of things.'

'Yeah. I just wondered why you went for Jock rather than Martina who was holding the gun. You realise we could both have been shot?'

'Sorry, I didn't really stop to think. I just recognised Jock here as the man who beat me up and I guess I lost my temper.'

Ian was just wondering if Molly had been persuasive enough to bring the police urgently when he heard a car crunching to a halt on the gravel drive and saw the flash of a blue light. With any luck it would be Duncan or one of his team. But there was a possibility it could be Kezia Wallace. Did chief inspectors respond to calls like this one? Apparently they did. She strode in with one of her sergeants. 'We really have to stop meeting like this,' she said to Ian with a grin.

Claude stepped forward, bowed deeply and kissed her hand. Ian could almost believe she was blushing.

'We've caught your murderer for you,' said Claude, pointing to Jock. 'There were a couple of women on a motorbike who left here a few minutes ago. One of them held us up with a gun.' He pointed to the gun, which was still underneath Craigie's desk. The sergeant dragged it out with the tip of his pen and sealed it into an evidence bag.

Kezia pulled out her phone and shouted instructions to stop and detain two women on a motorbike. 'Did any of you notice the number plate?' she asked.

They all shook their heads except Claude. 'I didn't catch the number, but it was a Triumph 1200 Tiger,' he said. Kezia looked impressed. 'Blue,' he added.

'Well, at least one of you was paying attention,' said Kezia, writing down the details.

Forgive me if I was a bit too busy trying not to get shot to look out of the window at number plates, Ian thought.

'What should I do with this?' asked Craigie, picking up the bundle of cushions that contained the manuscript.

'What is it?' asked Kezia.

'It's the cause of all this trouble,' said Ian.

'A priceless manuscript,' added Claude.

'Who does it belong to?'

'It was stolen from Tipu Sahib during the Mysore war and hidden behind the painting that was stolen from here,' said Ian.

'You can prove that you're the owner of the painting, Mr Craigie?' Kezia asked.

'I have all the paperwork, yes.'

'And this Tipu Sahib, did he report the theft?'

'I doubt it,' said Ian. 'He died in 1799 at the siege of Seringapatam.'

'And it was doubtless one of my ancestors who stole it,' said Craigie. 'Several of them served in the East India Army. There were a good many spoils of war that made their way back to Scotland. I must admit to feeling rather ashamed of them. I feel I should try to return it to someone who has a greater claim to it than I do.'

'That's really not up to me,' said Kezia. 'I suggest you take advice from someone at the British Museum. Until then, perhaps lock it away somewhere safe.'

25

Jock was arrested for the murder of Julian Grainger and for the attempted murder of Claude Lambert. He'd been seen boarding the train at Leuchars on the night of Grainger's murder and Claude identified him as the man who attacked him. Duncan was not sure that a murder charge would stick as Grainger had drowned. Although being beaten up and thrown from the bridge was certainly a factor in his death. Either way, Jock was likely to be locked up for a long time.

Claude now had his passport returned to him and was free to leave. Something he seemed reluctant to do. Ian could hardly evict him from his house, since he had probably saved his life. But he and Molly would be heartily glad to see the back of him and have the office to themselves again. They both dropped hints about how Claude's Paris office must miss him, not to mention his associates at the Didier Pierre. Ian promised to keep an eye out for the paintings that his French client had lost, but it all landed on deaf ears. Claude had become a fixture.

Until one morning when Ian was woken at six-thirty by someone banging on his door while at the same time pressing and holding down the doorbell. It was driving Lottie wild. She had rushed downstairs and was hurling herself noisily against the inside of the door. Ian dragged on some clothes and went to try to quieten things down. On his way he passed the closed door of the back office, where Claude was managing to snore at a volume audible above the racket of door banging, bell ringing and Lottie's barking.

Ian opened the door and found himself face to face with a woman he'd never met before. Around his own age, she was dressed in jeans and an oversized white shirt, and had a pale-coloured overcoat slung around her shoulders. *Camel,* Ian thought, although why he recognised it as camel he didn't know. It looked expensive so perhaps it was something his mother wore. He was fairly sure that no camel had suffered in its manufacture. In an idle moment he might try to find out where the name had come from. But probably not. Life was too short to worry about any more coat names.

Looking at the woman standing on his doorstep, Ian's first thought was that she was a new client. Another case of an untrustworthy spouse seemed likely. Her coat told him that she probably wouldn't quibble about his fee. But it was too early in the morning, and he was about to tell her that his office was closed and suggest she should came back later, when she smiled at him.

'Forgive me, for calling on you so early,' she said. 'And also for my poor English but it is about my 'usband.'

He was right. A clear case of marital suspicion.

'My name is Mariette Lambert,' she continued.

He'd give her his card and suggest she make an appointment. With luck he could get back to bed and grab another couple of hours sleep. Then he realised. The name. *Lambert.* And he was speechless. Again. Was this going to happen every time he answered his doorbell?

'Your local police tell me he is 'ere. I stay last night in St Andrews and take a taxi this morning.'

This was Claude's wife? Ian hadn't even known that Claude was married. He'd never mentioned a wife, but then Ian had never asked him about one. 'You'd better come in,' he said, leading her into the living room. 'Claude is still asleep.' He pointed to the door of the back office.

'Then I shall wake him,' she said. 'He is needed in Paris for a new case. He cannot be in two places at once.'

'No,' said Ian. 'Of course he can't.'

'We have a flight to Paris at eleven o'clock this morning. We need to take a train for Edinburgh so we should leave soon, no?' She smiled at him.

They'd need to do more than that. The train from Dundee took an hour to get to Edinburgh and then there was a forty-minute tram ride out to the airport, plus check-in time. 'I'll drive you,' he said. 'We can be there in an hour.' A couple of hours on the road would be more than worth it if it meant getting rid of Claude.

She smiled at him again. 'That is very kind,' she said.

'Why don't you wake him up and help him get his stuff packed while I make you both some coffee?'

Mariette hammered on the door of the back office and entered the room without waiting for a reply. Ian listened from the kitchen to the sound of Claude protesting about being woken so early, but then becoming quiet when he realised who it was waking him.

'He will be ready soon,' she said, returning to the office and sitting in Molly's chair. 'I know he has been valuable to you.' She picked up a cup of coffee and took a sip. 'I hope you will be able to complete your case without him and that you won't try to persuade him to stay.'

What had Claude told her? 'Our case is complete,' he said. 'Arrests have been made and I can assure you there is no need at all for him to stay in Scotland. He has been helping the local police with a murder enquiry, but I am sure they will have told you that he is free go now.' *The sooner the better.* 'If there is any news of his client's painting, I will let him know at once.'

She looked puzzled and Ian wondered if he had just put his foot in it when, to his relief, Claude appeared, looking sheepish but tidier than usual and with his holdall and laptop bag. 'Seems I'm needed back in Paris,' he said. 'Sorry.'

'Shame you couldn't stay a bit longer,' said Ian, hoping he sounded as if he meant it.

'It seems I have a new client who needs my full attention.'

'I'll let you know if your last client's Gunn painting turns up.' Ian glanced in Mariette's direction, but she showed no sign of interest in either Claude's client or Gunn.

'Now the secret is out,' said Claude, 'I doubt he will care very much. I predict that Gunn's paintings are about to tumble in value. There'll be a lot of red faces in the contract theft market.'

Good, thought Ian. It might just teach people to value art for art's sake, not as just another form of money.

He texted Molly to tell her he would be out of the office for the morning as he was driving Claude to the airport. Molly replied with several thumbs up emojis and a message saying she would spend the morning straightening out the office.

WATCHING as Claude and his wife disappeared into the international departure lounge, Ian reflected that the back view of the red coat was exactly the way he had first seen Claude in Felicity's photo of him. He felt a surprising tinge of sadness at his departure. He had been infuriating, untidy and full of himself. But it had been an experience and Ian was going to miss him. He walked back to the car and set off for home, Lottie standing in her usual spot with her paws on the back of the passenger seat, sniffing the air and probably expecting a walk. Ian looked at the clock on the dashboard. Plenty of time for a quick run, perhaps round the loch at Kinross. He called Molly to check there was nothing urgent, but she was quite happy sorting out the office.

The whole thing had begun with an overcoat and, in a way, it had ended with another one. An expensive-looking camel coat worn by the wife of the once-mysterious man he'd been contracted to find. A strange case, but no one could claim it was a boring one. As he walked around the loch, he reflected that this was the first time it had been just himself and Lottie for a long time. It was a thoroughly enjoyable feeling. Perhaps he wasn't that sorry Claude had gone after all.

26

A weekend away. Leave the laptop behind. Turn off the phone. Ian was looking forward to it. He and Lottie were driving up to Inverbank to spend the weekend with Elsa. The last time he was there he had been stinging from Mickey's comments about his uselessness. It wasn't certain that an evening with Elsa had been enough to dispel this, but she had invited him to spend a weekend with her in a cottage she had only recently moved into. It sounded idyllic. Just three miles from Inverbank, where she worked, it boasted a wood-burning stove and promised relaxed evenings with bowls of soup and very little to do. That had to be a good sign, didn't it?

The thought of his own dismal record concerning the women in his life reminded him that he should call on Douglas Craigie. It was not on his way, but he could leave early and make a small detour. Ian hadn't seen him since he'd called in with the news that Felicity and Martina had been detained trying to board the Cairnryan to Larne ferry the morning after the incident at Stonebridge House. He hoped Craigie hadn't been too downhearted after Felicity's betrayal. He'd been so happy that he had found someone to share his life with once more. There'd been no one, he told Ian, since his wife's death. Now he'd returned to being a lonely widower again.

Ian set out with Lottie and timed his arrival for what he hoped was mid-morning coffee time. As Ian crunched to a halt in the gravel drive, the door opened and Craigie appeared, looking sprightly and cheerful in ochre-coloured corduroy trousers and a dark green fisherman's jersey.

As Ian climbed out of the car, Craigie stepped forward and shook his hand firmly. 'Ian, dear boy,' he said. 'Welcome. Come in and get warm. You'll stay for a bite to eat?'

Ian accepted readily. Lottie didn't need to be asked twice. Neither of them would turn down a nice cosy fire and a plate of food.

'You're looking well, Douglas,' said Ian. 'How have you been?'

'Not so bad,' he said. 'Nice to have the old fish back.' He pointed to the painting, which now hung once more over the fireplace. 'Hamish Gunn may not have been the world's best painter, but this one brings back a lot of happy memories for me.'

'It's a great fish,' said Ian.

'Oh aye, old Hamish knew his fish. Mind you, I suspect he exaggerated the size of this one.'

'Any news of the manuscript?'

'Still at the V&A in London. It's causing a bit of a diplomatic stir. I've given up any claim to it, but it seems the British government are not being so generous.'

Ian had read about recent disputes over claims of stolen artifacts. The Parthenon Marbles being the best known.

Ian dipped a crusty homemade roll into his bowl of mushroom soup. 'This is delicious,' he said.

'Aye,' said Craigie. 'Janet's a good cook.'

'Janet?' Ian asked.

'She's not here right now. Popped out for a bit of shopping and a wee chat with her friend over in Glenrothes.'

'And Janet is?'

'My new lady friend,' he said. 'We met at a Lions Club function a week or so ago.'

Ian hoped she didn't turn out to have a criminal sister. 'Not too upset about Felicity, then?' he asked.

'Bless you, no,' he said. 'To tell the truth, Felicity was beginning to irritate. It's not been easy since Fiona died. I tend to mess things up where women are concerned.'

Ian could relate to that. But perhaps Douglas would have better luck with Janet.

'The company Felicity worked for have been very good to me,' Craigie continued. 'A full apology from the CEO, an offer of help to upgrade my alarm system, reduced premium for next year. Guilt, I suppose.'

'Have the police been in touch?'

'They have. I made a statement and may be called as a witness at Jock's trial. But better still, they found some of my wife's jewellery at a shop in Carnoustie. I can't tell you what it means to me to have that back.'

'There's one thing I don't understand,' said Ian. 'When Felicity got that letter, why didn't she and Martina just go and collect the package themselves?'

'I wondered that as well. But it would have been difficult for them to transport it on a motor bike or in Felicity's tiny car. And bringing it back here made sense. The house isn't overlooked. They could unpack the parcel, take the manuscript with them and leave the painting behind.'

'How did Martina know what time we'd be back here?'

'The police asked me if I knew there was a tracking app on Felicity's phone. My guess is that Martina was keeping an eye on her movements. She knew exactly where we were and what time we arrived back here.'

'So much for sisterly trust,' said Ian, pleased to have sorted that out. 'And thank you for paying my account,' said Ian. 'I'm sorry you had to take on Felicity's share as well, though. I feel I need to discount that.'

'Not at all,' said Craigie. 'I wouldn't hear of it. We made a contract with you and you earned every penny. Is Claude still with you?'

Ian laughed. 'No, his wife came and more or less frogmarched him onto a flight to Paris.'

'Good for her,' Craigie laughed. 'Best place for him. Didn't know he was married.'

'Neither did I until she turned up on my doorstep. A very glamourous lady. I'm surprised he stayed away so long.'

'You never know what's under the surface of a marriage.'

Ian couldn't argue with that. Marriage and any other relationship.

'And I suppose he took his coat with him?'

'Unfortunately, yes. Molly had her eye on it, although it would have been far too big for her.'

'Poor old Claude,' said Craigie. 'Remembered for his coat rather than his detecting skills.'

Ian agreed. 'All charm and little substance,' he said. 'But he probably saved our lives that day. Along with you and your letter knife, which I assume you'd hidden up your sleeve.'

Craigie nodded. 'So what will you be doing next?'

'We've a number of ongoing cases to catch up with. Nothing very exciting. But I'm taking the weekend off and going to visit a friend up in the Trossachs. In fact, I'd better be on my way.'

CRAIGIE WAVED him off at the door and Ian turned his car away from Anstruther and towards Inverbank. He had a fifty-mile drive ahead of him. Plenty of time to think. Work wouldn't be a problem. There was enough to keep him ticking over. New and exciting cases would pop up sooner or later. He had an invitation to spend Christmas at Drumlychtoun. An invitation which included Caroline, who would be back from California soon. And that was a problem. He was very fond of Caroline. They'd had some good times together. But he also had Elsa in his life, and he was very fond of her as well. Was he in love with Elsa? Or Caroline? He didn't know. He tended to favour whichever one he was with at the time. To be honest, he preferred his solitary life. Did that mean he had to give up either of both of them? He had no idea. He'd enjoy this weekend and then try to decide what the hell he was going to do.

ACKNOWLEDGMENTS

I would also like to thank my editor, Sally Silvester-Wood at *Black Sheep Books*, my cover designer, Anthony O'Brien and all my fellow writers at *Quite Write* who have patiently listened to extracts and offered suggestions.

COMING SOON

I would like to thank you so much for reading **The Man in the red Overcoat** I do hope you enjoyed it.

Check out my new series **The Breakfast Club Detectives**

Book 1 **Death in the Long Walk**
    https://books2read.com/u/mBV2wD

ALSO BY HILARY PUGH

The Ian Skair: Private Investigator series

Finding Lottie – series prequel

Free when you join my mailing list:

https://storyoriginapp.com/giveaways/61799962-7dc3-11eb-b5c8-7b3702734d0c

The Laird of Drumlychtoun

https://books2read.com/u/bwrEky

Postcards from Jamie

https://books2read.com/u/4X28Ae

Mystery at Murriemuir

https://books2read.com/u/mgj8Bx

The Diva of Dundas Farm

https://books2read.com/u/bMYMJA

Printed in Dunstable, United Kingdom